"Kenyon shifts smoothly between '80s-style supernatural horror and modern-day science thriller in this superb sophomore effort...readers, left breathless, will hope he makes good on hints of a sequel."
—*Publishers Weekly* (starred review)

"Kenyon skillfully escalates the suspense with teasing snippets of information...Those caught up by this multilayered exploration of trust and betrayal will want to read it in a single sitting."
—*Booklist*

"A gripping, thoughtful story that delivers the scares in spades."
—*Rue Morgue*

"Car chases, telekinetic destruction, and shifts in loyalties that could give the reader whiplash...Kenyon's first novel was nominated for the Bram Stoker Award. *The Reach* confirms his place as a gifted horror writer."
—Hellnotes

"Kenyon blind-sides expectations by delivering a terse, tense, and no-holds-barred dark science thriller...One of the best and most surprising novels of the year."
—Gary A. Braunbeck, Bram Stoker and International Horror Guild Award–winning author of *Coffin County*

"This intelligently written thriller is a delight to read—tense, surprising, and daring, it weaves an intricate trail of deceit and wonder towards a horrific climax."
—Tim Lebbon, author of *Fallen* and *Bar None*

"With *The Reach*, Nate Kenyon has...created a tense, twisted, and finely written novel full of betrayals, secret agendas, and lost innocence. Bravo."
—Christopher Golden, author of *The Boys Are Back in Town*

"One hell of a book...very detailed and well written. Kenyon is quickly rising to the top of the genre."
—The Horror Review

BLOODSTONE

"Stephen King's influence is apparent in Kenyon's debut spooker…an impressive panoramic sweep that shows the horrors manifesting subtly and insidiously through the experiences of a large cast of characters."

—*Publishers Weekly*

"Crisp prose and straightforward storytelling make *Bloodstone* a must-read!"

—Brian Keene, Bram Stoker Award–winning author of *Castaways*

"A dark, disturbing, white-knuckler of a page-turner!"

—Douglas Clegg, Bram Stoker and Horror Guild Award–winning author of *The Priest of Blood*

"[*Bloodstone*] delivers…there are chills and suspense and gripping action with characters you come to know and care about. A fully satisfying read that will hook you from page one."

—Rick Hautala, bestselling author of *The White Room*, *Looking Glass*, and *Follow*

"*Bloodstone* is a stunning debut. The writing is smooth and refined, the imagery striking and vivid…involving the reader and dragging him or her along for a very dark, very disturbing ride."

—Tim Lebbon, Bram Stoker and British Fantasy Award–winning author of *Face*

"Reminiscent of '*Salem's Lot*, *Bloodstone* is a terrifying horror novel that is action oriented yet doesn't neglect the development of the characters…This is the kind of horror novel that will make readers want to sleep with all the lights in the neighborhood shining brightly." —*Midwest Book Review*

"Tense and entertaining, this is one of the strongest debut novels to come along in years. Highly recommended."

—*Cemetery Dance*

"Kenyon's debut evokes an atmosphere of small-town claustrophobia…[a] tale of classic horror." —*Library Journal*

THE BAD MAN

When Helen finally awoke and left the dream world, the lazy feeling remained. She did not immediately think of the past week's events, or the doctor's words; in fact, she hovered for several long minutes in that state between sleep and full awareness. When she finally opened her eyes, she did it with a deep sense of regret

The clock beside the bed read nine thirty-two.

She had the profound and irrefutable idea that someone was watching her.

Feeling her heart begin to pound heavily in her chest, she sat straight up in bed, pulling the sheets close around her body.

Jessica stood in the doorway, holding Johnny Bear loosely with one hand. She looked tiny and lost, dwarfed by the doorframe. Helen let out a great sigh of relief.

"You scared me, honey." She smiled, and began to climb out of bed. Her daughter's words stopped her short.

"He's coming for us, Mommy," she said. "The bad man is here."

Other *Leisure* books by Nate Kenyon:

THE REACH
BLOODSTONE

THE BONE FACTORY

NATE KENYON

LEISURE BOOKS NEW YORK CITY

A LEISURE BOOK®

July 2009

Published by

Dorchester Publishing Co., Inc.
200 Madison Avenue
New York, NY 10016

ISBN 10: 0-8439-6287-9
ISBN 13: 978-0-8439-6287-1
E-ISBN: 978-1-4285-0698-5

The name "Leisure Books" and the stylized "L" with design are trademarks of Dorchester Publishing Co., Inc.

Printed in the United States of America.

10 9 8 7 6 5 4 3 2 1

Visit us on the web at www.dorchesterpub.com.

ACKNOWLEDGMENTS

There are always plenty of people who help pull a book together, and this one has a long history. I'd like to thank my family for their love and support, my friends from back in my State of Maine days, and my agent, Brendan Deneen, for all he does behind the scenes for me.

Last, but certainly not least, I'd like to thank the crew at Dorchester, including editor Don D'Auria, for continuing to have faith in me and for supporting my career.

As usual, I've taken plenty of liberties with geography, and more than a few with the inner workings of various government agencies as well. I'd like to think this makes for a better story. I hope you feel the same.

THE BONE FACTORY

And thus I clothe my naked villainy
With old odd ends, stol'n forth of holy writ;
And seem a saint, when most I play the devil.

—William Shakespeare, *Richard III*

PROLOGUE
BLOOD

Winter's frozen fingers caressed Joe Thibideau's face, his breath twisting in great clouds of steam to ice his eyelashes. The moon was bright as he moved as quickly as possible across the three inches of fresh snow that softened the ground. Little eight-year-old Melissa had been reported missing yesterday afternoon, and that was a long time in this weather. The night was brutally cold, and she was almost surely frozen stiff by now, a ghostly statue in the blue-white moonlight.

He immediately tried to wipe the image from his mind, but it kept coming back again, and chilled him more than the cold ever could. As the deputy sheriff in the small town of St. Boudin, Thibideau had never had to search for death until yesterday. Anyone dead was right out in plain sight, in the middle of a nasty car wreck, or perhaps a logging accident.

But this was different than anything he had faced before. This time, they had a killer in their midst.

The first victim, a local farmer named Eddie Brosseau, had been discovered yesterday morning about three miles away, stuffed inside the front end of an abandoned truck out in his field. He was missing his head, a right arm and part of a shoulder. The reason for this gruesome dismemberment was anybody's guess; Thibideau figured that whoever killed the old man had trouble fitting the whole body into that little import's engine cavity. Maybe there were other reasons, but he preferred not to think about it any more than was absolutely necessary.

Then the girl had disappeared from her home while gathering some wood from the shed. He remembered the desperate voice of the mother on the phone: *We usually fill the wood box together. I never let her go out alone, especially on a cold day like that.*

Joe Thibideau had a daughter of his own. If Melissa had fallen victim to the same brutal bastard who killed Eddie, he only hoped he'd have the chance to nail the son of a bitch. Never in all his forty-seven years had he wanted anything so badly.

Of course, the girl could be a simple runaway, or she might have gotten lost. And yet he couldn't shake the feeling that they were linked together by a single savage thread.

He moved through a thick patch of alders, and paused with his back against the rough bark of a tree. He had lost the others about twenty minutes ago. He should keep close by, he knew, but they had been searching in the cold for nearly two days. It was time to take a chance. He had a hunch. Just another hour or two couldn't hurt, right?

And maybe, just maybe, if the girl was still alive, he could do something to keep her that way.

A branch snapped and sent its burden of heavy snow thudding to the ground. He jumped, almost dropping his flashlight and hitting his head against the tree trunk, which only caused a fresh shower of snow to fall on top of him. Shaking snow from his collar, he pulled a compass and then the map from the left pocket of his parka and smoothed it out over his knees, holding the flashlight in his mouth. The areas already searched were circled in bright fluorescent green on the map. They had been over about four square miles directly behind the house. She could have been picked up by a car, could be fifty miles away from here by now. So far they had been betting against that, since the house was a good half mile off any provincially plowed road, and the driveway hadn't shown any fresh tracks. But they couldn't rule it out.

The map didn't have it, but the hydroelectric plant was less than a mile farther south. It was supposed to make use of the old mine shafts in the area to produce enough power to light up most of Quebec City and parts of Northern Maine into the twenty-first century and beyond. Construction on the new plant had been halted a couple of months back, but he was sure the old Jackson mine building was still there, and it might be just the place for a lost little girl to seek shelter. Or for a killer to hide a body.

The moonlight dimmed and a few fresh snowflakes began to filter their way down as Thibideau made his way through the bare patches and drifts. The trees here were spaced a good distance apart, their lower branches gray and stunted, and a snapped twig under his foot sounded as loud as a gunshot. He knew his way around well enough to keep from getting lost; in any case, the road down to the hydro compound was probably still impossible to get through by car. They'd stopped construction late that fall when the first heavy storm blew in. He never could understand the idiot who organized that whole project. Winters in this remote area of Canada were a bitch, and nobody but that special contractor (who was, incidentally, originally from California) thought they could get the place finished without building a quality road to it first. Now there was no doubt that contractor was out of a job, but it was too late for the road. The ground was rutted, frozen hard as a rock, and covered with a foot of snow. So the plant just sat like some huge, hibernating beast, waiting for the scientists and construction workers to wake it up in the spring.

A few more minutes of walking and he came to a break in the trees, and the entire vast, unfinished compound spread out below him, a huge and gaping hole in the earth with several small buildings scattered around it, including the old mining building beside the frozen river. The river itself cut through the woods directly below, at the foot of a steep bank scattered with small saplings and naked shrubs. It sat as a silent warning, like a line drawn in the dirt by a childhood bully. *Cross it and you're gonna get yours.*

The scope of the thing was remarkable. Until now he had never seen the place, and standing here at the edge, he found it lived up to the stories he had heard in town. Hell, it blew the stories out of the *water.* Trees had been cut down for what seemed like miles in every direction; the place looked like the center of an atomic bomb blast, the half-completed buildings dotting its edge like props for a toy train set.

Standing there gaping, it took him several minutes to realize that something seemed out of place, something more than just this alien blast site in the middle of dense woods. In another second, he knew what that thing was, and crouched behind the trunk of the biggest tree he could find on the upper slope, trying to calm his thudding heart. Partially hidden behind the old wooden mine building just across the river was a snowmobile, cleaned of snow and with what looked like fresh tracks behind it.

He killed the beam of the flashlight and slipped it into his coat pocket. The flakes had stopped falling again, and the light of the moon was enough out here. He felt the sweat inside his mittens and the shake in his legs, and the fiery rush of adrenaline lit up his body like an electric shock. *There's nobody else around; you could be dealing with the fucker right here, right now, just you and him, one on one.*

He scanned the entire complex slowly, watching for any movement, or light, or bit of smoke. Nothing.

Come on now, she could still be alive. He unzipped his jacket, and pulled his .38 out of its holster, trying desperately to keep his hand steady. There was no time to get help; he might have been seen.

Slipping out from the protection of the tree trunk, he made his way down the steep bank, stumbling and sliding until he reached the ice at the bottom. Nothing stirred, and he hurried across the frozen river towards the closest structure, a half-completed building along the right edge of the pit. Out in the open, he was painfully aware of how vulnerable he was under the moonlight, with the snow crunching under his heavy boots. He would have to move fast.

He made it to the corner of the building without incident, and leaned carefully around the other side. The complex looked like a ghost town. The entire side of this structure was open, and great drifts of snow filled the inner section, its surface completely smooth. Moving out and around it, he kept the gun held out at arm's length, like he'd seen cops do in movies. He'd never pointed the gun at anything other than the targets at the range, and it felt uncomfortably heavy and awkward now.

He walked quickly along the edge of the pit to the left, making for the old mine building. At the wall he crouched and crawled under a window, then slowly raised his head and peered into the darkness. It was lighter outside with the moonlight, and he had to cup his hands to the dusty glass and squint. Even then, he could see only shadows. His hand shook and rattled the gun barrel against the glass. Once again peering in, something caught his attention. One of those shadows, over in the far right corner, slumped over in some impossible position, looked like a body.

A little body.

Sweat began to roll in little beads down Thibideau's forehead, stinging his eyes. *What if it's her? Christ, what if the killer's standing right there, just out of sight, in one of the deeper shadows?*

But she could be hurt, unconscious . . .

He crouched and ran along the wall until he reached its edge. Blood pulsing impossibly loud in his ears, he stuck his head around the corner. He found himself looking at the door of the building, shut tight against the cold. Cutting off his fear as best he could, he tried the handle. It swung open with a dull scraping sound.

It was the smell that hit him first—an overpowering, rotten stench that clogged the nostrils and made him gag, staggering backward until he could get his parka zipped up to cover his face. Even then it was there, the unmistakable smell of death.

Right then, he almost turned and ran. But the thought of that little girl, maybe still alive and scared at least as bad as he was, made him take a step into the darkness.

The blackness surrounded him, swallowed him and welcomed him with the utter equality of the blind. He blinked stupidly, eyes adjusting to the deep black shadows around him, and stood frozen with his gun held out as things began to take shape. A dim patch of light from the window shone onto the floor, and he shuffled towards it, closer to the wall until his hands met with something hard.

Jesus the flashlight I forgot the fucking flashlight in my pocket.

How could he be so stupid? Holding the gun in his left hand, he pulled the flashlight out of his jacket and aimed it at the wall, switching it on.

The thing he had touched was an animal, or at least it might have been at one time. It looked to be the size of a raccoon, and it was covered in dried blood and frozen stiff.

There was no head.

Joe stumbled backward, and the beam of the flashlight lit up the entire wall. It was covered with the carcasses of animals and bare bones, a grotesque and sadistic trophy case. Blood ran in drips and blotches down the wood, staining it a dull, coppery brown.

He turned and saw the girl. She had been thrown into a corner, her body broken and battered and her clothes ripped to shreds. Her head was twisted at an impossible angle and her dead eyes stared at him vacantly.

The doorknob was slick in his gloved hand, old and slippery metal, and then the door opened and he stumbled into the cold. The smell would not leave him, it followed him as he struggled across the snow, and then he saw his tracks and there were *another pair, oh Christ, another pair,* and he spun around wildly, losing his balance and dropping his gun.

Joe Thibideau never had a chance to get up. A shadow fell across his path, followed by a searing pain in his shoulder, moonlight flashing on a silver blade that rose up and plunged down again and again, speckling the pure white snow with his blood.

PART ONE

PAST TRANSGRESSIONS

CHAPTER ONE

David Pierce walked into the office expecting the worst. A loud, balding man in an expensive suit, or an old bastard with nothing on his mind other than to keep a young guy like him from getting a job. The past few months he'd run into both; one he couldn't stand enough to work with, the other wouldn't give him the chance.

Third time's the charm. I wonder if they give out awards for this stuff? World's Greatest Ass Kisser, Professional Job Searcher. As long as they paid him, he'd be willing to get called just about anything.

But the guy was all right.

"Welcome to Hydro Development, David. Michael Olmstead. Call me Mike." He stuck out his hand, and David took it. The hand was smooth and dry, but the grip was firm. "Glad you could make it."

Olmstead released his grip and flipped through a file folder on a neatly organized desk. "Please, sit down."

David smiled and nodded, keeping his expression as neutral as possible. Showtime.

He sat in the wide, comfortable chair offered to him, and waited until Mike settled down in the leather seat behind the massive oak desk. He took a quick glance around, admiring the dark wood of the walls, the soft lighting and thick carpeting. Lots of money here.

"Let's get right down to it. We want to know what you can do for Hydro." Mike leaned forward and put his elbows on his desk, hands steepled in front of his sharply defined nose. *Every little detail of this man is sharp.*

"Well, I've worked on two other hydropower plants, one right out of school, and one for six years, which ended last July."

"EPC?"

"That's right. I was involved in development with them, primarily doing research on the possibilities of pumped storage and overseeing the reservoir construction plans."

"Well, this job will be overseeing exactly that kind of thing. We've been a little old-fashioned in the past, but now it's time to take the big plunge, so to speak." Olmstead smiled.

"You're going to harness a portion of the St. John River through an underground storage facility."

"Done some research? That's good, we appreciate the initiative." Olmstead tossed a folder across the desktop in front of him. "There's a lot of hydro activity up in Quebec and New Brunswick, make no mistake about that. Most of the rivers coming off the north coast of the St. Lawrence have a big dam or two. But a lot of that power goes to the pulp mills. With the Jackson project, we want to supply New Brunswick with all the power it's going to need for years. Down into Maine too. And pumped storage is a safe and effective way to get that power. It involves quite a bit of manpower, but if we can pull it off, this will be one of the largest successful underground pumped storage hydro facilities ever. If you do work with us, you'll be getting all you can handle."

David flipped through the folder's pages, past engineer's notes, schematics and technical summaries. "Selling to Canadian Power and Light. Big company."

"That's right. You'd be involved directly with the planning and development of the lower reservoir and tunnel, and getting us back on track."

They discussed the plan details for a while before Olmstead took the folder back and stuck it in a desk drawer. "There are plenty of men working on this thing already, but most of them are at our branch offices in Quebec City at the moment. This is a major project, and we want to make sure everything's done right. After that, there would be an opportunity to stay on in the area and work with maintenance and the lease agreement—that and figuring out how to keep the damn tunnels from icing up. That is, if you're not bored to death by that time."

"My wife and I are easily entertained. We both read a lot, watch movies. And Jessica—she's our little girl—she's got three or four make-believe friends by now, I think. Maybe this would give me some more time to spend with her. I don't do that enough."

That seemed to make an impression. "I know how it is. I was going to ask you about your family. It does get lonely up there, or so I hear. A close family unit is really important to us. We need to know you're intending to stay around for a while. Anyway, this place is pretty isolated. Bitch of a winter too."

"Yeah, I read about the problems you guys had keeping it going." This seemed for an instant a little too critical, and David winced.

Olmstead just smiled, running a hand through his patch of well-groomed hair and sitting back in the relaxed pose of the successful businessman. "You got that right. What we really need is someone to be smart and work with people, not against them. We'll have a big crew on-site eventually, and they all have to use each other to get things done. Know your stuff, and take advantage of it. Frankly, I think you can do it, looking at your job experience and schooling. You've been in and out of the business for what, ten years? You know what makes a plant tick by now. You've worked with pumped storage development. And your references are good, with the exception of the EPC job."

There was a sudden, uncomfortable silence. David cursed silently. Of course he knew it would come up, had to, but still he hadn't been prepared to face it so soon.

"I'm not going to lie to you. Your boss at EPC had some pretty loud ideas about how you handled yourself there."

"Look, I can explain all that." David paused, and found Olmstead had leaned forward again, studying him closely, waiting. He didn't look away. "The guy was a prick."

Olmstead raised one eyebrow in an almost comical expression of surprise, then laughed. "I admire your courage. I spoke with your supervisor myself, and frankly, I'd agree with you. Now I hope I'm reading this right. You had a difference of opinion, got tired of waiting around for real opportunity and decided to go out and get it."

David nodded. "That's about right."

"Again, I admire your courage. Not exactly what I would have done, not with the economy the way it is, but I understand. I think that shows some initiative that could be put to use. Of course, I'm not the only one that makes the decision."

David forced a smile. "I hope you'll put in a good

word for me. I really want this job. I know what it takes. I worked in Alaska on my first project, so I've had experience with the cold. As far as Hydro goes, this has always been the place I've wanted to be." *I just got three million interviews in other places for kicks.* "And working in Canada might be just the thing for my family life."

"Could be. And the scenery's beautiful, believe me. I went up there to check the spot out before we started construction last summer. Thick pine forests and lots of wildlife. There's a hell of a lot of logging going on too, but you'd never know it in most places. And the water coming off the peaks is just about the most pure thing you've ever tasted."

"Sounds great." Of course, he would be spending the winters there too. *Not saying much about those, are you?*

"Listen—" Olmstead stood up and stuck out his hand. David took it. "I have a couple other interviews, but I can say that you are the most impressive so far. If this works out, we'll need you to start right away. The place has been completely shut down for months, but we need someone to evaluate the current situation and advise on next steps. We'd take care of getting you a place to live, as soon as something opens up, and, of course, we'll pay for it. Salary's more than fair, but the benefits are fantastic—full health, dental, the works. Not that there are any dentists within a hundred miles of that place."

Olmstead grinned, and David felt a momentary touch of revulsion—just a touch, but nonetheless it was there. That grin had reminded him of the Cheshire cat in Lewis Carroll's *Alice's Adventures in Wonderland*.

"I'm ready. Thanks for everything, and give me a call if there's anything else you need to know."

David thanked him and left. The interview had gone pretty well, he thought. He had liked Olmstead, not counting that quick moment of distaste; nerves really, that was all. He had already dismissed it. His history with EPC was bound to come up, and with all the problems he had run into before, this time was a pleasant surprise. Olmstead didn't seem to care much about what McDougal had to say, which was lucky. McDougal could be a real son of a bitch.

As he walked out the doors and into the bright sun, he considered Olmstead's last comment. A hundred miles—a little exaggerated, maybe, but it got the point across. A skilled doctor could be fifty miles away for all he knew. What if someone caught the flu, or worse, broke a leg? Thinking about the possibilities made him nervous. If he got this job, he'd have to make sure Jessie understood the rules. *Have fun, kid, but don't play in the woods.*

CHAPTER TWO

He got home an hour later, pulling into their little cul-de-sac street in the suburbs of Rochester, New York, with a lot on his mind. On top of the thoughts of the possible job and the curious, smooth-talking man who would help decide his fate, it was another dull, overcast day. That did little to raise his spirits, though the interview was fine (even if it had seemed a little too easy) and for all intents and purposes he should be thrilled. At least today offered him a chance, which was much more than he could say for yesterday. Yesterday had been another in a growing string of bad luck, where the hours seemed to blend one into another until it was tough to say what time it was, never mind when he might find a break.

He had learned about the Hydro job through an old friend who still worked at EPC, Jake Edwards. Jake was a tall, thin man, balding and slightly hunch-backed from working long hours in the tunnels of various projects. He had called yesterday with news of the job in that gruff voice of his, telling about how he heard of the opening through one of his friends, who had heard from one of his, who had heard . . . the line was endless. But the voice on the phone had been positive, if a little sad. As if Jake Edwards almost wished he could apply, just walk out that door at EPC and into some new life this job might offer him, leaving his worn-out one behind like an old skin.

Hydro Development was a small but growing company specializing in pumped storage facilities, which used water reservoirs at different elevations to generate electricity, and the Jackson Hydro project would be their first step across United States borders in an attempt to generate business in other parts of the world. Personally, David thought the idea of building such a revolutionary project in a risky area like Eastern Canada was crazy, especially since it would be the first of their projects out of the States. But Hydro Development was known for taking risks, usually big ones. They owned five other projects, including the twenty-megawatt dam near the San Andreas Fault, and an underground facility in South Dakota. It was how they'd made their money, taking risks and investing in things nobody else would touch. "Crazy bastards," Jake had said on the phone. "But smart." Research was the key, and usually it paid off.

David figured that was why they might hire him after nobody else would. He was a risk, but he was also a damn good engineer and could get the job done. His other references were stellar, and nobody had ever questioned his work ethic. And he was willing to take on a troubled project like this; hell, he didn't have much of a choice.

He eyed himself in the rearview mirror and ran a quick hand through his coarse, unkempt hair. Two bleary, slate gray eyes stared back at him in silence. His alarm clock had not gone off that morning and he had rushed through the early-morning rituals in order to get to the interview on time. Michael Olmstead didn't seem to be the type to judge on appearances—at least he hoped not. This job might be his last chance.

Their little two-bedroom house was the last one on the left side of the street. Just past it, the road ended in an unexpected mass of greenery, where a thin wooden staircase disappeared into the brush. He had taken Jessie down through the little "park" several times. The staircase wound around several thick tree trunks and down a steep bank before ending abruptly in a caged lookout overlooking a highway. This was the Rochester council's idea of adding a touch of country to an otherwise urban setting. They moved to this place three months ago, after he had been unable to find a job and they had to sell their old house, located in a much nicer setting outside the city. The new place wasn't much, but it saved them some money.

He pulled their three-year-old Corolla into the driveway just as the sun managed to break through the heavy layer of clouds for the first time, painting a soft, pale glow across the tops of the bare shrubs that lined the edges of the house. As he walked quickly up the narrow path to the door, he caught just a glimpse of Jessie's little face peering down at him from one of the attic windows. He knew that now she would be racing to the front door to greet him, and it made him smile. When he was working, she had never let a day slip by without this greeting. He had missed that.

"Daddy Daddy!" Jessie flung herself up into his arms as he opened the door, and he fought for a moment to keep his balance.

"Oh, my little devil," he said, swinging her up onto his shoulders. "You frightened me."

She giggled and clung to him. This was their little game, and no matter how many times it was played, she reacted as if it had never happened before. If he didn't act surprised, she would get angry and pout through supper. So he played along, and occasionally allowed himself a moment to realize that these evening rituals did him as much good as they did her.

He walked over to the kitchen table, bent down and swung Jessie over his head and into a chair, taking a moment to ruffle her hair and give her a big noisy kiss on the cheek. She smelled faintly of attic dust mingled with the sweet child smell she always carried. "Where's your mother?"

"She's sleeping." Jessie gave him her serious look, and he smiled, keeping his real reaction to himself. In fact, this worried him. Helen had been spending more and more time in bed lately, and he hoped she was not having another of her migraines, which usually immobilized her for hours.

He fumbled into the tiny bedroom, which was shrouded in darkness. As his eyes adjusted, he was able to make out his wife's form on the bed, and he sat down next to her.

Come on, honey, he thought. *Feel good now. We should celebrate. The interview went well.*

All he said was: "Helen?"

She stirred, and turned towards him. "Is everything okay?"

"Just fine. I wanted to see if you needed anything."

"No, I feel better." She pulled herself up until she rested against the head of the bed. Her blonde hair was tousled, her normally pretty face worn and blurred with sleep. "How was it?"

"Not bad," David said. *A bit better than that, actually. Why don't you tell her the truth?*

He knew the answer to that one. The reality was, he

had been searching for a job for close to six months now, and every interview was the same. None of them had resulted in anything but a few terse rejection letters: "thank you for your interest . . ." and "we regret to inform you at this time . . ." And since he knew that the situation they were in was his own fault, he was leery of giving Helen any false expectations.

"I've got a good feeling on this one," she said. "Don't you?"

"Sure. We need every bit of good karma we can get." He stroked her bare arm lightly. "Feel like some dinner? I can go pick up Chinese."

"You know we can't afford that," Helen said. He stiffened. She studied him a moment, as if feeling for his mood, then took his hand. "Sorry. I don't mean to sound that way. I know how you feel. It's just that sometimes I miss the way things were."

"You think I don't?" He stood up abruptly, letting her hand fall to the covers. She looked at him, her eyes full of hurt. *Don't do this*, the look said. *We need each other right now.* And there was something else in that look, hovering only for an instant but as clear as day nonetheless. *I love you*, it said. *But I can't take much more of this.*

"I'm busting my balls out there," he said.

"I know you are. But something's got to change. I could give it another try—"

"No," he said, cutting her off. "We've discussed this. Jessie needs you home." *I need you home*, he almost added, but stopped himself. He needed her there with Jessie to make sure everything was okay, needed to know their daughter was in capable hands. But they had been over all that, and there was no use dragging it up again.

"You are so goddamned chauvinistic sometimes."

"It's not that, Helen, and you know it. I love Jessie, but you know how to handle her. And you've told me yourself that you couldn't go back to work right now if you wanted to, with the licensing board and the paperwork."

"I could." Helen sat, arms crossed, and glared at him. "I'd just be behind a little, that's all." They were both silent for a long moment.

"All right," he conceded. "Let's talk about it after I hear from this guy. If you still want to pick up the job search after that, it's fine with me."

She seemed to relax a little. "I just want to help."

"I know." He sat back on the edge of the bed and took her hand. This pointless argument didn't do them any good. They were scared. Both of them. That was what it all came down to, the fear of losing control of their lives. David could remember contemplating travel after college, when he was twenty, just being a bum, who knew? That was the point—back then, none of his friends knew what they wanted to do with their lives. But now there was Jessie.

"Why don't I just make us something? I know I'm not the best cook in the world, but I make a pretty mean hamburger."

Helen smiled. "I don't know if mean is such a good thing, for a hamburger. I'll get dressed and come out to help in a minute."

He nodded, and walked back into the kitchen, his mind on the growing rift between them. When Jessie was born and she had begun having the nightmares and then later, exhibiting signs that were dangerously close to OCD, they had both decided that Helen should quit her job and devote herself to being a mother. David was making plenty of money at the time. But now it was different. There had been too many of these confrontations lately. Their little nest egg, tiny to begin with, was gone. And the money they had saved selling the first house was gone too.

It wasn't that he had trouble with the idea of Helen working. He just worried that Jessie wouldn't be able to handle it. She was a special little girl, but she had problems that needed a lot of attention, attention he was afraid he wouldn't be able to offer alone. He admired his wife for handling Jessie the way she did. Her nightmares had been getting better lately, but it was impossible to know when they might come back stronger than ever.

He was in the middle of rolling the hamburger into little balls when Helen came in.

"Can I help?" she asked.

"There's some salad stuff in the lower bin, you know."

"I know, smart-ass. It's not like I never even look in the refrigerator." She opened the door and paused. "Which bin was that?"

The phone rang. He wiped his hands off on a paper towel, and didn't grab it until the third ring.

"David? It's Mike Olmstead."

"That was quick," David said, balling up the paper towel and tossing it towards the garbage. It hit the side of the can and rolled away. "I hope the news is good."

"Listen, I called the team together as soon as you left."

"And?" He glanced at Helen and held his breath, feeling the familiar knot tighten in his chest, feeling his breathing grow labored and short, the race of adrenaline along his limbs. The line was silent for a long moment, and for a second he thought it could only be bad news, that there was nothing else that would make a man pause in such an uncomfortable way. Then he heard Olmstead's voice again, and all the fear dissolved into blessed relief.

"When can you start?"

CHAPTER THREE

Jessica Pierce was an especially bright four-year-old. Sometimes she even surprised herself—things just seemed to come to her; like that day she found Daddy's drawings of THE PLANT and copied them in crayon, labeling everything like it was in the pictures—even though she couldn't read or write. Or the time she found the toolbox in the corner of the garage and took her tricycle apart, piece by piece, saving everything in neat piles for Daddy when he came home. He wasn't too happy that time, but he let her help put it back the way it was.

Sometimes, she felt the need to fix other things. Like her dolls that weren't lined up perfectly all in rows. Or her clothes that weren't stacked by the right shade of pink in her dresser. When that feeling came, she couldn't rest until she put things right. She knew Mommy and Daddy didn't always like that, but she couldn't help it if something needed fixing. It was a big deal, because she couldn't sleep until she was done.

And sometimes, though only once in a while, she could tell when things were going to happen. She would tell Mommy, and Mommy would smile and say she was PERCEPTIVE. She thought that was a good word, and practiced saying it over and over. She usually had fun on those days when she was PERCEPTIVE.

Today was one of those days.

Daddy had come home from the store in a very good mood. Jessie could tell because he had brought flowers for Mommy, and she laughed and he picked her up and swung her around and around, and then he grabbed Jessie and swung her around too, until she got so dizzy she couldn't stand up when he finally put her on the floor. Daddy had gotten his job last night, and they were moving to some place very cold. She knew it was a cold place because Mommy told her later to wear her sweater, and they didn't pack jackets, they kept them out for the trip. Jessie's was on her bed, waiting for her, her Care Bear jacket with its pink and blue hearts. She had picked it out herself last Christmas from the big store in the mall, and it was the best jacket she had ever had.

It was when they were packing that day when she felt PERCEPTIVE. Sometimes these things she saw were bright and clear, and sometimes they were just feelings that she got for no reason. She would get sad, and then something would happen, like the time when her friend Katie's hamster got lost, and Jessie was sad because it had gotten killed. She told Katie and Katie had screamed at her NO HE'S NOT DEAD HE RAN AWAY and then the next day her mom found it all the way downstairs, and it had been crushed by the leg of a chair.

But today she just felt nervous. It was like when she had to go to the doctor's or the dentist's office for a checkup, but then when it was over the doctor would give her a balloon and she would feel better. Today she felt like there weren't any balloons. Daddy and Mommy were nervous too, but it was the good kind of nervous, when you were happy and excited, and talked real fast and were ready to "get the show on the road."

When she told her mommy how she felt, she smiled and kissed Jessie on the top of the head like she did when she said good night. "It's all right, sweetheart. You'll meet new friends, and everything will be okay. Maybe we'll even get a puppy. Would you like that?" Jessie had just smiled at her and nodded her head. Sometimes it was better to keep things to yourself, if people didn't understand. That was something she had learned from experience, even though she was only four years old and hardly big enough to tie her own shoes.

They packed all day, putting the cups and plates from the kitchen in big brown boxes and their clothes in heavy suitcases. Jessie helped as much as she could, but sometimes she just got in the way, and after Daddy almost tripped over her while he carried one of the heavy boxes out to the car, she decided to play somewhere else. She didn't like helping to pack anyway; it meant they were leaving, and she didn't want to leave. She liked this house and especially its little dusty attic, with the Jessica-sized windows looking out to the neighbor's porch on one side and the driveway on the other. Mommy let her play up there on special days, when it was rainy and she couldn't go outside. She kept her most favorite toys among the boxes in one corner, the little yellow school bus with the red-faced driver in the funny hat and the people who could move from seat to seat, and the set of plates and cups for her dolls. All except Johnny Bear, but he wasn't a toy, he was her friend. He slept right next to her in her bed every night.

Johnny Bear was a gift from her grandma Ellie on Jessie's third birthday. Jessie had opened all the presents and blown out all the candles and Gramma had just kept sitting in that old chair she loved so much, the big purple one by the sofa in their old house. Whenever she visited them, Gramma sat in that chair and stayed there until it was time to leave. On this birthday, Jessie had been wondering when the present from her grandparents would appear, but when everything was over and Grampa had taken to the couch and Gramma was in that chair, still there was no present. Jessie kept quiet about it because she knew it was bad to ask for presents. Mommy had told her to always remember that, but still she was a little sad that there was no present from Gramma and Grampa because those presents were usually the very *best* ones.

And that was when Gramma had stood, her old joints creaking softly, and gone to the back room for a moment, coming back with a big box. Jessie's eyes had been wide with excitement, but Gramma had motioned for her to be quiet, as if this were their little secret and nobody else could know about it. Mommy and Daddy were in the kitchen cleaning up and Grampa was asleep, and after looking around carefully, Gramma had given her the box with a smile and whispered, "There, you see? We didn't forget, after all." Jessie had ripped it open and out came Johnny Bear. Even now, thinking back, it seemed as if he had come leaping out of the box on his own.

Gramma leaned over her then, and for a moment she was just a little bit shy as the old woman's breath settled over her in a cloud of cranberry and ginger. Gramma said, "He's yours to name, Jessie, and he'll be your very best friend forever. He's magic, you know." Her eyes were wet and heavy, and Jessie shrank back from them. Then Gramma smiled and sat back down again and everything was fine, and she forgot about that little quick jump of her heart. But Johnny stayed with her from that point on, because he really was magic, and he was her best friend.

She made sure to hold onto Johnny the whole day while they were packing so he wouldn't be left behind. When they were ready to leave (FINALLY, Daddy said—Helen, you have more stuff than Kohl's), they all climbed into the car. Most of their stuff was in a little trailer hooked to the car. Jessie got to sit in the back with Johnny Bear surrounded by boxes, right on the cushion and not in a child seat. Mommy had let her sit like a grown-up since the beginning of this year, but it still made Jessie really excited. It helped her forget about leaving for a while. She felt like everyone was looking at her when they backed out of the driveway. Daddy had said once that New Yorkers are funny that way— they'll just stop and stare for no reason one time, then walk right by someone in trouble the next. Jessie had never noticed that before. Daddy was pretty smart.

The drive was really long (ALL DAY) and she began to feel sleepy by lunchtime. Mommy and Daddy talked for a while, then they played the color game with her, and finally they turned on the radio and everyone was quiet. She looked out the window at the trees and houses, but the sky was cloudy and the road was so straight and long that her eyelids began to feel heavy as she watched the bit of rain roll in little drops across her sight.

She had just begun to dream about Johnny wearing her Care Bears jacket (give it back, she said, but he just shook his furry head) when all of the sudden she felt that jump in her heart again like she did on her third birthday when Gramma leaned over her, breathing cranberry and ginger. She fought against the dark that coated the inside of her head and then she was wide awake, staring, her heart pumping and her mind spinning and she was really SCARED, scared for no reason at all but just that she felt empty, black inside. She had opened her mouth to scream, and then choked it back; all that came out was a cough. And then all at once it filled her mind, overpowering her, like someone had snapped on a light. *Oh my God it's Johnny Bear, Johnny Bear and he doesn't have a HEAD* and then it was gone, just like that, and everything was okay again. She heard the scrape of the windshield wipers, and the hum of the motor, and the little drops of rain still rolled along her window, frosting the inside of the glass.

Mommy looked back at her then (Jessica, are you all right? You look pale, sweetie, what is it?) and she had forced herself to smile and say she was hungry. Sometimes, when she told her parents about herself and her feelings, they acted real funny, and once she had heard them talking about taking her to see a doctor. Now they were so happy, she didn't want them to be upset about her. So she kept quiet, and actually began to feel a little better by the time they pulled into Burger King for lunch. But something remained, a fear deep inside where she couldn't hide from it, no matter how hard she tried. What she had seen was real, that was what scared her the most. It hadn't been a dream, or at least she didn't think so. No, she was positive she was awake when it had come.

She made sure to take Johnny in with them to lunch, and put him in his own chair right next to her.

After lunch, the slight rain that had fallen since they left the house had changed to flurries, dusting the trees and roofs of houses along the highway. They had decided to take the long, scenic route to interstate 90 and finally up 95 through Maine. It would take them almost twice as long as the direct route near Montreal to Quebec City, but it was worth it. Neither of them had seen that part of New England before.

They were going over the Catskills in New York now, really more like hills than mountains in this part of the country with their long, rolling sides pushing out like the stomachs of pregnant beasts, and the tops blunt and weathered with age. And the snow continued. Helen thought it was one of the most beautiful things she had ever seen; something so cold and yet so full of life. There had been snow in Rochester, of course, but it was of such an utterly different kind she almost didn't recognize it. Their snow in the suburbs had been wet and heavy and often dirty, the kind of slush found in city gutters. It was all the same to her, noisy and crowded. She had grown up in the New York countryside with the cornfields and farms and had never felt comfortable among large groups of people. It had been the same with her father. He was a hard man, but as shy and awkward in social situations as he was strong and sure of himself in the fields. Yet he was given to moments of extraordinary gentleness and kindness when the mood touched him, especially with her. She had been his favorite.

She remembered a particular day late during her eighth summer. The harvests were short that year and money was tighter than it had ever been, and yet she remembered her father promising her that day that he would take her into town when the harvest was over. That evening, he came for her out of the corn he had been cutting, out of the yellow against the orange sky. Going into town was a big deal then, and this time, though she was sure his feet had ached and his back had stiffened up like a board, he had gotten into his best clothes and taken her to the store for a soda as he had promised. She had felt like a real lady, sitting up there in the front seat of the old Packard with her father on the way home. He had died in 1992, older than his years, the land spent and the cows gone, but she liked to remember him as he was that day, sitting up straight behind the wheel.

As for her own family life, things were looking up now that David had found a job. It was funny, she thought, how quickly things changed. Just a few days ago she had felt like her marriage was being sucked down a giant, spiraling drain, squeezed like a sponge until there was nothing left but a dry carcass. She had gotten another migraine; they had been coming faster lately. After their little fight, she had felt like crying, just burrowing deeper under the covers in the dark bedroom until she found a space away from all the frustrations that were staring her down. And then the phone rang, and in spite of herself she felt that little spark of hope deep in her belly. It had grown hotter when she heard David's voice, and blossomed into a true feeling of relief and joy when she realized that finally, finally it was over. No more cutting coupons. No more pressing that little sliver of leftover soap into the new bar to save a penny. No more worrying about money. His new salary would be more than enough to make them comfortable.

She remembered meeting David at a luncheon for financial aid recipients at college. Tall and good-looking, with light brown hair and a strong jaw, he had seemed so at ease among the heavyweights of the school, talking and joking, always ready with the right thing to say about grades or future plans or anything asked of him. She herself had no idea what she was going to do with her life, and did not at that point particularly care. Her grades were average, his were perfect; her social skills as inadequate as her father's, his impeccable. So she was taken completely by surprise when he asked her out on the bus ride home that night. They had gotten along wonderfully together right from the start, and by the end of the year she found herself accepting his proposal of marriage with an almost eerie feeling of unreality. If this were a fairy tale or a dream, she never wanted to wake up. They had a few fights as everyone does, but nothing ever came of them. Her friends loved him; there were no problems, and their life together began with no regrets. "Some people have all the luck," her best friend and maid of honor had said, not without envy. And Helen had finally believed it was true when Jessica was born.

But as she got older, things weren't always right with Jessie. She was stubborn and obsessive, and sometimes the way she knew certain things was just a little bit scary. It put a lot of stress on their marriage. And then David had lost his job. Things had started unraveling, slowly at first, then faster as the money ran out. She tried not to blame him because it wasn't his fault, not really. Still, it was his decision to quit, and the only thing she could really blame him for (though even that was unfair, wasn't it?); he could have swallowed his pride and continued on. They would have kept him. *But it was the right thing to do*, she reminded herself. *At least it seemed to be at the time.*

She realized that she still loved him. There had never been much doubt about that, but it was good to actually think it again. He still sent shivers down her back, and she got goose bumps at his touch. And he was a wonderful father. Jessie's problems had only caused him to heap more attention on her. Helen teased him about worrying that he was not good enough with her, but it really wasn't true. They were buddies from the start. And in the six months since he had been out of work, they had become even closer.

Her thoughts turned to her daughter, and she felt the familiar pangs of worry deep down in her belly. She had trouble remembering the exact time she began to wonder about her little girl. It was disconcerting to say the least. Usually she could pinpoint specifically when something began, and file it away in the deeper recesses of her brain, locked up for future reference. But when Jessie's strange premonitions began, she couldn't recall. The first few times she had dismissed them as coincidence. What they had here was an unusually bright child, nothing more. And that made sense. Jessie had shown remarkable ability to mimic and learn from others, almost from the moment she was born.

But gradually she began to realize that Jessie was not just a bright little girl, and suddenly that awareness had become unsettling, almost frightening. Once, when Jessie was less than two years old, she had been bouncing off the walls all day, saying "bike, bike" so loudly and so excitedly Helen had wondered how she didn't hurt herself. Sure enough, by suppertime David had shown up with a brand-new plastic tricycle, and while Jessie was trying to pedal the thing around the living room, her little legs hardly reaching the pedals, Helen had sat on the couch and wondered how she possibly knew it was coming. She asked David, but he swore it had been a total surprise even to himself, buying it on a whim when he saw it at the mall that day.

Perhaps even then, she thought, she had dismissed it as coincidence because the alternative was so utterly alien and unsettling to her that it was almost unthinkable. No, it was infinitely easier both as a human being and as a mother to ignore this, even when it was shoved rudely into her face to some extent every day. So she did: at Jessie's third birthday party, when her daughter told her that her grandparents were dropping by to surprise her, and they showed up two minutes later holding balloons; when Jessie had told her that Mommy's friend was angry with her because she had forgotten something, and two hours later she realized that she *had*—she had forgotten a school board meeting that started *five minutes ago*. These things would terrify her if she let them, but she refused with stoic persistence, beating back the incessant clamor and urgent whisperings of her conscience. She tried to dismiss it altogether at first, then later decided Jessie was picking up the stress in the house now that David was out of work, and her feelings had begun to surface in the form of these dreams.

She and David *had* talked about it, even before he had lost his job. It was one of the reasons they had decided it was better for her to stay home for a while after Jessie was born, longer than the three months of maternity leave she had planned to take. Even before Jessie could speak, they had noticed things about her. She was moody. She cried in her sleep, more than they thought was normal. She didn't like the feel of cloth on her skin, or unfamiliar textures of food in her mouth. She drew intricate patterns and shapes long before it was developmentally appropriate for her to do so. She wouldn't go to bed unless a very specific routine was followed to the letter. More than once they had talked about taking her to see someone. David argued (and she didn't really try to refute it) that Jessie was just an unusually bright child, and bringing her to a doctor would only frighten her and make the whole thing much worse. She seemed to be better when her mother was near her, and they had finally agreed to extend Helen's leave from work even longer, and that year had turned into two until suddenly she felt so out of touch that she couldn't have gone back to work if she wanted to, at least not to the same school where she had worked as an assistant guidance counselor. She hardly knew the kids there anymore, and starting over seemed like a mountain she was unable to climb. Jessie needed her at home, and so she stayed. Actually, she preferred it that way, at least until money had gotten so scarce they were about a week away from food stamps.

Slowly Jessie gravitated towards her father. David didn't notice it, but she did all the same. He was the one she would come running to when she skinned a knee, or when she wanted to stay up late. Helen supposed it was only natural, since Jessie saw her as the "boss lady," not so much as an ally.

But now, on the highway, with her husband holding onto her hand beside her, lightly squeezing, with her little girl asleep in the backseat, she was able to relax a little. The new job made everything easier. Already things seemed back to normal, as good as they used to be.

And now maybe, just maybe, this new place and new life will stop Jessie's nightmares. Then we can all settle in and truly start down a different path.

They pulled into the parking lot of the motel near Portland, Maine, at about nine thirty that night, a little over halfway through their trip. While Jessie helped

Helen check in, David busied himself with getting the bags onto the snow-covered walkway, and with thoughts of the work ahead of him trying to help clean up the mess that the last guy had left at the plant. He and Helen had decided that the best thing for them to do was spend the night in Maine, hit Quebec tomorrow and sleep in the hotel there until they got the housing situation under control. Olmstead had made a reservation for them at the Château Frontenac, a hotel that in his words was "very impressive." Any and all fees would, of course, be taken care of by the company. Someone named Hank (with an almost unintelligible Down East accent) had called just before they left, said he had been contacted by Hydro Development and that he had some information on a "place to settle down in" that was only about three miles from the hydro plant and had just been vacated. "Lucky for you too," he'd said. "There ain't many houses 'round that area." David didn't doubt that was true, but he wasn't sure that made them so lucky. *Not that there are any dentists within a hundred miles.* Somehow, the idea of leaving a suburban neighborhood near Rochester and moving to the great outdoors was more than a little frightening. But without a job, they weren't going to be able to afford suburbia anyway. They would get a little money when the house sold, but there were bills to pay already. So here they were.

After the bags were on the walk, and Jessie and Helen still had not returned, he decided to wander around a bit. The motel was your classic Motel Six setup. Not much of a place for a vacation. *And we're still three hundred miles from the hydro plant*, he thought grimly, *at least by road*. Of course, the last part of the drive been at night, so they hadn't seen much of the country. If it was as beautiful as Mike Olmstead had claimed, perhaps it was worth the isolation. At least his first meeting was being held near Quebec City, which was over two hours away from the plant according to Olmstead, but much more populated, of course. Evidently there wasn't a motel anywhere near Jackson. There wasn't even a general store; the closest to Jackson was at least five miles away in St. Boudin.

A dim, yellow bulb lit the outside door to each room, and David peered at the numbers as he strolled down the walk. The markings had been burned into the wood, and were faded and cracked with age. *Creepy*, he thought, turning up his collar against the cold. *It's like the Bates Motel out here.* The snow crunched beneath his shoes, and as he neared the end of the short walkway, he had a feeling he could just keep on walking, right off the end of the world, into the darkness beyond. *That's why they call it the great outdoors*, he thought, turning back towards the comforting, familiar image of the car. *No end in sight.*

He was still standing there when Jessie came running out of the office, yelling, "Daddy, Daddy!" at the top of her little lungs.

"She found the gumball machine," Helen explained, laughing.

"Can I have a piece of gum, Daddy?" Jessie looked up at him with her big, brown eyes and suddenly David could almost hear her thoughts. *I know what you're gonna say Daddy you're gonna say yes* and then he was saying it.

"Sure, honey. Go bug your momma for the money."

She ran over to Helen, and David was left with that peculiar feeling. *But of course she knew I'd say yes, why wouldn't I?* It was the end of the day's drive, after all, and he almost always got her something at the end of long trips. *Stop being so goddamned jumpy.*

They had checked into a small room with two twin beds, and an even smaller bathroom that harbored a yellow washbasin and a tub with a deep copper rust stain under the faucet. A half hour later they were more or less settled in for the night, and Jessie was in the bathtub.

"How long will we be living out of hotels, do you think?" Helen asked. She was unpacking her pretty blue robe, her back turned to him.

"I don't have a clue. I'm going to look at the house as soon as we get there, so maybe we can move in after a couple of days." David sat at the motel room desk, an old, shaky-looking thing. The summary file and the application for license for the Jackson Pumped Storage Project sat on the desktop in front of him, weighty and intimidating. He had picked them up that morning from a secretary in Olmstead's office.

Helen found the robe and snapped the suitcase shut. "I'd like to see the house too."

"I know, honey, but it's in the opposite direction from this damn meeting, and I've got no idea when that'll end. You don't want to sit around the lobby with Jessie for three hours. I'll tell you every detail about the place, okay? And you'll see it in a few days. You can decide if you like it then."

"You going through that whole thing tonight?" Helen asked, walking over behind him and lightly kneading his shoulders. He let himself relax under her touch.

"Most of it, or I won't know what the hell I'm talking about when I get there." He closed his eyes. He could feel the knots in his shoulders loosen, the tension of the day disappearing.

"Maybe later after Jessie falls asleep . . ." She pressed harder.

"You're kidding, right? I didn't think she ever slept."

"Well, I've heard that most four-year-olds are supposed to, sometime. Actually, she did sleep in the car on the way up. I guess that's not such a good sign for later."

"No, I wouldn't think so. A recharge like that should last for days." He stood and grasped her around the waist, pulling her to him. "As for now—"

Then Jessie was yelling something about soap in her eyes, and Helen gave him a quick peck on the cheek, raised her hands in defeat, and disappeared into the bathroom. He sat back down, a warm, tight feeling in his chest. It had been a long time since they were this close, this happy. It was hard to believe how fast and how easily it had happened.

He turned his attention to the file. The morning after next he was supposed to begin by attending the meeting at the branch office in Quebec City with the Federal Energy Regulatory Commission and the Canadian environmental board. He could only guess that they had some serious questions about why the project had to shut down in the middle of the biggest, dirtiest and potentially most harmful part of construction. Their job was to make sure everything went smoothly, that no part of the environment or the people in it were in danger, and that there was nothing illegal going on. Without the FERC, developers could do pretty much anything they wanted. It was good to have them around in many cases.

But sometimes, they could be a royal pain in the ass.

The file in front of him was well over an inch thick; it looked like an all-night job. As he listened to his wife and daughter splash happily in the bathtub, he flipped through the mass of papers, beginning with the executive summary for the project. Here he found a project description, and began reading. *The proposed power plant consists of the following major sections: Lower reservoir, constructed using the existing and abandoned Jackson copper mines, with extensive renovations and structural improvements . . . upper reservoir, currently containing approximately 70 acres of woodland, surrounded by a man-made earth bowl . . . power tunnel running for an approximate distance of 2,500 feet and 200 feet below the surface . . . powerhouse facilities, located below the entrance to the original mine, containing four 250-MW turbines . . .*

When he got to the small paragraph on the project's financing, he could hardly believe his eyes. *A construction cost estimate has been prepared in accordance with FERC requirements,* it read. *Total cost is estimated at $1,000,000,000, including purchase of land and mining rights.*

That was a hell of a lot of zeros.

Of course, he thought. *You've been around this stuff before, you know how much it costs.* But even knowing ballpark figures, the final sum was more than a little terrifying.

From the correspondence file, he pieced together what had happened to the access roads. The only original roads to the spot were the old dirt path previously used for the mines, which had not been kept up since they ceased operation, and a logging track running nearby, which was wider and in slightly better shape. They ended up cleaning and using the logging track, since updating the old path would take greater effort. He wondered how they had gotten around the permits regarding proper access. The engineer had probably been working towards a deadline, and bet on being able to use the logging track almost immediately, and so he worked around it somehow. He was probably right, but when the first heavy storm blew in, the track became impassable, and they got into trouble. Still, it would take an awful lot of work (and money, he figured) to get around those permits.

Right now, the most important thing seemed to be satisfying the FERC that the plant would continue to comply with their regulations regarding environmental concerns. According to the correspondence in July and August, there was a significant amount of sludge coming downriver from the construction by the end of the summer, and the FERC was also probably worried about the work that was to be done to get the road into shape. They had to comply with regulations in the license and environmental permits anyway, or they'd lose the project.

"Daddy, will you read me the story about the magic bone before I go to bed?" David looked up and his daughter stood before him, her dark brown hair still dripping from the bath. Helen appeared behind her in the navy blue robe, toweling her own hair.

"Don't you know that one by now, honey? We've read it every night for the past three days."

"But it's good, Daddy, and I can follow the pages," she said, obviously proud of her new ability.

"Come on, Daddy," Helen said. "You promised."

David took one last look at the summary file, and then dropped it onto the table. Hydro Development and the FERC would have to wait just a little bit longer.

CHAPTER FOUR

Jonathan Newman stood six-foot-five and his shoulders were broad and heavy, with a thick frame to support a slightly bulging stomach. He was one of those men that, though tipping the scales at just under two hundred and sixty pounds, would not be considered obese; the weight was distributed nicely, if a little generously, on his large bone structure. He looked like a linebacker on a football team.

He might have been more comfortable among groups of people, except for his mouth and cheeks. His upper lip curled towards his nose in the middle and ended in something like a harelip, which had been clumsily corrected when he was in his early teens. His lips and cheeks were lined with thin, white scars made long ago by a sharp instrument. Together these things frightened most people away at first sight, and made Jonathan a shy man in social settings. He was not, and never had been, a social man.

He had gone to the Vietnam War in his twenties, and that experience had triggered the onset of a serious mental disease. He had been in and out of institutions for most of his adult life, and had met many doctors who did nothing more than shut him away by himself and promptly forget about him until cutbacks in government spending forced a scourge of the mental institutions and he was set free. This had happened many times, for though Jonathan was troubled and mentally disturbed, he was not dangerous. His problems were those of perception more than anything else. If the time was taken to get past the physical outside of the man, he was a fascinating subject, and occasionally he ran into a doctor who tried to treat him instead of lock him away.

His last doctor had tried more than anyone else ever had. His life had been dominated by disordered thoughts and feelings, causing him to withdraw inside himself for protection. She tried to pull him out and unravel the cocoon.

He ended up in this particular hospital after several weeks on the streets of Boston, during which he lived on park benches along the Common and anywhere else he could find an empty spot. He had become convinced over a period of several months that the police who roamed the streets in their dark blue cars were actually after him, and that if he tried hard enough, perhaps with a sharp blade or other instrument, he could scrape the stenciling off of the vehicles' doors and underneath the words "crime enforcement" the words "people enforcement" would be clearly visible. So he tried to keep out of sight during the day. He never tried to hurt anyone, but frightened many people not expecting to encounter such a large and gruesome figure on their early evening walks.

Finally, there were just too many complaints for even the police to ignore, and after they became convinced that jail was not the place for Jonathan Newman (and it wasn't; he would die there just as surely as if he had been sent to the electric chair), they sent him once again to the hospital. So in the end, his delusions became a self-fulfilling prophecy—one gray blustery day in November the men in uniform *did* arrive to take him away, and he was placed a little roughly in the back of one of those dark blue cars he worried so much about. This did nothing to help his growing number of problems.

Once a day he met with the beautiful doctor in a small, tastefully decorated room with a couch and two chairs, and even a hanging plant in one corner. It's an experiment, she told him once. The people who run this place want to see how patients react to a soothing environment. This was one of the reasons he began to trust her. She made him feel like they were conspirators, together against the enemies outside that threatened him every day. He started to talk to her more freely as the visits grew longer.

"You have reacted," she explained to him in one of their sessions, "in a perfectly normal way to stress. We all develop defenses against threats in life, whether they are real or imaginary. Some people just lose sight of where they began. Think about a boy who is being chased by a dog. He runs away. Wouldn't you? That's perfectly normal, the right thing to do. But what if, later down the road, his father buys him a dog for a present, a cute little puppy. The problem is, the boy can't go near it, because he's too scared that the puppy will bite him. Now, he has a problem. But where did the problem begin? In a perfectly normal reaction to a frightening situation."

He listened to her carefully. She was intelligent, and she cared about him too. He wanted to make her happy.

"You might think that it's no big deal. Just get rid of the dog. But what if it's something more serious? What if later on the boy falls in love with a dog trainer and he can't even get near dogs? What if you say that the dog that chased him was not a dog at all, but a man? Now the boy is afraid of all men. When he grows up he can't work with others, he has trouble meeting new people. Now, you have a real problem."

He nodded. This was true; he understood it all.

"Something has happened to you, Jonathan, that has made you so afraid. Besides the war. That's part of it, but not all, am I right? What is it?"

But he was not ready to tell her that. He was not even aware of it himself anymore. He was an orphan, he knew, but beyond that his past was gone, the causes of his disease lost within the complexity of the defense mechanism they had triggered.

The thing that was always on his mind was the war. He had been sent to Vietnam towards the end of the conflict, had somehow managed to get past the medical board and into combat at a time when his illness was mild enough to be overlooked. In fact, in those days nobody knew about the suspicious bend in Jonathan Newman's personality because it had yet to surface. But it was there, all the same. And the war brought it out. He had wanted to go to war, had waited eagerly for combat, perhaps because in war (and in death?) he would be offered the chance to escape these ever-increasing voices in his head, these thoughts that troubled him a little more every day.

He was the perfect candidate for combat syndrome, and once he was under fire and among the bodies of the dead, he experienced a complete mental breakdown, which prompted the first of his extensive hospital stays. During the few weeks he had spent in Vietnam, he had slowly come to realize that the real problem was with the government of the United States. They were the ones who sent him there to die. Since then, his suspicions rested mostly with people in authority (like his fears of the "people enforcing" police), and he saw them as the enemy.

He and the doctor discussed all that. She helped him fill in the blanks as gently as she could, had done more than any other doctor had been able to do. She seemed encouraged by these stories and his reactions to them, and promised him that they were getting to the bottom of his problem. But they weren't, not really. She may have been fooled for a while, but it didn't take long for her to realize this was not the root of his sickness, only a symptom. There were other, perhaps more disturbing, things that lurked in his subconscious. He had felt the paranoia inside him long before Vietnam. Soon, she was asking him that question again (*And you, Jonathan. What has happened to make you so afraid?*), but he couldn't answer her. He just didn't know.

This lasted a year. By the end of it, he was talking more freely to her than he ever had to anyone in his life, discussing the world outside the hospital, his fear of people watching him wherever he went. His delusions about the government continued to haunt him, and he was convinced that the men in power were taking bribes from gangsters and drug dealers and that they all were aware that he knew what was going on, and wanted to "keep him quiet." Delusions of persecution, the doctor called it. A form of paranoia. Understanding the problem was the first step towards treating it, she said.

Finally, it all ended. She came to one of their sessions visibly upset, and he asked her what was wrong. Cutbacks, she said. The board has ordered all nonviolent patients into release programs.

He didn't know how to react. The thought of being back outside was as exciting as it was frightening. She had helped him a great deal, and he felt more confident than ever before. But he would miss her terribly.

"There is good news," she said, sitting him down. "We have been contacted by a group looking for a man like you. They want to give you a job. This one is special, like you. There won't be many people around, so you don't have to be scared of anyone. It's perfect, really. You're much better. I'm very happy with how well you're doing. I'll want you to check in with me by phone, and come in when it's over. It will last for a few months, and then after that we can talk again and see how things went. Would you like that?"

He thought about it, and nodded. He was ready.

She smiled, and stood up. "I'd wish you luck, but you won't need it. You're going to do great."

There was one thing he hadn't told her, though he wasn't sure why. During his time inside, he had watched a lot of television. There wasn't much else to do. The hospital paid for cable and set up a room with a TV and lots of chairs where the nonviolent patients could spend their time. It kept them out of trouble, and was a relatively cheap babysitter. Jonathan became fascinated by The Learning Channel and watched the documentaries on ancient civilizations with interest. He really was a fast learner, especially when the learning interested him. There was one in particular he admired and focused on, watching the program whenever it was broadcast. Finally, he had it taped by one of the staff so he could watch it whenever he wanted. It was called *The Secrets of The Mochai*, and it dealt with a sixth-century civilization that existed on the north coast of Peru. It was a violent and simple culture, but a beautiful one, filled with paintings and murals of colorful people. The program showed ancient burial plots and giant mud-brick temples pitted with grave robbers' holes.

He became fascinated by the culture. It was filled with worship and religion, gods and demigods. He began to look forward to the part of the show where they described "the decapitator," a demigod that was part spider, part man, and played the role of the sacrificer in the priests' ceremonies. The paintings of the creature were so beautiful. There was a certain painting he liked, only partially preserved. It showed a huge being with long, black arms holding a knife covered in blood in one hand, and a severed head in the other, grotesque but somehow so alive. He wondered if it were real. He wondered how the prisoners felt, lining up to meet the decapitator. He wondered how the knife felt touching their necks.

When he left the hospital, he missed two things, the doctor and the documentary about the Mochai. He could call the doctor, but there was no television. His job left him lonely and often afraid. Perhaps this wasn't the perfect place for him, as the doctor had thought. Perhaps he would be better back in the hospital.

As he worked in that cold, lonely place, something began working at his mind, digging its fingers into his skull. He could feel it, digging, digging. He didn't know what the thing was, but it made him more frightened than he had ever been. It seemed to him that someone was watching, spying on him. He stopped calling the doctor because they were listening. He kept most of the lights turned off so they wouldn't see him. He stayed away from the windows, and only went out when it was absolutely necessary, to get firewood or check the machine.

The fear of being watched got worse as the days went by. It had never been this bad. He was neglecting his duties, but he no longer cared. The thing working at his mind felt like a giant spider digging itself into his skull. He began to feel that only the decapitator could protect him from those prying eyes.

Not long after that he began to see shapes. Vague dancing dots of color at first, then geometric figures with vivid color; tunnels that spun and twisted in the air, dizzying combinations of pulsing reds and blues. The tunnels would convulse and turn into a giant spiderweb in the sky like a sign from God, and then he would see a checkerboard pattern covering the trees, the snow, buildings. He wept openly in awe.

His awe turned to fear as the images changed. The days went by and the brilliant patterns began to hide creatures in the mist of color, terrible things that watched him with giant saucer eyes like black holes. Dark Eyes, he called them. They watched him day and night, hunting him like an animal. Now he knew these feelings were no longer in his head, because he could *see* them, could see the disembodied eyes peering at him through the blackness. And through the fear he felt a strange sense of validation and euphoria because he hadn't been crazy after all; he had been right all along. They were out there, and they wanted him.

He hardly slept, and when he did his dreams were filled with the eyes of these creatures. He planned ways to get rid of them forever.

And dreamed of the Mochai, and the decapitator.

CHAPTER FIVE

The St. Lawrence is perhaps the most important water-way in Canada, and it is on this river's edge that Quebec City was born. The city stands as a testament to another time, enclosed by thick stone walls and crossed by steep, thin streets running down to the water. The houses are old and majestic in some spots, crumbling in others. Holes meant for battle guns dot the top of the old wall, and here and there a cannon still occupies one of them, waiting patiently for a battle that never comes.

The Pierces arrived outside the city just before dusk, when the sun was low in the western sky and the city walls were bathed in orange and red. It couldn't have been more beautiful. Spring was not due to begin in Eastern Canada for another month, at least, and close to a foot of snow still layered the frozen ground. Their little Toyota's heater was going full blast. They were tired, but relaxed. Customs had been a simple process of questions and answers. They were allowed to bring in personal belongings, and after a cursory check of the U-Haul, their passports and an explanation from David, the border patrol let them through.

Jessie was asleep in the backseat when they arrived at the Château Frontenac atop Cap Diamant, poised above the narrow streets of the city. It was an imposing old castle with high turrets and a drive that swept up the stone and brick to the entryway and circular courtyard out front. David pulled up near the doors, where a tall young man with a shock of curly reddish hair and a sharp-looking uniform was waiting patiently. Across the wide, flat stretch of Dufferin Terrace was the wall, and below that, the lower city and the river. They got out of the car and walked slowly across the terrace, past the giant statue of Champlain on their left, to look at the view.

"God, it's gorgeous," Helen whispered. The old buildings were clearly visible from here with their dusting of snow, and the long, thin streets that divided them split the city into parts of a complex and varied whole. They stood close together at the edge of the wall, their breath rising and mingling in clouds of white steam. Behind and to their right perched the Citadelle, in the light of the sinking sun, a fortress complete with parapets, bastions and cold, gray stone.

"Mommy, are we staying with Cinderella?" Jessie had gotten herself out of the car and stood next to them, tugging at Helen's sleeve.

"No, honey." She laughed, a high, girlish giggle. *She's happy*, David thought. He hardly recognized the sound.

"It sure looks like Cinderella's castle, doesn't it?" He leaned down and scooped Jessie up. "Let's go see who's inside."

The tall, young man in uniform had returned from parking the car, and held two of their overnight bags from the backseat in his hands. He set them down on the front steps to open the doors to the hotel, and Helen smiled warmly at him and walked through like a queen.

David followed her into the large hall, and promptly stopped short at the sight. The floors were richly carpeted, the walls a pinkish stone and layered with paintings in heavy frames. The ceiling curved away above them, dotted with several heavy-looking chandeliers, bringing the eye with it down to the far end where the elevators waited to carry guests into the heart of the old hotel.

Jessie was squirming in his arms. He put her down, and she ran immediately over to one of the bellboys who now held Johnny Bear in one hand and a suitcase in the other. Once she had retrieved the bear, Jessie smiled at the boy and promptly stuck a thumb in her mouth. David wandered over to the desk, which sat unobtrusively against the wall to his left, next to a set of double doors that he assumed led into the restaurant. There was a short man in uniform behind the desk and an old, gray-haired gentleman standing next to it, his manicured hands placed neatly on the counter.

"American?" the older man asked as David approached. The voice held a slight tinge of accent, though it was perfect English. David introduced himself.

"Welcome to the Château Frontenac. We are expecting you. I hope you will enjoy your stay. My name is Mr. Poisson. If there is anything I could do to make your stay a more pleasant one, please let me know." The man waited a moment, bowed slightly, and disappeared through the double doors.

How much do you have to shell out for this? David thought, and grinned a little. Whatever it was, he wouldn't be paying for it, and that was fine with him.

He turned to the man behind the desk, who had been waiting patiently, and signed the register.

"Please follow me," the bellboy said, after they had checked in. "I'll show you your rooms."

Rooms?

They crossed the lobby and entered the elevators. In a few seconds the doors opened on the third floor. "Champlain founded Quebec City in the 1600s," the bellboy said, "and the Château Frontenac was born out of the womb of his great fortress. In fact, he built on this very cliff. The Frontenac was built in 1892 for one of the greatest of the governors, and has had an extensive and colorful history."

They followed him down the narrow hallway, their footsteps muffled by the carpet. Jessie kept quiet by her mother's side, cowed with the respect commanded by such an awesome structure. David himself felt a similar urge to speak in whispers, in order to not offend the ghosts.

"Presidents have stayed here, many times. Kings and queens. Royalty of all sorts." The bellboy had stopped in front of room 218. "Here we are."

He slipped a key in the lock and swung open the heavy door, and David slipped him a tip. "If you need anything, please, the desk extension is double zero. Mr. Poisson will be glad to help you." With that, the bellboy was gone.

The rooms were breathtaking. The door opened to a sitting room as elegant as the one downstairs, with old polished chairs and thick carpeting. A door on the left led to a little bath with antique fixtures and tiny tiles, and through a door on the right he could see one of the bedrooms, lit with a soft light. There was another, smaller one next to it, where he could see a single bed with similar coverings.

"Pretty impressive," he remarked, though "impressive" didn't seem to do justice to the place.

"Yes." Helen's eyes flashed. She had walked over to a small window set into the far wall. "Look at this view."

He went over to her and saw the city from above in the deepening twilight. The snow sparkled in flashes of blue here and there from rooftops, and the lights were on now in most of the houses below them. Beyond Lower Town was the river, its center a broken line of black water surrounded by giant chunks of ice, vague shapes in the dark.

"Romantic, isn't it?" Her arms encircled his waist, and he felt the familiar pressure. She was as pretty as he remembered her in college, golden shoulder-length hair, dark eyes, smooth skin. She kissed him.

"This is how we got the first one, remember?" he said, pointing at Jessie, who had come out of the bathroom now and was disappearing into the smaller bedroom.

"I'd like another."

He looked at her, surprised. They had always talked about having two children eventually, but this last year had put that plan on hold. He wondered if she really meant it now, so soon. Only days ago he had been unemployed and the future had been slipping away. He remembered being in the hospital with her when Jessie was born, and how helpless he had felt just standing there doing those goddamned breathing exercises like they really did something and weren't just a quick and easy way to hyperventilate. When the head finally appeared and Helen squeezed his hand like a vice grip, he felt almost as if he were being born again, that somehow this life was going to help him do the things he missed from his childhood all over again. Only this time would be better because he would be there to make sure it came out all right.

What the hell, he decided. She was even more beautiful than in college.

"Well?"

"Let's start practicing," he said.

CHAPTER SIX

February 23rd dawned cold and crisp, but by nine o'clock the sun was shining brightly down on Quebec City as if determined to take on the thick layer of snow blanketing the town and break down the slush that sucked and pulled at the feet of the pedestrians on the street. David awoke feeling better than he had in weeks. His wife lay naked in his arms, the sheets slipped over her thighs as she slept.

He managed to extract himself from Helen's grasp and made his way to the window. The icebreakers were at work on the river in the brilliant morning sun, the huge boats using their prows to break the sheet of ice that had formed the night before. He remembered hearing about what could happen if the ice were allowed to build up, and shivered. The destructive power of the river was unnerving. Quebec had lost several bridges and many more lives to the ice and flooding over the years.

He turned from the window to find his jacket and tie and hit the shower.

By eleven o'clock he was walking up the steps towards the Quebec City offices of Hydro Development. It had been about an hour drive, first along the narrow streets, among the heavy traffic, and then through in a less-populated area to the office, which was located in a business center outside the city. Helen and Jessie were out sightseeing; he had left them talking animatedly to Mr. Poisson at the front desk about who and what to see.

The building welcomed him with a warm blast of air, prickling his skin and drying the little beads of nervous sweat that had formed on his forehead. A pretty, young woman ran by carrying a stack of papers, while other men and women in business suits walked past looking purposeful and sure of themselves. The area with all the activity seemed to be roughly the size of a city block. He straightened his tie and studied the best way to weave through the traffic, aware that the huge gold clock on the wall above him pointed to just past eleven.

He fought his way to the elevator and got off on the third floor. The hallways were thickly carpeted and the walls paneled with a rich, chocolate wood, which deadened any sound. He felt as if he were being swallowed whole. He found room 313 without any trouble, tried a quick knock, got no answer, and turned the knob.

He heard raised voices, but all conversation stopped as soon as he entered. There was an uncomfortable silence that lasted for a few seconds, then a white-haired man at the head of the table stood up, leaning his hands upon the tabletop for support.

"You must be David Pierce." This was said with a clipped, prep school accent, and David could only think *oh, shit* before he was told, "You're late."

"Sorry," he said. "I'm still finding my way around the city. And you are?"

"Peter Thompson, head of Hydro Development's engineering division here in Quebec City." He pointed to a worried little man in a rumpled suit on his other side.

"This is my associate, Ronald Stevens. And these"—he swept his arm towards the three men and a woman across from him—"are representatives from the FERC and the Canadian Government. The man in blue is Dan Flint from the FERC—" (the man at the far end of the table raised his hand in greeting) "—and he'll be reporting all of our discussions to the Commission. They have many, many questions, and at least one interesting thing to say. I'm sure they'll be glad to enlighten you."

"I'm sorry," David said. He hadn't even had the chance to move from the doorway. "I thought this was just a meet and greet."

Flint glared at Thompson and then slid a folder across the tabletop without a word. David picked it up and read the title on the first page.

"Preliminary Findings on Abnormalities Sighted Among Native Fish Populations." His heart began to pound. "What the hell is this?"

"You tell us," Flint said. "It's your project."

"You think this is linked to Jackson Hydro?"

"We're damn well going to find out."

David flipped through the file, which included a confusing jumble of figures and chemical formulas. "I don't get it."

Flint took back the file. "A week ago some kid caught two smelt fish from under the ice of the St. John, about six miles down from the plant. Both had growths on their head and gills. He brought the fish home, and his mother showed them to the police, who contacted Environmental Protection."

"Why didn't anyone mention this before?"

"They've just told all of us today, Mr. Pierce," said Thompson. "Did you think they would come find you before anyone else? Maybe they think we love surprises. I'm sure we'd all appreciate some advance warning."

"Why, so you could be sure to cover your tracks?" Flint was steaming. "That plant is an environmental hazard. There are numerous violations going on up there. You think you can buy off the locals—"

"We aren't in the business of buying anyone off, Mr. Flint," Thompson said. "Frankly, I resent your tone."

"Excuse me," David said. "I don't mean to jump in here out of turn, but I studied the files on this project pretty carefully during the past few days, and other than the access road problems, everything looked in order. Have you all had the chance to review Hydro's records?"

"Actually, no," Flint said with a grim smile. "Your company hasn't exactly embraced the concept of full disclosure."

"Look, Mr. Thompson can tell you more than I can. But I'm sure the company would be willing to share any documentation you wish to review. Why shouldn't they? It's a hydroelectric power plant, not a military facility."

The four men looked at each other like a bunch of trained seals. "Well, Mr. Thompson?" Flint said. "How about it?"

Thompson looked like he'd swallowed something very distasteful. "There are privacy and competitive issues. But I'm sure we can provide you with what you need." Ronald Stevens remained silent; only a swiftly pulsing vein on his temple kept him from looking like a corpse. His skin was gray, his face chalky. David realized that he hadn't said a word the whole meeting, not even so much as hello. *How does it feel to be a 'yes' man, Mr. Stevens?*

He glanced at Thompson and felt an icy chill prickle the hairs of his neck. Thompson stared back at him, little expression in his cold, watery gray eyes, except perhaps the slightest hint of—what? Anger? *Hatred?* In the full glare of his hard, unfaltering gaze, David felt himself tighten, his own anger come to the surface. This man definitely did not like him, and at the moment, the feeling was mutual.

One of Flint's associates whispered in his ear. He nodded. "I appreciate your offer," he said. "As long as it's full access. FERC is a large organization, but it's not a blind one. Anything going on in that plant that violates federal code must end, period."

"At the moment, there's nothing going on at that plant at all," Thompson said. "Mr. Pierce here has been hired to help reevaluate the site, but until we have more information, all development has ceased."

"I'd like to see what you have at this point beyond the filed permits and public documents. I'd also like to set up a meeting with you at a later date, to review your plan of action."

"Fine. I'll have my secretary make some copies for you of anything relevant, and you can call my office next week."

"I guess that's it then." Flint offered his hand to Thompson over the table. "Let's keep this meeting short. We all have plenty to do."

David watched the four men carefully as they picked up their files and left the room, feeling pretty good about himself for helping diffuse a tense situation. But as soon as the door closed, Thompson stood up, Stevens bobbing from his chair beside him like a shadow.

"Mr. Pierce." Thompson was visibly shaking now. "You have been a part of this team for less than a week,

and are not in any sort of position to be making prom-
ises to the FERC. You have no idea what's going on.
I'm in control of this situation, not you."

"I'm sorry," David said as calmly as possible. "It didn't
look like you had things in control when I walked in."

Ouch. He winced as soon as the words were out of his
mouth, but it was too late to pull them back. *Way to go,
hotshot.*

Thompson's face went bright red. "We don't tolerate
insubordination here, Mr. Pierce. The next time you
speak out of turn, it'll be your job. Mr. Olmstead has
obviously neglected to tell you that I'm your superior,
and you are to check all of your decisions with me. As
for this meeting, you were supposed to be an advisor on
the lower reservoir construction, not our representa-
tive."

The room was silent for a long moment. David took
a deep breath. "I'm sorry," he said. "I think we've gotten off on the wrong foot here. I didn't mean to cause
trouble. I was just trying to help."

Thompson smiled, and it was as if he slipped on a
mask. His face lost its color, and the hatred that dominated his gaze retreated, hiding behind the hard, gray
coldness of his eyes. "This is a very serious problem for
the plant. From now on, let me do the talking."

I know it is, asshole, David thought, but kept it to himself. Thompson's sudden change kept him off balance.

"David Pierce?" The new voice came from an older
man in worn overalls, standing in the doorway. He
looked to be in his late fifties. His face was deeply
creased from long exposure to extreme weather; these
lines seemed to define his features, so that while his
eyes seemed to disappear when he smiled, still his face
took on a warm and friendly glow. He had a pronounced

Maine accent, so that "Pierce" became "Pee-yes," rolling off his tongue in a heavy drawl.

David found he liked him immediately.

"Did I interrupt somethin'?"

"No, Mr. Pierce was just leaving."

David stared at Thompson for a long moment, then turned his back on him and walked over to the man in the doorway.

"You must be Hank Babcock."

"Ayuh. Got my Jeep out front, if you're all set."

"Great." Without looking back, David left the room.

As the door closed behind them, Hank let out a low chuckle. "Tense in there?"

"Yes, it was." David slowly let his fists unclench as they walked down the hall. His footsteps were swallowed by the deep carpeting. *Like I wasn't even here*, he thought grimly. *Maybe that would be for the best.*

"Met that guy once last year when I was working for the state. He was looking to buy a hydro dam in Bangor. Never liked him much. Seemed tighter than a whore's dress. You know what I'm saying?"

David smiled. "I sure do."

"Anyways, if you don't mind I'll change the subject. Don't mind me, I do that a whole hell of a lot. Now, Mr. Olmstead called me up and told me when you was comin', and where to meet you. I don't know much else, but that could be just as well. I got a tendency to run at the mouth a little." Hank chuckled again. "We better take my Jeep. It gets a little rough out there."

They walked out the doors and into the cold air. Hank led him down the steps to an off-white, much-abused Jeep Cherokee. Its sides were spotted with brown rust.

"Palomino," David said.

"She's my baby," said Hank, slapping the side of the Jeep. A cloud of fine brown dust puffed out from under the fender. "She may not look like much, but she'll get through just about any weather. Climb on in." He yanked open the passenger door, and slid across to the driver's seat. "Driver side door sticks," he explained. "In cold like today I got to get in from this side."

David climbed up beside him and shut the door. Hank twisted the key, and with a sick grinding noise the engine turned over and roared to life. They pulled out onto the narrow street. There was no traffic, and as they passed out of sight around the corner, he risked one look back at the building. No one came running after them waving a pink slip. He relaxed a bit more, feeling the rush of adrenaline that had electrified him in the office fade. He was still angry, but now he felt as if his reason had returned for good. And with that came more than a little confusion. Why had he been invited to that meeting? Where was the rest of the engineering team? *One hell of an introduction. Way to break me in slow, let me learn the ropes.*

But there was more at stake here than his own comfort, he reminded himself—this job was not just for him, it was for his family. And, no sense in beating around the bush, it was for his future family. He and Helen had been on the edge of something very bad lately (exactly how bad he would rather not consider), but just last night they had been thinking about another child. It was better to let the problem with Thompson rest. There was no sense in getting caught up in a battle he couldn't win—and that was exactly what he would get with Peter Thompson. He was sure the inquiry from the FERC would turn out to be nothing to worry about.

* * *

Soon they were on the highway, flying across a bridge at what seemed like two hundred miles an hour. Hank sat with one hand balanced on the top of the wheel, weaving the old Cherokee drunkenly from the yellow line to the shoulder. As he looked out the window, David was greeted by a truly beautiful scene of deep-green woods and majestic hills topped with snow hovering in the distance. It was nature as he remembered from his childhood camping trips with his father and hadn't seen since; so thick and healthy you could smell it in the air. For the past twenty minutes he had been unable to take his eyes off those mountains.

"So where are you comin' from anyways?" Hank asked.

"New York."

"I live down towards Bath myself, in the summers. But up here there's more work for me in the winter. Usually I'm cutting trails for the towns 'round this area. Lots of business for me here; it's just about the only way to get places in the winter, by snowmobile, that is. Doesn't pay much, but I like it. Know my way 'round pretty well. Should, I grew up 'round here as a boy."

David smiled. Though he tended to hold things back about his personal life, Hank seemed determined to bare most of his. In some people, the trait would have been unsettling, or at the very least too dull. But with Hank it was all right.

"Bath's right around where the pogies come every summer. You don't want to be around then. Me, I don't mind it, been living there so long. They all get into the coves, see, in schools—I've seen pogie schools some three four miles long, or more, twenty feet deep. They come feed on the algae that grows on the bottom 'round there." Hank had fallen comfortably into his story-telling role now, the words flowing out in that slow Down East accent like molasses on a cold day.

"Vegetarians, they is. Then these schools of bluefish—they're predators, see, like piranha—they come in and tear into those pogies, rip 'em up into little bits. 'Course that sends the pogies into some craziness, and they thrash around until they use up all the oxygen in the water and suffocate. That's those the bluefish don't get. They sink to the bottom, then in a few days they start to rot." Hank looked over and grinned, continuing quite cheerfully. "Gases in their stomachs make 'em rise, see. 'Bout that time it's not a pretty sight around Bath. Stinks to high heaven for three weeks or more."

"How far are we from the house?" David decided to switch gears. It was fine to hear about Hank's personal life, but the pogie situation in Bath, Maine, was a little too much.

"Oh, about thirty miles." Hank glanced over at him. "You're just itchin' to see it, ain't you? Well hold on, we'll be there in a half hour. Sure hope they plowed that road for us."

"Plowed . . ."

"You're talking about a mile-long driveway out there. Sometimes it don't get plowed right away, and there's close to two feet of snow right now. Don't worry, though—I made sure Jimmy knows we're comin'. He'll have checked it out."

"I hope so, or this will be one hell of a long trip for nothing."

Hank continued as if he hadn't heard. "My cousin Darren lives around here—you know Darren? Naw, you wouldn't, 'course you wouldn't—he just up and quit school to be a lobsterman, just like that. Smart as a whip, he was, too, straight A's, two credits from being a certified public accountant. Well, he got a deal on a boat and some traps he couldn't pass up. 'Bout three weeks later, he threw a party down at his house on fourteen, and some guy shows up there he hardly knew. Little scrawny guy he was, you know, one of those." Hank stuck up his arm and let his hand hang loosely. "Kind of ladylike. Don't bother me much, but Darren, he don't like it. Anyways, Darren gets up for a minute and that guy steals his beer. Grabs it right off the table. Darren comes back, you know, steamin' mad. 'Give me my fuckin' beer,' he says. Guy says no. Darren tells him he's gonna hit him if he don't, and that fairy just sits there an' says, 'Go ahead.' I was right there, saw the whole thing. Anyways, so Darren just up and slaps him, backhand like. That guy doesn't say a word, just hands him the beer. Next afternoon, Darren's wife calls him at work. 'Hurry,' she says. 'Your boat's on fire.' Sure enough, that guy had gone down and torched it with five gallons of gasoline." Hank grinned. "Well, they got him for arson, and Darren got as much money for his traps as he'd paid for the boat, plus insurance money. He quit lobstering for good and went into law enforcement. Darren's lucky that way. Smart as a whip."

David struggled to keep from laughing, then decided it was okay and gave in to the urge. Hank grinned and didn't seem too offended. When he'd wiped his eyes a little (Damn if that story didn't help him feel a *whole* lot better), he said, "So how did you end up with this house, exactly?"

"Well, I done some research. I been cutting a trail for the town up around that hydroelectric place up there, and I saw how it was just getting ready to go into high gear. I mean, there's a hell of a lot of constructin' that needs to be done. I started figuring, hey, I bet somebody'd pay good money for a nice house near that place. I was thinkin' of building one—but then I knew there was just no time for that. So I kept my eyes open." He glanced at David. "Oh, I know what you're thinkin'—how the hell could I afford to buy a house, just like that? Well, my grandaddy left me a little, and I used it for a down payment when this place opened up a few weeks ago. Like I said before, my finances ain't the best, but I been saving that little chunk for something just like this. It was dirt cheap, and I figured I wouldn't have to keep makin' payments, once spring came. Somebody was bound to snap it up."

"Pretty smart," David said.

"Got that from my grandaddy too. Was a lumber man, he was. Had a pretty good company going, before the Depression hit. He managed to save a little."

By now the road had dwindled down to two twisty lanes with no shoulder. Hank kept the old Cherokee at breakneck speed, its tires sliding softly on patches of ice, then squealing in protest when they hit dry tar. David clung to the door handle; this had become a genuine, white-knuckle ride. Hank still drove with one hand on the wheel, paying almost no attention to the road.

"We're about five miles from the border right here. The road runs past the house and then you can take it over the bridge and into the States, or left to St. Boudin. That there's the closest real town, you know. Got a police station, clinic, even a place to grab a sandwich. Right civilized, least out in these parts."

Then, finally, he began to slow down. "This is the driveway. Goes in about one mile." He turned the old Cherokee into the driveway. "See, it's plowed now.

Had to pay my friend Jimmy thirty bucks up front, and he's a drunk. Thirty bucks'll buy him a few drinks at the bar."

The Jeep bounced and lurched over the ruts in the road. David wondered if the Toyota would even make it down this far.

After a few minutes, they rounded a corner and the house came into view with the hilltops poised behind it. The brown of the stained wood stood out in sharp contrast to the white of the snow. A large, open deck ran around three sides of the house, and the south side was a wall of glass. The windows on the west were lit up in fiery red and orange with the reflection of the sun.

"Those windows will let in the heat in the winter, and there's a big wood stove too," Hank said. "Keeps the place pretty toasty, I guess. The inside's mostly open so the heat circulates. Makes for a nice look too. Little bit of heaven, she is. You look for a nicer spot, you won't find a one. These woods are just the quietest spots around too. Of, course, you got to watch your little ones. Last family here lost their little girl; they never found her. Woods run back 'bout forty miles some places."

"You said they just *lost* her?"

"Wandered off. Couldn't stand to stay around here after that, so they just up and left. That's why the house is open now. Sorry, thought you knew. Terrible shame, it was, but these things just happen sometimes. Why, my brother lost a dog just the other day . . ."

Hank continued to ramble along, but David shut him out. *Just lost her? Jesus Christ. This place gives me the fucking creeps.*

". . . and then I says, Bobby, you know you got to shoot her. Broken legs, they might as well pack it in."

Hank grinned, exposing two large, darkened front teeth. They had come to a stop, and David got out slowly, staring at the fiery red windows. The happy feeling he had watching the mountains and the woods was gone, just like that, and dark, worried thoughts worked their way around in his head. He imagined Jessie wandering off into the woods, the cold working at her, calling for her daddy and nobody would come—

Hank slid across the seat and jumped down beside him. "Worried about the little one? All you got to do is scare 'em a bit, then they won't go into those woods. Me, I tell my kids about the bogeyman, how he lives out there in the dark, waitin' for them to wander out alone. It's a bit hard on 'em, but sometimes you gotta do things you don't like. My boy won't leave the front yard for weeks, works every time. Every time."

"I don't know, Hank," David said. He had started walking slowly forward, drawn by the red in the windows, by the dark wood and white snow. His skin tightened and he felt a chill. The house stared back at him, silent in the swiftly deepening twilight. *Almost as if it has eyes.*

"It's the only place close by," Hank said. He was standing right behind David, his voice startlingly loud in the stillness. "The plant is about three miles through the woods as the crow flies. Nice house, decent price. We can discuss it."

"It's not the money." David turned and looked at Hank. "What happened to the girl?"

"Didn't I tell you? Nobody knows for sure. Most people figure she wandered off, it got late, you know. Gets mighty cold during the nights."

Deadly cold. David turned back towards the house. He couldn't explain it, couldn't discuss this feeling he got when he looked at it, like it was watching, waiting for something to happen.

"You want to look 'round a bit, I s'pose."

David didn't answer for a moment, then shook it off. It was only a house. Stupid to have come all this way . . . "Sure. Go ahead and open it up."

Hank walked up the front steps and slipped the key into the lock. "You'll want to see this." He waited patiently at the door until David joined him, then fumbled around in the dark until the lights snapped on.

The inside of the house was beautiful. The living room opened up all the way to the ceiling. Railings ran along two sides of the second floor, and in the center of the house between the living room and kitchen sat a large, black woodstove on a square of bricks.

"You see what I mean about being open. Feel it too, come nighttime with a fire goin'. Heat really gets circulating, up to the ceiling and through them open rooms on the second floor.

"Come on upstairs, I'll show you the bedrooms."

He followed Hank up to the second floor, down the hall and past two small bedrooms until they reached a large open space that looked out over the living room. It was about a fifteen-foot drop. A Christmas tree in that living room could be a full two stories tall. *You could stand up here and put the star on the top.*

The master bedroom was a bit more private than the previous rooms. It was also done in deep brown wood, and through a generous skylight he could see the bright dots of the stars overhead.

"Pretty view at night," Hank remarked with a grin. "Gets the little lady in a romantic mood. I had one put in down at my place; haven't got any sleep since. There's another room downstairs. Could be a guest bedroom, I guess. Kinda smallish. All the furniture's sold as is, by the way. Figure you'll need it."

David followed Hank out of the bedroom and back downstairs. The kitchen was a nice size, divided in half with one side near the windows serving as the dining room.

"The wood for the fire is piled up next to the back door, and there's a tool shed or some such thing out back." Hank pointed out the kitchen window.

"I like the house, Hank, but I'm not sure about the location," David said, peering at the dark shape of the shed on the edge of the woods, a guardian against whatever lurked in the deeper shadows. "It's so . . . isolated."

Hank frowned. "Yessir, I understand. But you've got to do some thinkin'. Any place out here is going to be the same, the way I figure it. If you want this job, you got to put up with these woods. I'm not trying to pressure you or nothing," he added quickly. "Lord knows I wouldn't do that. But you just got to do some thinkin'. I'd talk it over with the little lady, if I was you. I learned a long time back not to do much without checkin' with your girl first. Makes 'em less ornery."

David smiled. "You're right, and I will." He *was* right; there was no way to avoid the dangers of living out in the woods, and that was one of the job requirements, like it or not. He had to be close to the plant. And how would it look to Hydro if he refused the first place offered to him, especially after this afternoon's spat with Thompson? He might not be the one to make the ultimate decision of whether or not David kept his job, but he surely had a say in it.

Hank nodded. "All right then. I'd take you on out to the plant, but we need a snowcat for that, and it's pretty dark now. It's right through them woods out back." He went out the front door. David stood for a long moment in the center of the living room. The house was still now, its ghosts asleep or in hiding, and he wondered again about the girl. Who was she, and what had happened to her? Was she Jessica's age? He shuddered momentarily, imagining himself as the parent, sick and frantic with worry. *I will never let that happen,* he thought with conviction. *Never.*

But as he stood in the emptiness of the living room, watching the darkness beyond the glass, he felt alone and infinitely small in this wilderness, a tiny speck of human life. *How could I stop it? Jesus, who would even hear her scream?*

CHAPTER SEVEN

Hank dropped him off in the parking lot behind the Hydro Development offices about three hours later. David told him he would discuss the house with his family and decide things within the week. The feeling that had overwhelmed him at first sight of the place he was unable to fully articulate, and after giving himself some more time for rational thought, he had all but dismissed it as a bad case of the nerves. The FERC meeting had been hell, and he had brought those feelings with him, that was all.

Hank's voice came back to him: *Last family here lost their little girl; they never found her. Woods run back 'bout forty miles some places.*

It was getting late now, and the wind had picked up, sweeping the snow from the drifts along the curb. David got into his car quickly, slamming the door before the snow and wind followed him in. The Corolla started up with a protesting whine.

It wasn't snowing yet, but the visibility was almost as bad. Gusts of wind shook the little car, and now and again sheets of blowing snow came up and blinded him, causing that quick second of panic before the windshield cleared and there was the road, stretching out beyond the glow of the headlights. The last time he had been in anything like this was the big storm that hit New York the previous winter. He remembered the storm clearly because that was the night of the fight with McDougal. Over the past few months he had tried to block out the memory, but now it came flooding back at him all at once, filling his head like the sheets of blowing snow outside the Toyota; that look in the man's eyes, and the feeling of rage that had welled up within him until he could hardly keep from swinging his fist and punching McDougal in the face.

He had decided long before that night that he was going nowhere in his current position with pumped storage research and development, because McDougal was on a power trip. McDougal, it seemed, could not get enough of it. Ate it, drank it, rolled in it. Although David was supposed to have as much to do with the plan and design of the holding reservoir as anyone, he was handcuffed by McDougal, who refused to allow anyone else's ideas to cross the drawing board. Or if he did, he claimed them as his own. David had finally complained to the CEO, Marc Killingly, but Killingly had shown an obstinate refusal to listen, and he decided it was time to get out. But the economy was bad and his job was their only source of income (We *made the decision that I would stay home with Jessie,* Helen had said, the one and only time they talked about it before the trouble really started. *We need the money.*) And he had remained mute, unable to make her understand the impotence he felt when he was at work, his self-image (say it, yes, your pride) shattered by McDougal's refusal to recognize his potential contribution to the company. He knew he was good at what he did, but he wanted to prove it, he wanted to design and help build the plant, not continue to turn over his ideas to some scavenger who claimed them as his own.

And then he had seen the problem. Even now he felt the urge to reaffirm to himself that he had been right, that there *had* been something wrong with the plans and that he was not just looking for revenge. He had seen a structural weakness one night, purely by accident. The lower section of the reservoir simply would not hold up under the pressure of a continuous flow at peak rates, no matter how many times he figured it. It didn't add up. Of course, he didn't try to deny the rush of triumph that had flowed quickly through his limbs, but that was all right. Because the mistake was there in plain sight, for anyone to see.

Anyone except McDougal, that is.

McDougal was dismissive, all but throwing him out of his office. But David wouldn't walk away that easily. He showed the man the figures, shoved them in his face when he refused to see them. Finally, he stormed out, intending to go to Killingly the next morning, but by the time he got back to the office the plans had been corrected with his suggestions. And McDougal didn't say anything to him at all; McDougal took the credit for it, even going so far as to tell Killingly the change was his idea, and that it had been to correct the mistake of one of the younger engineers.

Even then, he could have stayed on. He could have swallowed his pride and shut his big mouth, and kept his job. But he didn't.

The second confrontation with McDougal was much nastier, and that was when he had to use every ounce of restraint to hold himself back. He had threatened to ruin McDougal, but the man had just smiled at him.

The fact was, David had no proof. All copies of the earlier plans were gone. He had nothing.

The worst part of it was, McDougal was going to win. If he kept it up, not only would he lose the EPC job, he wouldn't be able to get a job within a thousand miles of a hydro plant, other than janitor. So he had just walked away, his fists clenched, the bile in his throat burning with anger and frustration.

When he got home and told Helen about it, she wanted him to go back and apologize. He wallowed in self-pity, becoming angrier at her than he had ever been in their marriage, all the time knowing that it wasn't Helen he was upset with and that he shouldn't take it out on her.

"Your daughter needs you," she said. "*I* need you, David. We can work it out. Don't turn away like this." And that was when he'd said the thing that had eaten him up inside and was still eating at him long after it had had been forgiven by her, words he'd regretted even as they were coming out his mouth.

"I don't have the fucking time for you right now."

She turned away with tears in her eyes. He stood there, aching to take it back, and said nothing, couldn't say it, couldn't open his mouth except to utter those few words which had hurt so much.

He went out for a drive to clear his head, and there was the storm. It snuck up on him without warning, and he found himself out on the highway in the middle of gusts so powerful they threatened to send him skidding off the road and over the embankment. He pulled over and the storm started in with a vengeance; the wind rocked the car and heavy snowflakes blew in crazy patterns around and across the windshield. He sat there in this world of white and resolved to make it up to

Helen, and to Jessie. His own world was too fragile and precious for such ultimate decisions; he couldn't afford to make enemies in the business when he was just a junior engineer.

When he got back home, Helen had forgiven him, but he had never forgiven himself. And neither had McDougal. The following day, he asked for David's resignation, citing long-standing conflicts and subpar work. For some reason, Killingly had gone along with it, and David was out of a job. He had trouble finding work; the days stretched into weeks, into months. Worst of all was knowing he had the experience and the training but there *was just nothing out there*, not for him.

When he pulled into the circle in front of the Frontenac it was almost nine o'clock. The wind had died a little, but as he stepped from the car, gusts blew tiny spirals of snow around his feet and along in front of him until they disappeared over the edge of the terrace. Off the edge of the world. He felt a strange urge to follow them, just step off that edge and welcome with open arms whatever lay beyond. *It's only a thirty-foot drop*, he reminded himself sarcastically. *What do you think you'll find? China?*

Upstairs, he opened the door to their room and Jessie flung herself on him immediately. He picked her up and swung her high above his head, marveling as always how incredibly light she was, and the thrill he felt knowing she was his own flesh and blood.

"Welcome home, Daddy," Helen said, coming up behind him and shutting the door. She put her arms around his waist, squeezing. "Jessie's been waiting for you all evening. Me too."

David pulled her to him, with Jessie between them.

"Daddy, you're smushing me," she protested with a squirm. He laughed and hiked her up on his shoulders so he could give his wife a quick kiss.

"So, how did it go?" Helen asked. "Did you knock 'em dead?"

David swung his daughter down and plopped her into a chair. "It was hell. The FERC was there. They threw some report at me that I couldn't make heads or tails of, and practically accused us of single-handedly poisoning the universe."

"I'll kill 'em," Helen said, putting up her fists in a mock boxing pose. "Let me at 'em."

David laughed. "Calm down, Wonder Woman. I think I did okay."

"I'm sure you did just fine." She sat down on the edge of the bed. "How's the house?"

"Not bad," he said carefully. "It's very pretty, actually."

"And . . ."

"And nothing. Not much else around except woods."

Helen frowned, her lips pouting prettily. "Well, what are we going to do, man-of-the-house?" she asked.

"I thought I'd leave the final decision up to you two."

"Some man you are," she teased. "If it's pretty, let's do it. Why not? We're not paying for it. And it's probably the only thing we're going to find in the area."

"Jessie?" He turned to his daughter. "What do you think?"

"It sounds okay. I just want a house," she said seriously, "with my own room."

"I think we can do that," he said, bending down to kiss the top of her head, and breathing in the sweet, freshly washed scent of her hair.

"So we've got a house?" Helen asked.

"We've got a house. Of course"—he added quickly—"you can change your mind if you don't like it."

"I'm sure I'll love it. We'll love it," she corrected herself, looking at Jessie with a smile. "As long as we're together, we'll be fine."

CHAPTER EIGHT

Jessica was alone in a world of white. She didn't feel particularly frightened, though it was lonely and unfamiliar. She felt curiously at ease, like she was floating above the clouds. And yes, here was Johnny Bear at her side, so she wasn't really alone at all. She felt peaceful and happy, and she didn't wonder where Daddy or Mommy were, or even where she was. This was enough, this soft white puffiness. It didn't matter; nothing mattered but the floating.

She reached out for Johnny Bear, and watched her hands swim slowly outward, then her wrists, then her elbows, and it was like they weren't even attached to her body, didn't belong to her at all. It was all in slow motion, like the way you felt when you were floating in the pool or the lake and you watched your arms with those big fat floaty things on them push outward, and then you were moving through the water. But slowly, and no matter how hard you tried, you couldn't go much faster, but it was okay, it was fun.

The change happened so slowly that she didn't even notice it at first. The bright, soft white around her began to gray, darken, and then she noticed the cold (*can you feel cold in a dream 'cause that's what this is a dream*) and her flesh prickled, her hair stood out from her skin and she got goose bumps. And Johnny Bear was being pulled away, gently but firmly, with a force that was constant and unshakable. She held him as tight as she could but felt his furry arms sliding through her own, then the cool smooth glass of his eyes against her skin for a moment and he was gone. She watched him float into the black clouds, away from her, and felt sad and lonely.

She began to drift downward.

Slowly at first, then her heartbeat picked up and she felt the prickly rush of fear as she fell faster, faster until the darkness was whipping by and her hair was slashing her face. The wind pulled at her and it got louder and louder and she opened her mouth and screamed as hard as she could but nothing came out. And she was falling so fast now her breath was being pulled from her lungs, the wind was shrieking in her ears and she closed her eyes tight, the sickness rising in her throat.

When she opened her eyes, she was on the ground. She was in a dark place that smelled like wood, a deep, damp smell like outside after a thunderstorm. And it was different, very different from before. This felt sharp and mean, this felt *real*. It was night but she could see; the light was from the moon through the window, yes, that was it. She looked all around for Johnny Bear but he wasn't there; there was no one anywhere. It was still very cold. This was a different kind of cold, though, not a windy cold but an ice cold, something that climbed deep inside of you and settled like a sickness. She felt it, probing her arms, her legs, her private parts, chilling, searching. She shivered from the inside out, crossing her arms and hugging herself. This was not home. This was someplace scary.

There was a sudden noise like a whimper, and she

realized it came from her own mouth. Backing up slowly, she found a corner of the room and slid down the rough wall until she was sitting on the floor, and it was like falling down on the ice skating pond. The numbing cold crept up her back and spread all through her body, and she shivered uncontrollably. Then her mouth opened to scream, but she held it back; she must stay quiet because something was moving; there was a shadow on the wall in front of her.

The long, dark shadow on the wood slid forward. It looked like a hand and arm holding something large and round.

She waited in desperate silence, her breath coming in soft gasps of fear and her teeth chattering. She wrapped her arms around herself and squeezed, trying to stuff everything back inside and keep the nasty thing away, shut out this horrible creature made of black arms and shadow limbs. *Wake up Jessie wake up wake up I want to go home—*

The hand and what it contained slid out from around the corner into view. It was a huge and roughly muscled arm, and it held a head, someone's furry head with a round button nose and glassy eyes.

She found her voice then, and it was with explosive power, leaping out of her like a living thing, and suddenly she was sitting upright in bed and the room was still dark but different, warmer, real. The scream went on and it sounded so loud she felt her ears would split and she threw a hand across her mouth to stop it. Then the lights snapped on and Daddy was in the doorway, frightened, his blue robe thrown over his shoulders and still open to the waist. She sat there with her hand on her mouth and the tears welled up and spilled over onto her cheeks. *I'm going to cry and Daddy will think I'm a baby*, she thought, but he didn't; he only came over and gathered her up in his arms, and she sobbed into his robe.

"It's okay, Jessie, honey, it's just a bad dream, everything's okay now," he said, and the sound of his voice made her feel better. The thump in her chest faded and the dark pictures of her dream receded, although they didn't disappear. Johnny Bear was next to her on the chair but she almost didn't dare look at him, didn't dare pick him up because it might bring back the dream. But he was probably scared too; she had frightened him with her screaming. And he didn't have anybody to hug.

"Daddy, will you hug Johnny too?" she asked, and he smiled and reached over, picking up her bear and adding him to their close little circle.

"Somebody hurt Johnny," she said, and saying it made the tears well up again. "Somebody hurt him, and it was in a dark cold place and I was really *scared*."

David looked down at his daughter's tear-stained face and rocked her gently. "I know, honey. But it's all right now, everything's okay."

They sat together in the bright lights of the motel room, rocking softly, and David Pierce really hoped it was all right, that all the troubled events of the day would pass them by and they could be happy.

Because if I ever lose this family, I don't know what I'd do.

CHAPTER NINE

It had been almost two weeks since she'd heard from Jonathan Newman, and Dr. Amanda Seigel was worried. He was not technically due to check in until tomorrow, but he usually called before check-in time, sometimes twice or even three times a week.

Jonathan was someone she definitely wanted to keep tabs on, more than any of her other fourteen patients currently on release programs. "Reintroduced into mainstream society," as the hospital board put it. Some of these patients had colorful histories, a few even violent ones, but none of them, *let's be frank here*, she told herself, interested her as much as Jonathan did. He was a one-in-a-million patient, a closet (and then not-so-closet) paranoid who could recall most of the trauma that had landed him in the hospital in the first place, *and* was willing to talk about it. Unlike most paranoids, Jonathan had opened up to her (though it had taken awhile, she would admit that).

In many of these types of cases, the problem could be traced back to childhood, but that took months and sometimes years of therapy. Many paranoids never had the luxury of assuming the world was a friendly, stable place. They could not trust others, patients would often say, even before the disease became prominent.

And they couldn't react to different situations with a relative shift in emotion; that is, most would react to something very simple and hardly threatening in the same way they might react to a uniformed police officer snapping on the handcuffs.

She remembered a patient of hers she had treated a few years ago, Ron King, who ended up in her care after weeks on the run. He had gone to work at a butcher shop run by an Italian owner several months before, and that was where all the trouble started. Ron had always been a pleasant, quiet person, but after several weeks of work, he had a minor argument with his boss over a paycheck that was a little short, and ended up storming out of the place on a Friday afternoon, the busiest time of the week. Upon getting home, he began to obsess over what had happened and became convinced that the little butcher shop was run by the Mafia, and that the Italian owner was really a trained killer. From that point on, things worsened rapidly; the next day, Ron didn't dare go to work, and began to realize that there were suspicious-looking people lurking outside his apartment. He pushed a bureau against the door and went out the fire escape. On his way to his car, he decided the police were always taking bribes and probably knew about him already. So he drove out of the city.

Over the next few days, he was sure they were following him, kept seeing them in every face at the truck stops and fast-food places. He kept driving. Finally, a week later and across the country, he attacked a young woman who he was sure had been following him and was "one of them."

Ron was treated and eventually released but continued to have trouble outside the hospital. *That's the prob-*

lem, Amanda thought, not without a pinch of distaste. Mental hospitals were overcrowded and understaffed. *There's just not enough time and money.*

The same thing had happened with Jonathan. She had found him easy to work with, receptive, open about his experiences in the war. Still, she had searched for something else. She sensed he was holding something back. Exactly what that thing was remained unclear, and he was released before she was able to break through.

Her head ached dreadfully, and the paperwork was piled up high on one corner of her desk, but she couldn't concentrate. *Nothing has happened yet*, she reminded herself. Not technically, no; but she knew he liked her very much (was well aware of it in fact, and used that to get close to him—something she did not mind doing), and thought surely he would have called by now, simply to talk with her.

It's just your pride, Amanda, she told herself with a thin smile. *You just don't want to admit that one of the patients is leaving the nest and doesn't need you anymore.* That type of recovery was rare in these cases, but it could happen, she supposed. He had been doing very well, especially in the last couple of sessions.

She would give him a few more days, and then if she still hadn't heard from him, well, then she would get in touch herself somehow. It couldn't hurt, right?

Dr. Amanda Seigel took the first of the heavy folders off the pile on her desk with a sigh, and started thumbing through it, letting Jon Newman slip back into a far corner of her mind. The amount of work was unbelievable; new patients to familiarize herself with, old files to be closed, meetings to attend. She was giving a talk on erotic paranoid disorders in another week, and she had hardly begun preparing for it.

It would be several days before she thought seriously of Jonathan again, and by then, it was very nearly too late.

Dan Flint, in the offices of the Federal Energy Regulatory Commission in Washington, rocked quickly back and forth in his chair the way he did when he was doing a lot of heavy thinking. Upon brief observation, someone not familiar with his moods might have supposed that he was picking out the scores for this week's basketball pool, or maybe just holding back the cramps from a bad case of diarrhea. But in truth, he was working hard on the Jackson pumped storage problem, turning the figures over in his head.

The team had returned with new water samples from the river near the plant, and the samples had been turned over to the lab for testing. Flint imagined the men stepping out onto the frozen surface of the river, and shivered.

He used to love the water. Hell, he'd grown up in Cairo, Illinois, where the Mississippi and Ohio rivers collide, and he and his friends were always stealing down to their favorite spot on the riverbank for a dip. Until one day during his twelfth year, when spring storms had swelled and quickened the rivers just as the entire town had turned out for a carnival near Fort Defiance State Park. At the height of the festivities, a drunken townsman had wandered too close to the crumbling banks and tumbled in. Another man had gone in to save him, and Flint's father jumped onto a flat-bottomed fishing boat and went after them both. Flint and his friends watched as the two men in the water went under, and his father, reaching down to try to save them, was pulled in too.

All three bodies were recovered two days later, a mile downriver where the water calmed itself in the shallows, the three of them tangled in tree roots and moss, minnows darting in and out of their open mouths.

Ever since then, he'd been unable to swim. It was more than a phobia to him; it was like a curse that he knew would catch up to him eventually. All those years ago he'd come to believe that the river had really wanted him, but had taken his father instead. Some day, that debt would be paid.

And there was something else too: whenever he imagined jumping in, he thought of bodies bumping into him in the dark, bloated limbs caressing his flesh as they drifted with the current.

Now the great irony was that he was dealing with water all the time. This Jackson Hydro project alone meant he would in all likelihood be staring at rushing spring rivers and streams for months to come. But hell, this wasn't just the Jackson problem any more, it involved all of Hydro Development's projects scattered from Fort Kent in Maine to San Diego. The FERC and the EPA were keeping a close eye on the company, and had been for the past six months. There were some funny things going on at a couple of the major sites. Jackson Hydro was just the latest of them. In truth, the Commission had been shying away from granting a temporary license to build in the first place, but in the end they had gone ahead with it under heavy pressure from the boys in Washington (who, of course, were getting heavy pressure of their own from the lobbyists of Fortune 500 members who had financed their campaigns).

It was times like these that Flint just wanted to get out, go find a job picking potatoes or moving furniture somewhere. The nature of the political system in America made him sick. Everyone was bribing everyone else, and then when the time came to call in the favors, nothing could get done. The fact was, there was a lot of money changing hands out there, and money in an election year, or anytime else for that matter, could work miracles. Whatever kind of miracles you wanted.

Hydro Development had a lot of money.

Flint spun his chair around to face the window. He had a corner office now, and the view was a hell of a lot better than the old cubicle. Views tended to be pretty lousy when the room had no windows. But he had been at the FERC now for six years, so he supposed he had earned the window, if not a better raise. He had done some damn good work, too, mostly investigating little problems like water temperature changes and silt downstream, stuff like that. If there was something more criminal going on, the investigation got turned over to the FBI sooner or later.

Flint wondered when the Jackson Hydro case would be turned over to them.

Actually, he was only guessing. Actually, he had no goddamned *idea* if anything was going on at all, not to mention anything criminal. But he had a hunch. Over the past year, three of the four pumped storage plants owned by Hydro Development had shut down temporarily. One of these shutdowns had happened over a supposed "chemical spill," according to the company, though the FERC (or anybody else, for that matter) had never found a trace of anything. After the spill was cleaned up, the plant reopened and everyone was happy. The really funny thing about it was, in all three of the shutdowns, somebody had died, at least one under strange circumstances, or so it seemed to Flint. In one case, a man had fallen to his death, and in another, somebody had been crushed by a flood gate. Tragic accidents, really. But in the third case (and this had been the one involving "the spill"), someone had gotten shot. According to the management, one of the maintenance men had downed a few too many beers one night and gone berserk, killing his best friend and partner on the night shift, and then killing himself. The FBI was involved in that one, but only briefly. It looked like an open-and-shut case, or did at the time.

Now, Flint decided, he wasn't so sure. Something smelled funny, and it wasn't the fish. If they could get the FBI in on it, maybe he could find out what that was exactly.

Of course, a simple chemical spill was hard to prosecute using the letter of the law. The sad fact was, the big money boys had been at it again. Whenever some environmental group came along and tried to get a bill through Congress ending a case of toxic dumping, or use of cancer-causing sprays, the congressmen would turn to big business and say, "What do you think?" and big business would say, "We're not really sure about this bill. It's just not quite right. We think you should kill it. Remember, you owe us a favor."

That was what pissed off Dan Flint. It was common knowledge that big companies like Reardon Chemical had been squashing environmental bills for years, then turning around and paying millions for some advertisement on TV that told everybody what great guys they were and how many ways they were helping make the world a better place to live. It was all a load of bullshit.

If someone died, though, it was a little different. There were plenty of laws against killing someone.

He sighed and turned back to his desk. The sky had turned gray, and it looked like they might get a few snow flurries. Later today, he was supposed to fly to Texas and sit in on a study or two out there, to make sure the bass population was holding steady downstream from one of the new hydroelectric dams. He didn't have any real doubts of that being true, but it was important to check anyway. After he returned, he would look in on the new samples from the Jackson Hydro project again, and see if the lab had found anything. They were busy right now trying to isolate whatever it was that had caused the growths on the smelt fish, but so far they hadn't been able to get much. Once they isolated a sample or two (and he had confidence in them; they were slow, but good), they could start the testing. That was where the fun would begin; if it turned out to be toxic, he could tighten the screws on the Jackson Hydro project and that Thompson guy, who he didn't particularly like. Squeeze a little more and see what comes running out.

He would have to be careful, of course, as much as it irked him to do so. Hydro Development was becoming a powerful company, and they had friends everywhere, even in the FERC.

Flint decided, after a moment's reflection, that they should go after the new guy first. He might be able to tell them something, and he seemed to be more receptive. Maybe they could get him to spill his guts, and once they had an "in," it would be much easier to crack Thompson. If they uncovered whatever was going on (and there was something, he could feel it), they could order a major cleanup at least, which would probably cost Hydro millions.

And maybe, just maybe, it would save someone's life.

He decided to buzz his secretary and make sure the plane tickets to Texas were all set. And after that, maybe he would take a trip down to the lab before he left. One more check wouldn't hurt; maybe they had finally found something in those fish. It seemed clear that he wouldn't get any extra sleep that night, though he was exhausted. He couldn't afford to sleep. He still had a lot to do.

CHAPTER TEN

They remained at the Château Frontenac for four more days. David spent most of the time at the Hydro offices sorting through the massive files on the project, and Helen and Jessie spent the time sightseeing. The options available to tourists seemed endless, as was the work at Hydro Development: stacks of construction plans, environmental documents, legal papers, licenses, financial documents, stock purchase agreements, leases, deeds, and power purchase contracts in various forms. Not all of them fell under David's area, but he felt more comfortable knowing as much as possible about the business and the project itself, especially with the FERC breathing down their necks.

He worked with Thompson briefly over those few days, and nothing more was said by either of them about the meeting and the argument that followed. He couldn't exactly say the man was friendly to him, but he was at least polite. It was almost as if the strange outburst had never happened at all, and after a couple of days, David felt it fading away like a bad dream. As far as he knew, nobody at the office had heard from the FERC, so maybe they had realized their mistake. Maybe they had found somebody up there on a snowmobile dumping pesticides, or discovered something seeping down from one of the Canadian mills.

The Pierces spent the nights lounging in luxury, eating dinners in the hotel restaurant (which was quite good; the waiters and waitresses dressed in Elizabethan costumes with puffy trousers and tights, and they even had lobster tails the last night, which Jessie ate eagerly, butter running down her chin), and eating out once in a tiny hole-in-the-wall place Mr. Poisson had recommended. The house remained on David's mind, but only in the irritating, nagging sort of way things with no real consequence did; he had made a decision, they all had, and it seemed like the right one. It was only a house, after all. What he really should be thinking about was how to make Jessie understand that the woods were dangerous, and not just a nice place to play hide-and-go-seek. He didn't think he was up to the Hank Babcock method of scaring-the-kid-till-she-shits-her-pants, and secretly he wondered if Hank himself were up to it, or only talking a good story. In any case, the woods were dangerous and would have to be dealt with in one way or another. He would figure out exactly how when the time came.

Jessie seemed to be feeling much better in the days since her nightmare, which was a good thing; he didn't know if he could handle much more of that. Her high-pitched scream had scared the hell out of him that night. It had pulled him out of a dream, and for a moment he hadn't been sure where he was in the dark; for just a quick second, before the dream faded completely away, he had been sure it was the other girl who was screaming, the one who had gotten lost in the woods and never made it home. He could almost see her, little black pigtails, pale face with eyes huge as saucers and wet with tears, and the branches closing in on all sides like hands in the dark.

His dream had faded quickly, but now and again during the week that followed, the thought of that little girl returned to him; when he was in the office, bent over a file, and once just as he had drifted off to sleep she had hovered like a ghost on the edges of his mind.

They ended their last night in the hotel by drinking a little too much wine, which always sent Helen into the giggle-fits, and thanking Mr. Poisson for being the "best damn host anyone could hope for." He, being the perfect concierge, responded modestly that he was only doing his job. But David had caught a little smile from the man as they had gone up to bed, and a nod, and he hoped sincerely that Mr. Poisson would not forget them any time soon and would welcome them back for a vacation when the time was right.

Jessie fell asleep as soon as her head hit the pillow, and David drifted off an hour later with his wife pressed naked against his stomach, dreaming about the following day's move.

In the morning, they drove north through the most desolate and yet beautiful country Helen had ever seen. The road cut a narrow, two-lane strip through the thick woods. Plump, icy pines stretched their needles outward into skirts to hold a lacy trim of snow. Even the trees looked as if they had fattened up for the winter. Under the thick branches she saw patches of dry brown earth surrounded by a circle of white snow that built its way upward until the drifts reached great heights of three feet or more, before thinning again and dropping to the edge of the next trees' protected circle of ground.

So threatening yet so stunningly beautiful, she thought. And the bare branches of the birch trees scattered among the pines bent down to touch the tops of the drifts like a lover's fingers.

They had not seen another car in over twenty minutes, and she supposed with some apprehension that they must be getting close. She could tell by the way her husband's fingers tightened on the steering wheel. What had bothered him about the new house eluded her with the faint qualities of a dream—she felt she almost had it, then it skipped away, taunting her. But it *had* bothered him in some way, of that she was sure. Perhaps he was simply nervous about the newness of everything; it had become painfully obvious to her over the past few months that he blamed himself for their recent financial trouble. She supposed that it was at least partially her fault. It had been wrong to pressure him to stay in a job he hated, but she had been driven by what felt right at the time. Now David felt he had to prove himself to her and Jessie; she felt it, felt his need. Maybe that was just as well; whatever happened, she would support him.

But Helen felt something more from him today, a tightness that hadn't been there back in New York, even when his job searches came up empty time and time again. It seemed to her like a kind of hesitation, the feeling you get on a dark night when you're alone on the street, and you pause just one fleeting instant before rounding that next corner, thinking about what might happen if there was someone or something there, just out of sight, waiting for you.

Jessica has been having those dreams again, her subconscious whispered. *Your baby girl had another nightmare.* She let herself drift back to the events of a few nights before. She had shot upright in bed, Jessie's scream echoing around in her head, but David had been already gone, the spot beside her still warm from his body. Like he knew it was coming. She remembered the look on his face when he returned twenty minutes later. Jessie's hauntingly accurate dreams would scare anyone a little, she reasoned, especially a parent. Maybe that was what had been bothering him today. It made sense, she supposed. Jessie's dreams had been less frequent in New York, it was true, but that last one had been a doozy.

One of her good friend's husbands was an intern at a nearby hospital, and Helen had asked him once for an informal opinion of night terrors in children. He suggested that they try a psychiatrist, but that more than likely Jessie would "grow out of it." Helen had resented his comments and suggestion for psychiatric help (if her mother couldn't help her, then what could some stranger do?), but embraced the idea that the dreams were just a phase; perhaps they would fade away like pictures in an old album. And for a while they had.

The next challenge, she supposed, would be making sure Jessica had a chance at a normal life. There was (according to Mike Olmstead) a one-room schoolhouse in St. Boudin, some sort of throwback to the turn of the century with thirty or so kids in grades one through six all mixed in together. Jessie would learn French as well as English if she attended there, and that would be good. She *was* going to start school next year; it was just a question of where. Helen supposed she could tutor her at home, but what about friends and a normal social life? What happened to a young child who never had to adjust to kids her own age?

Social retardation, Helen thought with a half-smile. Is that good or bad? And the one-room schoolhouse; the chances of getting a good education out of there, not just learning a different language but getting the new math, practicing the arts, things like that, were pretty slim.

The day had gotten a bit darker, and the trees along the road seemed closer together now and hunched over their treasures of pine needles and dead leaves. The deeper woods beyond the first layer of pines were shrouded in shadow. Occasionally they passed a logging road or a brief open space cluttered with stumps, but other than that there was nothing. Even the tiny wooden shacks and old trailers that had populated the edges of road near the border were conspicuously absent here in the deeper woods. *And they want to build a power plant out here*, she wondered, her eyes following the unbroken line of trees like so many fence posts along the road's edge. Why build something so immense and with so much potential out in a wilderness that doesn't want it, in fact would be better off without it? Transporting the generated power such a distance had to be expensive. But the land was cheap, she supposed, and it might be easier to get around the governmental regulations that surely surrounded the city and populated areas by moving out here to a place that had no need for those types of things.

Whatever the reasons, the plant was here now and that was what was important; it meant a job and a new sense of self-worth for her husband. A new sense of self-worth for her, she realized. For just as surely as day followed night, her fortune in life (or misfortune, as the case may be) followed David Pierce's every move. When he lost his job and could not find work, she died a little inside; and when the call finally came last week, she felt a new beginning and new hope blossom somewhere deep inside of her just as she saw it reflected in her husband's gray eyes.

Life was funny, she decided wryly. Just when you felt most comfortable with your role in life (whether it was in a mansion in Beverly Hills or a trailer in Canada), you got tossed something new, a scrap from God's table. In their case it was a job, but for others it could be a new baby, winning the lottery, losing a close friend. When it happened, your role was adjusted, skewed, and sometimes reversed.

There were many times when she felt an urge to just say "no thanks" and keep things as they were. But every once in a while she gathered the courage to embrace the unknown.

In this case, it was easy. There wasn't much to lose.

The gloom overhead had now turned threatening, and she watched through the spotted glass of the windshield as the heavy cloud mass heaved and writhed above them. David had turned on the headlights, but the frail beams extended no farther than a few feet before dissipating. A few lonely snowflakes fell here and there against the glass, but the full fury above them waited, pregnant and powerful. When had it moved in? Helen felt the icy fingers of fear run along the base of her skull and down the back of her neck. It had come on so *fast*. This was reality, right here in the middle of this storm, and reality was dangerous. Their new home was not a vacation spot but an isolated house in the middle of mostly unexplored wilderness, and the weather was often brutal and unforgiving.

Right now it's just giving us a taste, she thought, *but at any moment it could hit like a ton of bricks. And no matter what we do, no matter how hard we try, we can only go along for the ride.*

She found herself tensing up, as if waiting for something. She looked over at David, but he stared straight ahead at the road, trying to pick out the yellow markings that stretched out before them like a lifeline. She didn't dare say a word, didn't dare break his concentration for one instant. The atmosphere in the car had gotten tense. She felt it pressing down and around her. Jessie was silent in the backseat; Helen turned to look at her, and noticed for the first time her stillness, the almost hypnotized look in her eyes. She stared out the window, her shoulders hunched forward, making her look small and helpless.

"Jessie?" she whispered. "Honey, are you all right?"

Jessie didn't answer, and Helen noticed now how slack her jaw was, how her eyes fixed glassily on the clouds above them. Her instincts made her reach out, twisting around in her seat to touch her daughter, even as her thoughts told her *don't be silly, Helen, she's just a kid and a tired and bored one at that.*

And then her fingers touched the bare skin of Jessie's arm. It was ice cold, covered in gooseflesh, and crawling almost as if it were a separate living thing.

"Jessica?" Helen raised her voice now, the tiny alarms spreading outward through her body, raising her heartbeat a notch.

"What is it?" David took his eyes off the yellow line for an instant.

"I—I don't know—"

He glanced back at Jessie, a look of concern slowly spreading across his face, his annoyance at the sudden interruption gone. Helen looked from him back to her daughter. She was white, the finest traces of blue about her lips.

"What the hell?" David reached back behind the

seat, twisting into a position that looked so awkward and so unnatural Helen wondered how he did it: left hand still on the wheel, shoulders turned and dipped, right arm groping blindly. His fingers reached Jessie's arm and he grasped it and shook roughly.

Jessica screamed.

The piercing noise split the tiny confines of the car, and Helen tried not to flinch as David turned and slapped both hands on the wheel, the car and trailer behind it weaving dangerously on the slick pavement. He wrestled them back under control and pulled over onto the edge of the road. There were no other cars in sight, nothing human at all, no houses or even fences—just the flat stretch of pavement, whipping, snowy gusts, and the dark, eerie depths of Maine woods.

David got his seat belt off and got out quickly, letting the wind into the car. Helen followed, her mind a whirling mass of confusion and fear. He already had her out of her seat belt and sitting on the edge of the seat. The color rushed back into her face in an instant, and she flushed red.

Helen felt Jessie's forehead. It was cool, almost cold, and she heard the warning bells again in her mind. Something was very strange here, but she couldn't for the life of her figure out what.

"I saw it in the clouds, Daddy. I was there again and the man hurt Johnny!" Jessie was crying now, great racking sobs, tears coursing down her cheeks.

"It's okay, honey, I'm here." David rocked her in his arms, and Jessie gripped his shoulders fiercely. He glanced back at Helen, and she saw the confusion in his gaze. The dreams had never been this bad, never this powerful and certainly never in broad daylight, on a harmless car trip with her mother and father not two feet away.

"We want to help you, honey," she said, leaning forward and brushing the stray hairs from her daughter's forehead. They were sticky with sweat. *Funny*, she thought, *she seems so cold*. "We want to help you but you have to help yourself. There's nothing to be afraid of, I promise." A gust of wind rocked the car and sent a whirl of snow spinning around their heads and through the open car door.

"We've got to get back inside and close the doors," David said. "She's freezing."

The blue tinge had spread out from Jessie's lips, coloring her cheeks and forehead. She shivered visibly, huddled against her father's chest. David put her in the backseat and Helen climbed in after her, shutting the door and grabbing a scarf from the front seat that she wrapped around her daughter's neck and cheeks. She rubbed at Jessie's little hands, trying to warm the icy fingertips as David climbed in the front and slammed the door, cranking the little plastic knob for the fan up as far as it would go.

The welcome rush of warm air filled the car, and Helen sighed, feeling the tremble in her own fingers for the first time. The crazy speed with which the cold snuck up on them hadn't given her a chance to realize how frightened she had been, but now in the warmth of the car's interior, she felt weak and shaky. Jessie's fits (dreams, she corrected herself sharply) had slowly worn down her stamina, and now she felt exhausted.

"Christ," David muttered from the front seat. "I thought this storm would hold off a while longer." He turned around and studied his daughter carefully. Jessie looked up at him, the tears drying on her cheeks, and nodded. Color crept back into her face, and her tiny fingers warmed under Helen's touch.

"I think she's okay," Helen said. The car's wipers scraped softly against the glass, and the busy hum of the fan felt soothing after the cold and wind of the storm. "How close are we?"

"Around fifteen, twenty miles. It'll take us about an hour in this stuff." At that, the wind seemed to soften a bit; the tiny flakes of snow slowed their frantic dance against the glass.

David reached out and cupped his palm against his daughter's cheek. "Are you okay to go now, honey?"

Jessie nodded, and Helen felt a great blast of relief flow through her tired body. She really did look better. After a long moment, David snapped on his seat belt and pulled the car back off the shoulder and onto the road.

The driving was much easier now. The wind had eased considerably and the sky had lightened to the point where David could shut off the headlights. The storm was gone, as fast as it had come.

Just get us there, Helen thought, *just a little farther.* The full impact of what had happened tried to register with her exhausted mind, but she pushed it away roughly. *I will not worry. There is nothing wrong and I will not worry . . .*

But it was hopeless; she did.

She felt her daughter's fragile web of sanity being torn away like a mask, exposing something that had only to this point been touched upon. She had never seen anything like it before, not in her own mother, who had simply stopped talking two years ago at age sixty-one; not in her uncle Steve, who had killed himself ten years ago by jumping into the path of a Greyhound bus. These were people she knew, close family members who had snapped in some way, refusing to face the real world that they found too harsh and unforgiving. *But they knew where that real world was*, she thought, *they just decided to leave it while they could.* Was that what her daughter was doing? Had her young mind given up already, taken one punch too many and thrown in the towel?

She'll grow out of it.

Would she? Uncle Steve chose the front end of a bus over the constant jabs and cheap shots of life in New York City. He had always been like a child trapped in a grown-up's body. She remembered visiting him with her father in his plush downtown office just a week before his suicide, making the trip from the country she loved into the strange hurried life of the city; his eyes had been far away, vacant. *What was the last thing you saw before it hit you? The terrified face of the driver, the two headlights bearing down like pathways to heaven? Or just the deep and throbbing red of your own blood?*

Stop it!

She brought herself back with a jerk. Her daughter needed her more than ever before, and here she was acting like a scared teenager. But the image of Uncle Steve as he stepped calmly in front of that bus refused to leave her. *What if it runs in the family? What if you're just one nightmare away from a padded room?*

She turned to study Jessie. The scarf had dropped to drape loosely around her shoulders, and the heat seemed to be doing more good. Her eyes had regained their brilliance and her breathing had returned to normal.

Helen looked at her husband. David continued to concentrate on his driving, but she saw the twitch of muscle under the skin of his cheek. He was worried, she knew.

And why shouldn't he be? The stresses of a new job were hard enough. Her love for him rushed through her like a wave, washing out her fatigue and loosening her tense muscles. They would have to get through this together. If Jessie needed a doctor, she would get one, it was as simple as that. Right now they were moving to their new home, and it should be a happy time.

We will make it work, she promised herself. *Whatever it takes.*

She turned to look out the window and the woods stared back at her, deep and silent, watching, waiting. For what, she wasn't quite sure.

Half an hour later, they crossed the border back into Canada and turned onto the snow-covered track that led to their new home. There was a fine dusting of new snow on top of the old crust, but nothing more. The sky had almost completely cleared, the power of the storm gone as quickly as it had arrived. David felt as if they had been offered a reprieve, and issued a warning. *Don't mess with me*, Mother Nature said. *You're free to go, but watch your step.* He decided that was fine with him. If Mother Nature was a control freak, he was humble enough to respect that.

Jessie's problems made him feel like turning around and heading back to New York to find help. To hell with the job. But he knew that such a rash decision would be both professional and personal suicide. Without Hydro Development he was a dead man, any way you looked at it. So he continued on, while that illogical, emotional side boiled within him, and thought perhaps that this would be the last one, that such a crazy series of outbursts would turn themselves off suddenly like a light switch. If they didn't . . .

He preferred not to think about that.

Perhaps the light dusting of snow had softened the ruts a little, because the driveway seemed easier to manage. They turned the last corner, and the house came into view. The urgency of Jessie's situation had kept his mind off the place for a while, but now it all came rushing back to him, filling his mind with the bloodred light of the sun, the glare off the windows making the entire place seem ablaze . . .

The house stood empty.

It stood alone and small against the vast forest, a house and nothing more. And as he glanced back at Helen, he saw only hope and pleasure in her eyes, and the tiny hint of a smile twisting the corners of her mouth.

"It's beautiful," she said from the backseat. She had Jessie cuddled against her breast. "I love it."

They pulled up to the porch and he cut the engine. The silence seemed overwhelming.

"Let me show you around," he said.

They climbed out and he went to the back to unload the U-Haul. Jessie shuffled up beside him as he pulled out two of their smaller suitcases and set them on the ground. She grabbed one of the handles and tried to lift it, then frowned. "Here, princess," he said, smiling. "Carry your pack." He found the little red backpack where it was hiding near the back of the trailer, and helped her arms through its straps. She shifted Johnny Bear from one hand to the other as he did it, refusing to release him for one second.

"You feeling better?" he said after he had finished.

She nodded. She seemed tired, but there was a set to her shoulders that reminded him of Helen when she had her mind made up. "And you?" He reached out and scratched the stuffed bear behind its ear. "What do you think, Mr. Bear?" He waited for Jessie to respond, but she said nothing, hands against her hips. Her foot traced little designs in the snow.

"Does Johnny Bear like the place?" he persisted.

"I don't know," she said. "He won't talk about it."

Helen walked around the open car door. "Just because it stopped snowing doesn't mean you can't freeze to death," she said, hands on her hips. They stood side-by-side, mother and daughter, amusing if unintentional mimics.

Hank had supposedly hung the spare key on a nail under the front step. David groped blindly behind the first riser and felt a sharp pain in his palm as he touched the keys. He withdrew his hand quickly and stared at the splinter that dug deeply into the soft flesh. The damn thing looked the size of a toothpick. He picked at it, but only succeeded in driving it even deeper.

"Daddy, you're bleeding," Jessie said. Bright red drops ran down his hand to the sleeve of his jacket and hung from his wrist, the snow below him spattered with tiny dots of crimson.

He gave the keys to his daughter (who took them cautiously while making a face), grasped the top of the splinter firmly with his fingernails, and yanked. A sharp pain made him grit his teeth, and then it slid out smoothly, leaving an angry red wound behind. He slipped a few Kleenex from his pants pocket and wrapped them around his hand.

Inside, with the lights on, the house seemed almost cheery.

"It's beautiful," Helen breathed again, looking up at the deep brown of the railings that ran along the edge of the second floor. He slid his arm around her waist, pulling her close.

Jessie wriggled impatiently out of her backpack and dropped it on the floor. "I want a room up there," she said, pointing to the second-floor balcony. All the sadness and fear seemed to leave her in a rush. He leaned over impulsively and kissed her on the cheek, and she brushed it away impatiently.

"You can have any room you want," he said, and Helen pinched him hard. "Any room except the big one, that's ours." Jessie ran for the stairs, with Johnny Bear grasped tightly under one arm.

"She's fine, isn't she?" Helen asked.

He nodded. "I think so. She just fell asleep or something, and had another nightmare."

"I was so scared." She rested her head on his chest.

"Me too." He held her for a long moment, touching his lips to her hair. "I love you."

"I love you too." She looked up at him. "We're going to be fine too, aren't we?"

"Smashing."

"I really do like it," she said. "The house, I mean. It couldn't be better." She stood up on tiptoe and kissed him lightly on the lips, her breath warm on his cheek.

He laughed, and took her hand. "Wait until you see our closet. Jessie's probably already hiding in it." He led her towards the stairs. It felt good to him. Maybe everything would work out fine after all. The thought warmed him, and he embraced it gratefully.

Helen stopped suddenly at the foot of the stairs and raised his hand to eye level. "Honey . . ." she looked at him, concerned. The Kleenex was soaked with blood.

"Jesus." He unwrapped his palm and more blood welled up quickly. He tried to staunch the flow with more Kleenex.

"Let me find some bandages," Helen said. After a

moment of searching the suitcases, she pulled out a blue plastic case. "Give me your hand."

He extended it to her obediently, and she wrapped a long piece of white gauze around it from the case, securing it with medical tape. "There." A faint pink stain spread slowly outward. "How does it feel?"

He shrugged, ignoring the thumping ache and dropping his hand to his side. "It's fine. Let's see the rest of the house and get the things from the car."

Helen studied him for a moment, then smiled and took his hand gently. "A medical wonder. I'd better lead, man-of-the-house." She pulled an imaginary gun from her hip, and pointed it around the room, scowling. "There's splinters in these parts."

He slapped her behind, and she giggled. "Let's go get our daughter," he said. "Before she gets into trouble."

CHAPTER ELEVEN

Pete Winegold wound his truck through the hairpin curves with one hand on the wheel and the other on his bottle of Coors Light. *The Silver Bullet.* Tasted like warm piss, but he wasn't one to drink those prissy micro-brewery beers with names like Moon Lake or Jackson Hole or some such bullshit. Half the time, he figured, they were made out of someone's basement, and with labels just slightly more professional that what you'd get from an inkjet printer. At least with Coors, you knew what you were going to get. There was something to be said for that.

Pete had recently separated from his wife of fifteen years, and although they'd had no children, he had found it a remarkably complex process all the same. It was amazing how much crap you accumulated over those years together: anniversary gifts and furniture and piles and piles of paperwork, joint checking accounts, broken iPods and DVDs and jewelry and camping equipment. Hell, even friends had to be divided up like consolation prizes. *You can have the Davises, but I get Joan and Mark Price.* Pete shook his head, and a little beer sloshed onto the F-150's bench seat, speckling the gray material with a pattern that looked a little like fresh semen across a bedroom comforter. *Divorce is kind of like a high school orgasm*, he thought, with a wry grin. *You feel both an over-whelming relief and a lot of guilt—and you're never quite sure where the stuff's going to end up.*

His wife (soon to be ex-wife) Jerri was a grade-A bitch. Her nagging had built slowly over the years, and Pete was reminded of the story someone had told him about frogs, where if you threw one into a pot of boiling water it would jump right out, and yet if you put it in cold water and slowly turned up the heat, it would just sit there until it boiled to death. His marriage had been like that.

Finally he'd had enough, and apparently so had she, because when he announced he was leaving her, she hadn't shed a single tear. He imagined that she might have even thrown a party, although he had no proof of that. It just seemed like something she would do.

Jerri had wanted to meet with the mediator this afternoon, but he'd told her he was feeling under the weather. He told his boss at the Lowe's where he managed inventory the same thing. And then he climbed into his truck and headed north with his hunting rifle and fishing gear in the back, along with a tent, pack, sleeping bag and a cooler full of booze and cold cuts.

It was high time to escape for a little R & R (*my little divorce party*), and Dana damn well better be right about this spot up near the border. Dana worked stocking shelves in kitchen and bath, and he was often, although not always, drunk. Pete had resisted firing him the first time he'd smelled the booze on Dana's breath, and the two had formed a friendship of sorts over the past few months as Pete's marriage had gone south. Dana could sympathize, as he'd been twice divorced himself. The two of them had gotten to talking about hunting, and Pete opined about how when he was just a kid growing up in Waterville, his father had taken him out into the woods every other weekend with a couple of rifles and a box of ammo, and they'd shot at deer or bear or anything else that crossed their path for the next six hours. No permits, no wardens, no waiting for the right season or some such foolishness. These days you couldn't even go fishing without applying for a goddamned license. As far as Pete was concerned, the only things you should need a license for were driving or getting married, and the former ought to be a damn sight easier to get than the latter.

On a slow day at the store a few weeks back, Dana had started talking about how he'd been up in the deep woods near the Canadian border with some high school buddies a couple of years ago, and how the woods around there were full of wild game of all shapes and sizes. Hell, they'd brought back three carloads full of deer meat and the head of a 600-pound black bear. Pete knew this last was true, because he'd seen the head himself in Dana's basement, mounted on a piece of plywood. The only reason they hadn't brought back the moose they'd killed was that they couldn't fit it in the trunk.

The area, Dana said, was some sort of wildlife paradise. It was completely unmonitored by game wardens, there were almost no humans around at all to spoil the experience, and it was only about three hours' drive from Bangor. The two of them had started talking about going up there together, but Pete knew how these things went; there would be a lot of talk and nothing would ever happen. That's the way it was with work buddies, a bunch of back-slapping and tall tales and the occasional shared beer once or twice a month. So on a whim, he'd decided to go himself. Sure, it was winter, and hell, it would be cold as a witch's tit, but he'd been in worse situations more than once. He prided himself on his wilderness skills, and his gear was rated to twenty below. One thing was for sure: there wouldn't be anyone else up there to spoil the experience.

He killed off the Coors, tossed the empty bottle on the floor, and cracked open another. Foam ran over his hand and he sucked it off the neck of the bottle before it could wet his jeans. He had to be getting close to the logging trails now. Dana had said they were all over the place. He glanced at himself in the rearview mirror and thought again about hair plugs. He had a nice enough face, friendly, a little soft, but his hairline had receded enough that he'd just shaved it all off completely last year and gone with stubble. Now he looked older than his forty-two years. If he was going back on the market, he would have to make some changes. Nobody wanted to see a middle-aged man sitting alone in a bar, trying to pick up women.

He saw a break in the trees up ahead, and slowed the truck down to a crawl. Sure enough, a logging road wound off into the woods, and he pulled onto the shoulder for a better look. Not another car in sight, and the road looked to be in pretty good shape. He got out of the truck and walked a few paces through the foot-deep snow, testing the ground underneath. Frozen solid and flat enough. He got back in and drove the truck up into the woods, just out of sight of the road. Anyone passing by might see the tracks, but chances are they wouldn't think anything of it.

Three hours later, he was sweating profusely in his heavy coat and gloves and wondering if this trip had been such a good idea after all. He had to admit he wasn't in the same shape he had been as a younger man, and the beer buzz was wearing off, leaving him with a slight headache and a twinge in his right knee that was getting worse by the minute. In fact, now that he was sober, he realized that the wilderness skills he liked to brag about had not been used for over ten years now, and they were a damn sight rusty, to say the least.

For the first time, he started to think that this might be the beginning of that dreaded thing called a midlife crisis. If so, then he'd spectacularly overestimated himself. His plan had been to hike out far enough with his pack and guns to find a blind somewhere and wait for game, and then return to the truck before dark to set up camp. But right now, he was seriously considering just heading home and never speaking of this trip to anyone. Maybe, if he drank enough, he could convince himself it had never happened at all.

That was when he came across the bear tracks.

They were no more than a few hours old, he was sure of that. Big, too, judging by the size of the paws and the length of the creature's stride. Probably over 600 pounds, and in a black bear that was pretty rare. Pete removed his rifle from his pack and made sure there were rounds in the chamber, and then he slogged through the deeper snow to a tree where the bear had paused to scratch himself. The marks on the bark were nearly seven feet off the ground. Full-grown male, and a monstrous son of a bitch at that. He mentally increased his size estimate to 700 pounds plus. Curious that he wasn't hibernating at this time of the winter.

Pete felt the old tingle coming back. God, how he would love to bag a bear even bigger than Dana's trophy. A bear that big would be impossible to drag home, but he could saw off its head with his bowie knife and get that back to the truck without much trouble. He scanned the woods, looking for evidence of the bear's presence. At that size it was almost certainly a male, which was good, since females could have cubs, and with cubs they became a lot more unpredictable. You did not want to piss off the females, which, Pete thought, was a pretty good rule for any species, come to think of it.

The tracks continued through a break in the trees up ahead, and Pete followed them as quietly as possible, rifle at the ready. He did not want to get too far from the logging path, but there was no sign of a storm coming, and it would be easy enough to track his footprints back to where he started. Following the prints made him think of how each person followed their life's path, and whether that path was already set for them from the start. Had his path always included divorce? What if he stepped away from it and chose something different? Would the footprints change, would they lead him to another place? Or would he be forced back around again to the same result, nothing more than a pawn in a much larger game?

This wasn't like him, Pete thought. He was no philosopher. Hell, he'd barely earned his degree in history from the University of Maine, and if it weren't for his college girlfriend at the time, he probably would have dropped out and started working for his father. But long hours alone in the woods did something to a guy, there was no doubt about that. Maybe that was the real reason he'd decided to take this trip today. Maybe he was already off the path and trying to find his way back.

The opening in the trees turned out to be a river. Pete stood on the bank for a long time, looking out over the frozen expanse in awe. Winds had swept the ice clean in the middle, but along the edges were drifts three feet high in places. Now this was more like it. He could hike back to the truck to get his tent and make camp here, under the trees where it was warmer, and do some ice fishing tomorrow.

In his excitement, he'd almost forgotten about the bear. Now he turned to the tracks again, to see if he could figure out where the animal had gone. They led along the edge of the river and then back up near the woods. It was there that they crossed with another set of prints.

These were made by a human boot.

Pete crouched to study them. A big boot too. Probably a man's size twelve or thirteen, or larger. Pete was a size eleven. He put his own boot into one of the prints, and had plenty of room to spare.

"Hello?" he said. "Anyone there?" His voice sounded hoarse and strange after so many hours of silence. A slight breeze rustled the branches of the trees above his head. For some reason, the hairs prickled on the back of his neck. Someone wandering around out here, chances are, they didn't want to be found. It wasn't a place you went for human company.

The human had followed the bear back into the first line of trees, then towards the river again. Pete walked alongside the set of tracks and struggled through the deeper snow at the river's edge. Despite his best efforts at sealing off the gaps, snow found its way into the tops of his boots, and he felt an icy trickle down his thick socks as it melted. Felt sort of good right now, but he knew it could be trouble later, if he didn't dry them out.

Once out on the open ice, the snow was nearly swept clean, and he had difficulty following the prints. It didn't matter though, because he could see something on the ice near the middle of the river. A darker spot staining the expanse of blue-white. He hurried towards it, but before he got there, he already had a very bad feeling.

The feeling deepened into full-blown panic when he reached the blood.

There was a lot of it, just speckles at first and then arcing across the ice in a sweeping spray, and finally, a large pool full of gore. He crouched next to the pool and touched his finger to it. Still wet.

"Hello?" he said again. His voice echoed back at him from the far bank. He had no way of knowing whether this blood was animal or human. But there were two possibilities; this man had either bagged big game, or gotten himself into a heap of trouble.

"Anyone there!? Do you need help!?"

A crow, rousted by his voice, lifted off from a pine tree in a flurry of cawing and flapping wings and soared over the river. Pete jumped and swore. *Okay, Grizzly Adams, think. If the guy's hurt, there will be a trail of blood to follow.*

In fact, there was a thick line of blood leading away from the larger pool, towards the opposite bank. There were bloody boot prints too. He followed them across the ice, but before long, they faded and then disappeared well before they reached land again.

On the one hand, Pete thought, that was good news. If the man had been badly wounded, he would have kept bleeding. But then again, if he'd wounded or killed the bear, what happened to the carcass? It didn't make any sense.

He crouched and studied the last boot print. It was strange. Faint but still visible enough, and yet the prints just ended there, as if the wearer had grown wings and flown away. He could try to find this guy, or he could just turn around and go back to his truck and pretend like it never happened. There was nobody here to judge him; nobody, that is, except one man who may or may not be lying somewhere with his intestines hanging out and a bear's teeth marks in his skull.

WWJD—What Would Jerri Do? He smiled grimly at the familiar joke, referenced many times during the years of his marriage. At first it had been light-hearted, but more recently he'd said it with real bitterness. His wife really did feel as if her word was law, and that was the problem as far as he was concerned. Being tied down didn't suit him. He was a man, and men needed their freedom.

Jerri, he decided, would leave the guy to die. *It's his own damn fault for going out here in the first place*, she'd say. *If there's an angry bear on the loose, we need to find someplace else to go.* So Pete decided to stay.

He looked for any more marks, but there was nothing. Still, the general direction of the prints had been towards the far side of the river, so he headed in that direction, holding his rifle tightly in both hands. His entire body was tingling, and he felt more alive than he had in months. This was why he'd come out here in the first place, to find his balance again and remember what he used to be like, before life had gotten in the way.

When he reached the far bank, he walked up and down the drifts, looking for more prints or any other sign that something had passed through. But he saw nothing. Finally, he found a place where the snow was not as deep and climbed up to the tree line. The woods were thicker here, and he stood in silence for a long moment, then slung his gun and pack to the ground and took a drink from his water bottle.

That was when he saw a glimpse of blue through the trees.

Pete picked up his gun again and walked in that direction, ducking under the pine branches and pushing others aside, losing sight of what he'd seen for a moment before finding it again. The blue thing, whatever it was, did not move. As he got closer, he saw that it was a tarp, and something big was rolled up inside of it. The tarp sat under one of the largest pine trees in the general vicinity, and the snow around it was swept clean.

He scanned the area. Nothing moved. He reached down with trembling fingers and pulled down one edge. The snarling, gore-smeared face of a black bear leered back at him.

The creature's eyes had been dug out, leaving bloody sockets.

Jesus Christ, Pete thought. *Who the hell would do that? And what sort of man would be strong enough to pull that kind of bulk across two hundred feet of ice, up the snow-covered riverbank and through fifty feet of woods?*

The attack, when it came, was brutally swift and silent. He heard only a swish of something falling through air, and had the chance to look up just as a terrible weight came crashing down on his shoulders. His knees buckled and he fell to the ground, pain lancing through his back. His legs wouldn't move anymore, and something warm and wet ran over his body. He tried to cry out, but quickly descended into blackness.

When Pete came to, he was upside down and hanging from his feet from a rough-hewn beam in the ceiling, some kind of rope cutting cruelly into the flesh of his shins. His pulse thundered in his ears, and the pressure made his head scream, his vision tinged with pink. It took him a few moments to remember what had happened: the blood and finding the tarp and the dead bear, and then something falling on him . . .

A horrible smell assaulted his senses and he gagged. He tried to pull himself up, but his legs wouldn't work properly at all. Panic flooded through him and he tasted metal in the back of his throat. He had no idea where he was or what was coming next.

He realized something else: he was naked.

Jerri, I'm sorry, please do something call someone please help me . . .

He sobbed aloud, and it was very loud in the quiet room. He heard the sound of a slow, steady dripping. What was happening? Who had put him here, and why had they taken away his clothes? *WWJD, should have listened to her in the first place and I wouldn't be here I'd be home drinking a beer in front of the ball game and waiting for dinner oh God please, please help me.*

He was being punished for his sins; he had not been a good husband or a man; he had not gone to church or worked with those less privileged or donated money to good causes. He was lazy and a drunk and he had no friends except Dana and even he wasn't really a friend at all, but an acquaintance. His sister lived a thousand miles away and he didn't visit his mother in the home or own a dog and he didn't eat well or give out candy on Halloween to all the kids in their costumes—

Somewhere, the sound of a door opening. Pete Winegold realized two things in the ensuing silence of the room: everything he thought he knew about his life was wrong, and he did not want to die.

"Hello?" he said. He tried to twist around to see what had come in behind him. His entire body began to shake. "Whatever you want, you got it. I—I got a truck, it's parked down the road, it's almost new, you—you can have it. I got a couple thousand in the bank too."

Pete's vision swam in and out of focus, and he was feeling very light-headed now. He was so cold. The dripping sound continued. It sounded very close. He tilted his head enough to see the floor, and there was a pool of blood underneath him. *Drip.* A bright crimson drop fell into the pool. *Drip.*

A figure stepped around into his line of sight. It looked like some kind of monster carrying a hunting blade. Pete tried to look up into its face, but could not; it was as if he were peering into a distance far greater than a few feet. Peering into the abyss.

"Please," he whispered. "Please. Don't."

But the knife did not falter.

And the abyss stared back.

CHAPTER TWELVE

They settled into the new house with almost uncanny ease—the quiet of the surrounding woods seemed to be an elixir for Jessie—and by the afternoon of March 3rd it felt almost like home to David, who had already decided to set up an office in the spare room downstairs and make the shed outside into one hell of a workroom, though he hadn't yet had time to inspect it. He had always wanted one of those sparkling clean little areas with a place for everything—the hammer, screwdrivers, saws, drills, all hung in their rightful places. He knew it sounded old-fashioned, not to mention stereotypical, but he wanted a *tool shed*, plain and simple. And never had he wanted one more than now, out here in the depths of the woods. It seemed somehow natural for him to work with his hands.

"A regular pioneer," Helen said, grinning, when he mentioned it. The sad thing was (and he hoped fervently to change this with practice), he was a lousy carpenter. He had the desire but none of the skills. He had spent most of his childhood in Seattle, Washington, after all, and not in the great outdoors, building tree forts.

His father had kept a workroom downstairs in the basement, where he had tried valiantly to play the man's game, but all Neil Pierce had ended up doing was putting together a few "snap-rite" airplane models and making a mess of the place. Still, David realized that his father's basement was probably the reason he wanted a tool shed of his own. It had something to do with childhood memories that were always larger than life. He wanted to have a great tool shed, and he wanted his father to come visit in the spring and help him build things. He didn't at the present time know exactly what those things would be, but that didn't matter.

The spare room downstairs made a perfect office. He had brought several boxes full of files from the office in Quebec City as well as all his drafting tools from home, and figured to do a lot of work right here for the first few weeks. After that, he would have to spend some more time in Quebec City, and then they could all move in after the thaw. He felt confident that the plant would be a smashing success. Hell, maybe he would even get some recognition for a job well done, or at least move up in the ranks. For the first time since college, he began to feel good about his job and his future.

Later that afternoon, before Hank was to stop by with some papers to sign, he and Helen had a snowball fight in the front yard by the Toyota. He crouched as the fight became more intense, and the U-Haul, which was now unhooked and parked by the side of the house, became Helen's fortress (he had arranged to return the trailer to a rental store in Fort Kent next week; until then, it seemed to have found a purpose).

As the snowballs whizzed by, and he snuck a peek at Helen's flushed and laughing face from behind the car's front bumper, he was reminded of the first time that he knew he had fallen in love with her. She had taken him to a James Taylor concert for his twenty-second birthday, and on the way back they had stopped in a jazz club for a drink. The club was nothing special, just a hole in the wall, but when they walked in, Louis was singing the blues while the Duke played behind him with his big band, and for a moment it almost seemed as if they had stepped through time to the fifties. Of course, the music was canned and coming from the loudspeakers mounted on the wall, but the magic in the air stayed with them as they found a table in the dark and smoky rear of the club.

They ordered a couple of long-neck beers and leaned back, watching the people, feeling no need to talk. The concert had been great, holding hands and feeling each other close, even better. Halfway through the show, Helen had leaned to whisper in his ear, "I just *love* his voice," and then let her head remain on his shoulder. The words weren't important, but the touch on his shoulder was. He smelled the clean, soft scent of her hair and felt the softness of her cheek, and something stirred deep within him.

Later, as he watched her across the table at the club, she turned to him and smiled in the dark. It was then that her face had shown that childlike happiness, and he had realized with an almost shocking surety, *I'm falling for this girl. Falling hard.* He had leaned across the table, sure that he would be shot down, but full of recklessness, and whispered, "I love you."

To his surprise, she had replied frankly, with no hesitation. "I love you too."

They had spent the night together, and a month later he had proposed.

A snowball exploded on the silver curve of the bumper right in front of his nose, and he was shocked out of his trance. Snow was in his hair and eyes, and as he shook it off, laughing, he heard her running across the driveway towards him.

"Where were you, soldier?" she asked. "I've been shouting at you for an hour, it seems like. Hank's here."

He looked up and saw Hank parking his rust-colored Cherokee near the U-Haul. David gave Helen a quick kiss and a hug and went to meet him.

As they sat at the kitchen table, David was reminded again of how much he liked the older man. Even Jessie, who played with her crayons on the kitchen floor as they talked, seemed to be listening with half an ear to their conversation, as if Hank's slow drawl pleased her.

"I've got a cabin about five miles from here," he said. "Good fishing in the pond out back, ice fishing, of course, in the winters. You ought to take a gander at it sometime."

"Maybe I will."

"Always welcome. That pond sure knows how to grow 'em, sure does. It ain't much to look at, but that don't mean nothin'. Fish don't care much for looks."

Hank had brought a six-pack of Molson Light, and they both sucked at their beers comfortably. "I guess you don't have much company around here?" David asked.

"That depends. Used to have a good friend name of Joe Thibideau, worked in the station with Bobby. Hell—" he glanced down at Jessie to see if she had caught this blasphemy, then, deciding she hadn't, kept on. "We used to go fishin' 'bout every weekend in the winters, when I was here. He was a decent guy all around. My old lady liked him a lot, my boy too. Say, Michael and Jessie, they might get along. Didn't think about that. Mike's about six now. I'll have to drop by with him sometime."

He seemed to have forgotten what they were talking about. "So what happened with Joe?" David asked.

"He went missing about a month ago now. I was one of 'em that helped look, but we never found his body. Didn't figure we would. There's a lot of land out there to cover."

David nodded sympathetically, feeling like an asshole for bringing it up in the first place.

"He was lookin' for that little girl I told you about, the one who used to—"

David threw a quick glance at him and shook his head sharply. Helen was upstairs, but Jessie might overhear and understand. This was the wrong time for that to come out.

"—well, you know, he was one of them," Hank continued, with only a slight pause. "The only one in the search party we lost, thank God. It was bitter cold last month."

"It's bitter cold right now."

"Aw, this ain't nothin'," Hank grinned, accepting the obvious bait. "Why, when I was about ten, we had a storm . . ."

The conversation drifted off onto other things. Hank stayed for over an hour, they finished the six-pack, and when he left David had forgotten about Joe Thibideau entirely.

By the time he thought of him again, it would be almost too late for it to matter.

CHAPTER THIRTEEN

Robert Babcock (Bobby, to his friends) was having a hard time with his tie. He had never been much for suits, ties or sports coats (this was at least partially because they would not allow sufficient room for his enormous belly, and made him feel light-headed), and now that the town had finally decided to go ahead with this funeral, he wasn't sure he wanted to go. Joe had been his friend and a damned good deputy, too. His funeral would be a pretty goddamned bitter experience for everyone. At this point, Bobby didn't know how many of the twenty-seven-man search party blamed themselves for Joe's death, he just knew he did, at least a little bit. On top of all that, he had to get into this goddamned jacket and tie.

And the bitch of it all is that we don't know he's dead, he thought, though that wasn't true. Nobody survived out in those woods for a month without food or shelter. Still, there was something inside of Bobby Babcock that just wouldn't let go.

He sighed, giving his stomach one last gasp of freedom before he donned the blue blazer, and turned away from the mirror. He looked like shit anyway. Why bother? It had been one hell of a February in St. Boudin, and he had bags under his eyes the size of pumpkins to prove it. First Eddie, then the girl, and now Joe. Too many deaths for such a small town. And the only body they'd come up with was Eddie's; Joe and the girl would not turn up until spring, and maybe not even then. They just didn't know where to look.

Whatever the hell was going on, he didn't like it. People were acting strange lately. He'd seen cabin fever before, but this wasn't it. Besides, the winter hadn't been any harder than usual, and if people weren't used to the snow by now, well then they had better get the hell out and go find Florida, because the sun wasn't due in St. Boudin for another few weeks at least.

And whoever had killed Eddie, whatever sick and pissed off son of a bitch had done *that* little bit of late Christmas carving, was still out there. It had taken them a day just to get an ID on his body, and they had never found the head. Privately, Bobby prayed they never would. Maybe he had made a mistake sending Joe and the others out looking for the girl so late at night. Maybe he should have called in for backup a long time ago. Maybe . . .

Fuck the maybes, he thought. *Don't be stupid*. The truth of the matter was, if he had called for help, St. Boudin would be a war zone about now. And that would mean trouble politically. That would mean even more pressure on him, and with that he just might go under. The new hydroelectric facility meant jobs, money, *life* to this town, and he couldn't afford to screw it up by bringing in some bad publicity. Besides, for all he knew, whoever had killed the farmer had moved on a long time ago, or died out in those woods. He had no reason to suspect foul play with the girl or with Joe. Just because they hadn't found the bodies didn't mean a goddamned thing.

At the moment, Bobby Babcock was doing a very good job convincing himself that he had done something right, though with every passing day that became harder and harder to do. He had spent most of his childhood in St. Boudin, moved there when he was six from Fort Kent in Maine, been promoted through the ranks until he had finally reached the top (or as close to the top as you could be in a small town), but he still felt like he didn't quite measure up, like the town watched him a little more carefully than they might anyone else. He was an American. And though the cultures seemed to mix here in St. Boudin, an American was still a foreigner. He had to watch himself all the way, or he would step in something that smelled real bad, and would make him smell real bad too.

He prayed to God this February wasn't it.

"Ready to go, Bobby?" His wife, Mary, stood at the corner of the bed, a tall, unusually thin woman born and raised in St. Boudin, a woman who had married an American but had never given up her French roots. She still spoke French to the people who would listen, still visited the graveyard where her father and mother and distant relatives were buried, still observed the Saints' days that came and went without much celebration.

Goddamn her, Bobby thought suddenly. *Goddamn all these people*. He took her arm, all bone and loose skin, and guided her towards the door. The funeral would begin in an hour, and he hoped to sneak out early. *Joe wouldn't mind*, he thought. *He'd understand*. Funerals were more for the living than the dead, and Bobby didn't want to be a part of all that today. He was too busy thinking about how he'd screwed up and let the pressure get to him, and how maybe that had caused Joe Thibideau to die.

Before they reached the car, he tried to convince himself again that he had done the right thing, that the killer had moved on and that he would only be risking his job if he had called anyone else in. But he couldn't quite do it.

The old arguments weren't working very well anymore.

CHAPTER FOURTEEN

Around noontime the following day, Helen decided to go shopping and explore the local area. David had some work to do, and Jessie decided she would rather stay with him than ride around with her mother, which was probably a wise decision. So, with her bright and happy dreams of a family excursion fading rapidly, Helen climbed determinedly into the car and cranked the engine. It turned over lazily for several moments before finally catching. Even the car wanted to stay home, it seemed.

At the end of the long driveway, she held up for a moment and then turned right impulsively, away from the highway and the way they came in. The only thing she knew was that St. Boudin was around here someplace, and she could find some sort of general store there where gas and groceries were available, for a price (a very high price; Hank had mentioned that yesterday).

David had sat with Hank long after he'd signed some paperwork and the deal was done. It was all too easy. The company was handling all the difficult stuff (as well as the check).

In fact, it seemed to her like Hydro Development was eager to get them settled in, like they were almost begging them to take the house, medical and dental plans, everything and anything as long as David was happy. And that was funny, for though she didn't like to admit it, competition for David's services had not exactly been banging down the door.

The house really was wonderful, she was sure of that. After a long nap yesterday, she had spent a full hour sitting in the living room admiring the sunset through the generous glass on the western side. David started a fire that kept the house warm through the night. They would have to get used to checking it in the early mornings, but it had its own kind of rustic charm.

Jessie had claimed the bedroom next to theirs, a small but bright little room with a pretty view of the woods and hilltops out the back. And their bedroom took her breath away. The very first night, David held her, soft and naked, one hand idly stroking the side of her breast while they watched the stars through the skylight. The rooms were still sparsely decorated, cluttered with the boxes and the organized mess of the move, but they felt comfortable and the newness of everything settled down upon her like mist from a fountain on a hot summer day. The drive up was already fading to an old memory, lost among the stuffing of twenty-eight years.

Now the sky was a brilliant blue, the rare depth of color peculiar to the heavens on a clear, cold winter's day. The sun beamed down brightly, but without any warmth, a token gesture. The snow sparkled, so white it was hard to look at without squinting.

A few miles from their house, she came to a fork in the road and took the left turn, following the river. Occasionally, she passed what could be a driveway or logging road running off to her left into the woods, but there were never any tracks, and it was tough to tell with the deep snow.

She passed a trailer that spewed a long, lazy spiral of gray smoke from its chimney into the sky. After that was a farmhouse, then two more. She guessed she had hit the outskirts of town (whatever town it was), and a minute later she came over the crest of the hill and the village spread out below her, nestled in a shallow river valley.

On the right along the riverbank was a small general store and gas pumps, and beyond that rose the steeple of an old, white church. Just across from the church was a post office flying American and Canadian flags. Scattered about were houses of various sizes and shapes. On her right as she went by she noticed a small, hand-painted sign in both French and English: WELCOME TO ST. BOUDIN, EST. 1876. And underneath that, in English, in smaller letters and handwritten: "Like it or leave it."

I don't have much of a choice, she thought. Though to be fair, the place *was* pretty with its light coating of fresh snow and little country houses. It looked to her as she imagined an isolated Canadian town would, content to stay the way it was and let the rest of the madly rushing world pass it by in a blur.

She stopped at the store and grabbed some groceries. A woman in her sixties punched in the numbers and took her money without a word, but she refused to let it kill her mood—the sun was shining, it was a fine day. When she got back into the car, she took a left at the next fork, since ahead of her the ground rose again and the houses grew farther and farther apart, the woods thickening until even the road disappeared on its twisting, turning way.

Several more houses faced each other across the narrow street, then a volunteer fire department in what looked like an old barn, and the police station where a couple of beat-up old trucks sat crumbling in the parking lot. As she drove past the station, she found a deli called the Railway Cafe with a Coors Light sign in the window and a half-full parking lot. Maybe this was where the action was in St. Boudin, she thought. As good a time as any to find out.

Inside, the place was more pleasant that she would have predicted. A counter ran along the left wall and several people sat on stools, talking quietly. She sat down in one of the little booths by the window. In a moment, a young, pretty waitress walked over and handed her a menu. "Give you a minute?"

Helen nodded, grateful that she spoke English, and the waitress smiled and continued about her business. A quick glance at the menu told her it was nothing special, your basic soup-and-sandwich deal. She settled on a bowl of New England clam chowder, which was probably out of a can but would be good and hot, she hoped.

After she ordered, she let her eyes play over the walls around her. They were covered with all sorts of quotes and sayings—from a syrupy-sweet crocheted "Home Sweet Home," framed with braided string, to a print of the Norman Rockwell painting with the little girl in pigtails outside the doctor's office. But what intrigued her most was a bulletin board down near the far end of the counter covered with newspaper clippings and flyers. She got up and walked over for a closer look.

The clippings were mostly from the *St. Boudin Gazette* (this seemed to be a two- or three-page flyer), and they surrounded a large sign and picture in the center of the board. MISSING, it read. HAVE YOU SEEN THIS LITTLE GIRL? The picture below was of a girl who looked to be about Jessica's age, with straight, jet-black hair held up with bright pink elastics, and a large, gap-toothed smile.

"Marie Kennedy disappeared from Jackson Jan. 25" was written in French and English in dark marker below it. "Please call 555-9238 if you have any information. We miss her."

The room felt a bit darker than before. She glanced around nervously, but the sun was still shining brightly through the windows, painting little yellow squares across the tabletops.

How many people disappear from this area in a year? One, maybe two? And one of them just happens to be a little girl from Jackson?

"Sad, ain't it?"

Helen spun around. A young man stood before her, leaning an arm casually against the counter, long, greasy hair swept back from his forehead. She hadn't noticed him when she came in. He wasn't much taller than she was, but he was thick through the shoulders. He wore a faded, plaid shirt with the sleeves rolled up, and on one meaty bicep she saw the edge of a bluish silver tattoo.

Helen took a step backward.

The young man grinned. "That was the Kennedy girl, lived up near route 15. Got lost a few weeks ago, never found her. Sad, like I said. Her mom used to run this place. She headed out west somewhere after it happened, couldn't stand being around here anymore."

Helen nodded in what she hoped was a pleasant manner, trying to hide the shake in her knees. "I hadn't heard."

"You're new in town, ain't you? My name's Mike." The young man stuck out his hand, letting his shirt-sleeve ride back farther on his arm and exposing the tattoo fully. It was a thick, silver web with a spider in the middle, its white fangs bared and dripping red. She shuddered and tried to smile.

"My husband and I just moved into a house in Jackson. That's why this picture interested me."

"You bothering that young lady, Mike?" A second waitress stared at them from the other end of the counter, where she was pouring a cup of coffee for one of the men seated on a stool. Her sleeves were rolled up as well, and though the tattoo was conspicuously absent, her arms held the same bulk and solidity as the young man's. *A worthy adversary*, Helen decided immediately. *Thank God.*

"She looked curious, is all. Thought maybe I could help out. Always aiming to please, you know me, Angie."

"Well, you let her alone now, you hear? I don't want to have to call Bobby down here again."

"Relax, why don't you, for Chrissakes." He turned to Helen and grinned. "Just being neighborly."

After he retreated to the far end of the place and sat down, Helen realized she had backed herself slowly into the corner. She walked forward purposefully and sat down at the end of the counter, ignoring the shake in her knees. *Silly to get so worked up*, she thought. *What am I so worried about anyway?*

"Sorry about that." The waitress had made her way down to where Helen was sitting. "He used to be a harmless little schoolboy, if you can believe it. People are changing mighty quick around this town. Don't know what it is. MTV rock and roll, or something." She sighed, her large bosom rising like twin boulders within the uniform top. "Don't worry, he wouldn't cause any real trouble or we wouldn't let him set his foot any farther than the welcome mat."

Helen, though she wasn't completely convinced, smiled and nodded.

"Name's Angie Fisher. I sort of run the place here, such as it is. Haven't seen you around, have I?"

"No." Helen waited while the bowl of soup she had ordered was delivered, thick and steaming. The younger waitress set it down in front of her, smiled, and left.

"That there's homemade."

"Really?" Helen hoped she didn't sound too surprised.

"Yes, ma'am, I do it myself. Old family recipe, you know. We get the clams fresh from the coast. There's a man who comes around driving a truck of seafood, selling it to us inlanders."

Helen smiled, took a spoonful and sipped it gingerly. The creamy liquid warmed her throat and sent welcome shivers of heat to her arms and legs. It was buttery and thick, reminding her of the big, soft pieces of fresh-baked bread her grandmother used to make when she was a kid.

"It's excellent."

"Good, love to hear it. So where are you from, if you don't mind me asking?"

"My husband and I just drove up from New York. He's got a job at the new hydroelectric plant in Jackson."

"That place?" Angie frowned, her brow creasing. "I guess I don't know much about it, other than it being shut down this winter." But her demeanor had changed, her voice hardening.

"Sorry, I don't mean to be rude," she continued after a moment. "It's just that there's been some strange things going on out there in Jackson lately."

"Really?" Helen glanced at the bulletin board. The girl stared back at her from the photograph.

"That's Marie. I suppose you know all about that."

"No, only that she got lost."

Angie leaned forward, her voice lowered as if about to convey a deep, meaningful secret. "She disappeared from her mother's house just about a month ago now, and they never found a trace of her. Her parents were divorced, and her daddy lives out in Montana some-where now. He was an overhomer, you know. Came out of St. Stephen in New Brunswick as a boy and married an American. Anyway, her mother used to own this place—Jaimie, her name was. I was her head waitress, took over after she left. We were told she just couldn't handle the idea of her little girl dying alone out in those woods, so she moved down south. But the story around town is she lost it, ended up in a padded room."

Angie hunched even closer then, and Helen for one second had the strangest urge to laugh like a madwoman herself at this absurd lady in a country deli whispering like she was telling the country's greatest and most harmful secrets.

"The interesting part is she lost it *before* the girl wan-dered off, or so they say."

"You mean she went crazy and Marie ran off because of it?"

"Maybe, maybe not. Everybody around here's got cabin fever, like you never know what they'll do. Mike there's a good example." She pointed to where the young man with the tattoo had settled into a booth. "He was headed for college with a football scholarship, some Ivy League school, believe it or not, then he just up and dropped out senior year of secondary school, about four months ago now. Been hanging around here ever since."

Something clicked, and Helen suddenly felt as if

someone had punched her in the stomach. "Where did they live?"

"Who?"

"The little girl's family. The Kennedys."

"Off of route 15, near the plant. Nice place. I saw it once last year when Jaimie's car broke down, and I had to drive her to work. It's one of those solar type of houses, all open inside with railings along the upper floors. When I picked her up that day, she says . . ."

Angie continued on in that low whisper, but Helen wasn't listening. She threw a crumpled five-dollar bill from her pocket onto the counter, grabbed her jacket off the hook and ran for the door, leaving Angie in mid-sentence and the others in the deli staring after her curiously.

Screw them, she thought. Though part of her knew that something like that happening didn't have to change the way she felt about the place they were now calling home, she still felt like her stomach was being twisted into knots by some powerful, unseen hand.

Can houses think?

No. But people can. *And all I want is to get my little girl and get the hell out of that place.*

The door slammed shut behind her as she walked out into the cold. She spared one glance back and saw Angie's plump form at one of the windows, and then she reached the car, searching through her pockets for the bundle of keys. Nothing. Growing frantic, she opened the door and sat on the edge of the seat, rummaging through the big pockets of the ski parka. Finally, when she was just about to go back in, she saw them dangling from the steering column, and only then was aware of the insistent buzzing of the ignition warning system.

What am I thinking? Good thing we're not in New York anymore.

The thought of New York made her think of David, and she paused for a moment, hand on the keys. What was he going to think about this?

Or did he already know?

CHAPTER FIFTEEN

Jessica stood on the hard-packed snow of the driveway, little pink jacket zipped up to her chin and her hat with the bright yellow ball on top tucked down over her ears. Inside the wrappings she felt like a marshmallow, but it was warm and she had done it all herself, without even worrying too much about the seams in her socks or whether her pockets were zipped up exactly the same amount. That made her proud. It was one thing to *want* to go out to play, quite another to get ready and go do it, especially when the cold yucky wind tried to blow down your neck and made you shiver.

Her breath felt warm and wet on her cheeks. She tried to blow smoke rings like she saw people do in the movies but it didn't work; it all just came out in a big puff no matter how hard she pushed, and it made her dizzy. The day was bright and sunny and it looked nice from inside, but out here it was only cold. She wondered if maybe she should have stayed inside to play. But Daddy was busy in his office and she was bored. Her room was set up (her picture of Barney was on the wall, and she had made a bed for Johnny near her own, out of towels, in case her bed got too small for both of them) and the TV wasn't connected yet, so the picture looked like snow.

She had seen enough snow. That was why she wondered what made her want to go outside. After all, there was more snow out there than anywhere else. But she felt curious, and something tugged at her like a puppy on a leash.

These woods are not a playground, Daddy had told her.

She stood on the edge of the driveway, and looked out at the woods. They were a funny dark green color with all the needle trees, but the snow made it all right, lighter than she thought. It was possible to see into them a little way, just a little.

We're going to have to be very careful with the woods.

Somehow, Daddy's words made her want to go out there even more. What made them so special anyway? They looked like any old woods to her, a bunch of rough prickly trees and branches that caught your shirt when you walked. And out here in the bright sunshine, her scary dreams seemed almost silly. Almost.

She took a step off the driveway.

Around the corner of the house, she saw some kind of little building on the edge of the trees. It looked like just the right size for a child. What was in it, now that was a question. Visions of a tricycle or maybe a room full of toys filled her head. Daddy had given her old tricycle away to a little boy who had lived next door because it wouldn't fit in the car, and promised her a new one as soon as they were settled in. Maybe he had put it in the shed.

Another step.

She was off the hard-packed snow of the driveway and onto the deeper drifts. Her boots sunk in a few inches and hit a solid, icy crust. She tested it softly, then a little bit harder. It held. The shed was in full view now, its light brown wood looking new and shiny in the sunlight, like it had just been built. It sat a few feet out from the nearest tree, silent and beckoning.

Come over here, Jessie, it said. *There's plenty of toys, and lots of things to do. Don't mind your silly old daddy, he's just being GROWN-UP. He doesn't care about toys or other fun things like you do.*

Another step.

She was past the edge of the porch now and on what must be the front lawn, and felt the first little prickle of fear. It was so quiet and lonely out here. She wished she had gotten Johnny Bear out of bed to come along, but he had been tired and was happy in his new room. Besides, she felt a little more daring without him. That didn't usually happen; usually she felt empty without him and he was up and begging to come with her wherever she went. Maybe this meant she was becoming more GROWN-UP, like Daddy. She didn't know if that was a good thing or not.

She stood still on the crusty snow. The sun still shone down brightly; the woods remained silent. There was nothing to be afraid of, nothing at all. Then why was she just standing there now? Why weren't her feet moving?

It was important to make *sure* everything was okay, she decided. Because if there were wolves or big monsters in the woods, well then that would be dangerous. If she stood here, near the house, and nothing came to get her, then it was simple. She was safe. And besides, it didn't look very far from the shed to the house, not far at all, she didn't think. She could probably run to the porch if anything bad happened.

Another step.

She had reached the middle of the front lawn when she thought she saw something move in the woods near the shed. A glimpse of blue. She stopped short, her breath coming faster now and her legs wobbly. Nothing else moved. She was being silly, she thought. There weren't any monsters around here, because Daddy wouldn't bring her anywhere that had monsters.

Another step.

The door to the shed was on the left side, and just her size. A large, shiny padlock hung from the handle. It was unlocked. Now she was sure there was something neat in there, something that would be fun to play with like a big rubber ball or even better, a sled. Daddy had explained to her that the people who used to live there had left the furniture because it was too heavy or too old and they didn't want it. Maybe they decided they didn't want their toys, either. She hadn't seen any in the house, so the people must have kept them out here. Some things would be too big for inside.

Another step.

She neared the corner of the shed. Drifts were piled almost as high as her head, and little tracks marked where snow had fallen from the slanted roof. *Like little bird tracks*, she thought. *Or mice.* She had seen those tracks around the house in New York lots of times.

But here there were no animals. Not a sound broke the heavy stillness that surrounded her, except the soft hiss of her breath and the crunch of snow under her feet when she moved.

One more step.

Now she stood before the door, the lock winking in the noontime sun. And she saw, with a great deal of disappointment, that the snow had piled up here too, so that the bottom of the door was blocked with it. But it was funny, she thought, how the snow looked. It looked almost like someone had tried to pull the door out already, pulled really hard and had pushed the drift back a little bit. Yes, she could see the mark where it had moved. Daddy had been out here already! He wanted to see what was in here too.

But she didn't see any footprints.

This time, she took a step back. And caught movement again out of the corner of her eye—a quick flash of blue between the trees that was gone before she could even turn her head and follow it to wherever it was going.

Johnny Bear I wish I had Johnny, she thought, imagining his furry arms on her shoulders. Now she realized just how far she was from the porch. *If there was a big wolf after me and I was running as hard as I could I couldn't make it, he would catch me and eat me up.* She didn't like that idea at all, in fact it started to make her feel a lot more scared than before. She thought that there could be monsters out here, after all, and that monsters weren't always big purple creatures with giant teeth and sharp claws, sometimes they were wolves or bears or even *people*.

The sun was so bright and it lit up the snow into tiny sparkling bits of white that hurt her eyes. She squinted, feeling the tears well up. She wished she had never come out here, because now she was so scared she could hardly move. Daddy had been right. The woods were so close she could smell the sweetness of the pine trees, and she could see the branches moving deep within the darkness *like there was something in there watching her*.

Now she remembered clearly the blackness of her dream, the terror of that freezing room and the shadow on the wall of the head with little glass eyes and the huge muscled arm and rough shoulders as they moved against the wood.

And then it hit her like a bolt of lightning, the picture of a monstrous blue man holding a head JOHNNY'S HEAD and it was clearer and more intense than anything she had ever felt before, it was like she was right there with him.

Dimly she felt herself falling, but by the time her body hit the snow with a soft thump she didn't feel anything else.

CHAPTER SIXTEEN

It was the beginning of March, and the latest tests from the last batch of samples had finally come in.

Flint was sitting at his desk playing with a set of Ace cards. Flipping them, one by one, into the air and watching them fall in sweeping patterns to the desktop, his lap, the rug at his feet. A colorful pattern of fallen cards, some faceup, some facedown. Guess the suit on those. One of them stared up at him from the center of his desk, its cap tasseled and face painted white; the Joker. That was how he felt right then, like a big joker with nothing more up his sleeve. He had been on the road for three days, in Texas, then South Dakota, then Boston, but his mind kept switching gears back to the Jackson Hydro case. It was driving him crazy. Soon he would be a genuine lunatic, as obsessed as Lee Harvey Oswald or Booth. He only hoped he wouldn't do anything as drastic as they had. It just felt like he was missing something, that there was one more thing he could catch to make the whole mess clean itself up. He couldn't shake the feeling that something very bad was about to happen if he didn't find that one last piece of the puzzle.

He called down to the lab for the third time that day, and this time they had something for him on the samples collected from the most recent trip to the plant. They had already run some additional tests. Regardless of his impatience, he hadn't expected them quite so soon and was so surprised, it took a few seconds to register. Then he was out the door and on his way, thinking that maybe this time the catch had been made. He would call Pierce and put on some pressure if they had found something concrete.

As it turned out, what they had found was more than concrete. It was explosive.

In his new office, David was looking over the plans for the reservoir. Someone had already done a lot of work on them, but there were problems, and he meant to correct them fast. Now that he had the chance to be responsible for his own work, he wanted to make the most of it.

After a few minutes, he got up to grab a drink from the fridge (he thought that there might be one last Coke from the trip up) and stretch his legs. As he made his way across the living room, he studied the boxes that were stacked high by the closet door downstairs, a veritable mountain of cardboard, and thought bemusedly of his and Helen's promise to each other before the move to take only the most necessary things with them. It had not turned out that way in the end, and how she had managed to pack even used candlesticks escaped him.

The Cokes were gone, and he filled up a glass from the kitchen tap instead. It was nice to get clean, unfiltered water like this, when you could drink it without fearing for your life. And it tasted better than the water in New York too. He was beginning to think that this place would suit him just fine.

If he had turned to the window, he would have seen his daughter tottering slowly across the snow-covered lawn towards the shed and forgotten all about the plans and the project. But at that precise moment, the phone rang. He grabbed it off the counter with one hand while balancing the glass in the other, favoring his injured palm.

"David Pierce?" the voice asked. He hesitated a moment before answering. Somehow the voice didn't sound like someone he was particularly interested in talking to, especially now on a Sunday afternoon.

He was, unfortunately, right on.

"Dan Flint. From the meeting the other day?"

"I remember."

"Good. Listen, we went into the plant by snowmobile a few days ago, like we'd hoped. The samples we collected were contaminated with an unknown substance. We've done some lab testing over here, spent half the week, in fact."

"And?"

"It's not really something I can share over the phone. But we have every reason to believe the contaminant is coming from your power facility."

David waited, but the line was silent. "You're going to have to give me more than that, Mr. Flint. And why are you calling me? I'm not in charge of environmental concerns."

There was another long pause. David was beginning to think he had lost the connection when Flint spoke up again. "We think you can help us."

"What do you mean, help you? I told you, I'm not in charge—"

"I'm aware of that. What I mean is, we think you can

give us some inside information that might help us decide whether to shut down the project."

"What the hell is going on?"

"Again, I'd rather not talk about it over the phone," Flint said. "I'm coming to meet with you. I'll be at the Railway Cafe in St. Boudin at nine thirty next Friday. In the meantime, I'd like you to do a little digging into anything unusual. Anything at all. You've got a few days. I'd prefer it if you didn't tell anyone about our conversation."

"What makes you think I won't just call up Quebec City—"

"You won't," Flint said, "because I'm telling you not to. If you know what's good for you, you'll listen. I don't need to tell you how serious this is. I'll see you on the ninth."

The phone went dead. David slammed it back into its cradle, feeling the rattle all the way down to his feet.

He knew exactly what Flint was doing, and it wouldn't work. Maybe they felt he would be the easiest to crack, but he would not be intimidated.

None of this made any sense. The FERC wasn't the Mafia. Since when did they use spying and scare tactics to get their way? No, something was going on here, something that he didn't understand quite yet.

That was when he finally glanced out the large picture window in the kitchen and saw Jessica.

He didn't wait to pull on his boots. As he jumped from the porch, the cold snow shocked his bare feet, but he kept moving.

Jessica lay on the outskirts of the woods near the shed. He called her name. She did not stir. He struggled through the knee-deep snow, feeling the icy crust cut at his bare shins, and kneeled next to her.

"Jessica," he whispered, touching her cheek. "Jessie, please. Talk to me."

She opened her eyes, and they were calm and questioning.

"Daddy," she said. "I saw him."

CHAPTER SEVENTEEN

Helen arrived back at the house at two o'clock. David heard the car in the driveway but it didn't register to his preoccupied mind until the front door opened.

He had Jessie lying on the couch, a blanket over her feet. She had insisted that he get Johnny Bear from her room and bring him to her immediately. After David had carried her back into the house, she had seemed to be unharmed, but he couldn't shake the feeling that had come over him. Something was very wrong.

She had seen him, she said. In her head. He was a big, bad man, a mean man, and he wore blue trousers. The way she said those words, so calmly and truthfully, sent chills down his spine.

By the time Helen walked in, Jessie was dozing off. David pulled her into the office room and shut the door. "She's had another problem," he said, unsure of any other way to say it.

"What do you mean, another problem?"

David told her about the incident as simply as he could.

"Jesus," she said. "I'm scared."

"Me too—"

She took him by both forearms. "David, someone *died* here. A little girl."

He stood there for a long minute, wondering how to respond. "I know," he said finally. He felt her push away from him, and there was anger in her eyes.

"You *knew*?" Her voice went up a notch.

"Helen . . . I didn't want to upset you. It doesn't have anything to do with us or the house."

"It has everything to do with us, damn it!" Her voice rose still further, and David began to worry about Jessie waking up.

"Helen, please," he said, reaching for her hands.

"No!" She pushed him away again. "I want to get out of here, now. I want to take our baby away from these woods and I don't care about anything else. Her mother . . . her mother went *insane*, David. Do you have any idea how that makes me feel?"

He nodded. "I understand. I felt the same way at first. Jessie, she . . ." He struggled for the right words. "The house seemed so perfect in every other way, and I thought about how stupid it would be to let something that happened months ago affect our decision, because we're going to have to live out here *somewhere*, there aren't exactly a ton of choices, and we're going to have to deal with the isolation somehow. Or else we go back to New York and live on breadsticks. I don't want that, and neither do you."

This time when he touched her, her eyes had softened (though she looked like she could cry at any moment), and her body relaxed against him.

"When I saw the picture of that little girl . . ." She shuddered and closed her eyes, resting her head against his chest. "It could have been Jessica."

He held her close and tried to calm her trembling body. *What can I say? Let's run from here and end up on welfare, begging for meals? Or stay with the job and ignore the problems it causes?*

Then there was the phone call from Flint. He wasn't quite sure how to bring that one up.

He kissed her forehead. "Look, I'll do whatever you decide. If you want to look for another place, we will."

"No. You're right, I'm being irrational. We'll make it work. Just don't keep anything else from me again, okay?"

A noise at the doorway made them both turn. Jessie stood there rubbing her eyes, Johnny Bear clutched in one pudgy hand. "Daddy," she said, "did you try to get into the shed?"

"What do you mean?"

"I thought you did because the snow's all pushed away from the door."

"I haven't been out there." He looked at Helen, who shook her head.

"Then he did it," she said.

David felt a prickle of fear run along the base of his spine and tighten the flesh around his skull. He forced himself to relax, clenching and unclenching his fists. It took an incredible amount of will to keep from glancing out the kitchen window.

There's nothing there. It's Jessie's psyche you should be worried about.

"How about if I go look around a little? If there's anybody snooping, I'll find him."

"And call the police?" Jessie looked doubtful.

"And call the police." David smiled and ruffled her hair. *See, nothing to it. Now just go on out there and bring back a snooper. Don't come back until you do.*

He went to the closet, pulled out his boots, coat and

gloves, and slipped them on. Inside them, he felt uncomfortably hot and clumsy, but he knew he would be grateful for it outside.

"I'll be right back," he said. Helen followed him to the door. "Keep her occupied while I'm gone, will you? I don't want her to see me out in the woods. It might freak her out."

"I . . . Just be careful," she said. "Please."

Outside, he blinked in the brilliant sun, now low in the sky. Any wind that had been blowing had died, and in the dead calm of the late afternoon it was warm enough to keep his jacket unzipped.

He saw Jessie's footprints leading off the hard-packed snow near the front steps to the white expanse of snow-covered lawn, and he followed them towards the shed, struggling through the knee-deep drifts while the crust bit at his ankles through his pants.

About halfway across the lawn, his own madly stumbling tracks met hers and they continued together for several feet before stopping just to the left of the shed door. The rest of the lawn was perfectly smooth. If anyone had been near the house, they had either covered their own tracks or the fresh snow and fierce winds of a few days before had done it for them.

Or there was never anyone here.

That was, of course, the only reasonable answer. And yet he couldn't shake the feeling of unease that had crept over him. Jessie's strange behavior had apparently affected him more than he realized.

He stomped towards the shed, trying to ignore the difficult footing. The padlock on the shed door was unlocked, the snow around it unmarked, except around the door. There the drift was pushed back a bit, as if somebody had yanked the door and realized it was stuck. The marks were not fresh; a small dusting of powder had drifted down into the crack, bits of dead grass sticking of out of it from below.

Suddenly, he felt eyes studying him just as surely as he felt the warmth of the late afternoon sun on the back of his neck. He whirled around quickly, heart in his throat, but there was no one in sight. The woods remained silent and dark, the close-knit branches heavy with snow. Nothing moved.

There's a perfectly logical explanation for everything. Some animal tried to get into the shed during the last storm, a stray dog or raccoon. Christ, you'd try it too if you were out in that stuff. And it's probably watching me right now, that's what I feel. Some poor, skinny stray.

Or I'm going crazy like my daughter; she had to get it from somewhere—

He cut the voice off with an almost audible snap, and a moment later a branch cracked like a firecracker in the utter stillness and let its heavy load of snow fall to the ground with a thump. He spun towards the noise, but there was only the branch, swinging on its broken hinge of bark, and a soft-looking mound of powder below it.

Jesus, he was spooked. He tried to force a laugh, but it wouldn't come, and instead a strange memory overtook him. The pile of snow reminded him the time in third grade he and his best friend Chuck Howard had spent a full hour shoveling snow into a big pile, and when the time came to climb to the roof of the garage and jump, he had chickened out, wobbly legs and all. Chuck pulled himself up the trellis to the roof without a backward glance, and when he jumped it seemed to David that he hung in the air forever, arms waving in the lifeless dance of a puppet.

Chickenshit, go on and do it, he thought, and inside his head the voice sounded like old Chuckie. *Check out the woods, you big baby.*

David willed his feet to move. When he reached the outer trees on the edge of the clearing, he pushed back the lower branches with his arm, causing more snow to fall in clumps to the ground. A dim and narrow passageway between them opened, and he crept into it, still feeling those eyes on him. He felt like a trespasser in someone else's world. Inside, he paused, momentarily disoriented. The needles had swung back into place, and the way out was abruptly cut off. Branches closed in on him from all directions, thick and choking. He felt his heart pound a heavy beat in his ears, and the silence pushed down on him like hands.

Forcing his mind to remain calm, he turned in a full circle around the tiny space, searching for the best way to proceed. Yes, light filtered faintly through the branches where he had come through; he felt a bit better. *Christ, but it's thick in here. No wonder that little girl got lost. It's a maze, that's what it is. And I'm the mouse looking for the cheese.*

Only he wasn't quite sure he would like the cheese if he found it.

He moved forward cautiously, feeling a little ridiculous, his head bent low, almost in a crouch. He had to watch for ends of branches and needles that seemed to poke at his eyes of their own free will. It was slow going; he kept switching his focus from the branches to the ground and back again while trying to remain aware of where the edge of the front yard was; the last thing he needed to do was get lost and have to be led out when safety was mere feet away. Or worse, wander off into the deeper woods and get really lost when night closed in.

After several minutes of searching laterally, during which he moved twenty or thirty feet, he realized how pointless it really was. Nobody could move about in these woods without a chain saw, at least not around here. The trees were as squat and thick as linebackers on a pro football team, spaced within a few feet of each other. How they could survive that way was a mystery. The snow around their roots was much thinner, and in some spots he could see bare ground with its coating of brown needles. What snow remained was smooth and unmarked.

He decided to work his way inward, hoping it would thin out and he could move about easier. He tried to keep his mind focused on the ground ahead of him and the poking needles, not wanting to think about what he would do if he did find something.

Or worse, find someone, the Chuckie Howard voice said inside his head. *What are you going to do if that happens, Davey boy? Pull off your mitten and slap him to death?*

A few feet more and the woods thinned out, while the snow got progressively deeper. He saw the sky above him now in little pieces of blue, but the sun was too far down in the sky to penetrate through to the ground. It was colder in here, and he shivered, pulling his jacket inward and zipping it up halfway. Now that he could see better and move about more or less freely, he decided to try to circle the house, or at least the lawn. If anything was there he would find it, and if not then he would at least be certain he had searched the area completely, and that would make Jessie (*and*

you, you chickenshit, the Chuckie voice reminded him)
feel better.

As he walked, he began to breathe easier, as if the
eyes that had been haunting him had slipped back into
the shadows and he was alone again. But he watched
carefully for any movement among the trees. The snow
around him remained unmarked, not even the track of a
bird to scar the even surface. He kept the thicker woods
on his left, thinking that they would ring the yard and
keep him from wandering too far into the depths. He
felt the sun sinking deeper towards the horizon as he
walked, its light fighting through the heavy branches
and becoming more slanted and filtered. The bits of
sky visible above him took on a darker blue, with a tint
of orange. He was alone in a silent world; it was as if he
had been completely cut off from the last vestiges of
civilization and now moved among the dead.

That was a little too morbid, he decided quickly. All he
needed to do was look for footprints, not dead bodies.

The trees were almost exclusively pine in here, tall
and majestic towers of brown bark and green needles,
the lower branches of most of them gray and stunted.
He noticed where the ends of several had been broken
off; the inside looked brown and fresh, and around a
few he saw bits of wood scattered below on the snow.
*Like somebody passed through here and broke them. And not
too long ago, either.* In fact, the top of the snow just to the
left of the nearest tree looked scratched, as if something had been dragged along it.

He crouched and studied the marks. Yes, something
had passed through here. The snow looked as if it had
been wiped clean. The marks continued in a wide path
for about ten feet, then led up to a tree where they disappeared into the bare ground at its base.

What now, hotshot? the Chuckie voice asked. The silence around him seemed to deepen in reply, becoming more complex and intricate somehow, as if it was all part of some master plan with a key that hung just out of his reach. If he could only find the missing piece . . .

One step at a time. What the hell are these marks? Perhaps they had been made by a branch bending in the wind, or some kind of animal. Still, he felt uneasy again, like the eyes had returned to study him.

He suddenly felt like a rabbit with one foot in the trap.

Backing away from the tree trunk, he searched the woods around him frantically, straining to make out the vague shapes that hovered in the swiftly deepening shadows. Fear had crept up on him with ferocious speed, and now his pulse hammered in his head and his palms became wet with sweat. He felt the hair rise on his scalp.

Get out get out get out get out!

He turned and stumbled through the trees towards the thicker growth that ringed the yard, not knowing why he ran and not caring. Branches whipped at his face and he struck at them with his hand, wincing as his injured palm was slapped again and again. They clutched at him as if they were alive, catching his jacket, his pants, his hair, slowing him down *and he could swear he heard something coming through the brush close behind him, an echo of his thumping footsteps and harsh gasps.*

Then he burst through the last of the thick needles, almost tripping as branches grasped at his legs. He pulled violently loose and kicked away the twigs and needles sticking to his clothing, feeling himself sinking into the snow as he struggled to the center of the wide lawn. In the middle he paused, and fought the urge to keep going. He turned and stood facing the woods, breath rasping painfully in his throat, watching and waiting for his pursuer to burst through the brush.

The woods were silent and still.

He waited there for a long minute as his heartbeat slowed and his breathing returned to normal, and the trees did not move.

It was nothing you stupid shit nothing at all you just lost it you CHICKENSHIT!

"Shut up, Chuckie, goddamn it," he muttered, and let himself sink down until he was sitting on the snow. He tried to think. What had gotten to him back there? Nothing had actually happened at all; he had allowed the isolation and the silence to rattle him until he had fled in terror from his own shadow.

But what about those marks?

Those he couldn't explain.

The sun was painting gold and orange highlights on the tops of the trees as he finally struggled back to his feet. He felt defeated, physically drained, his limbs heavy and sluggish. The air had cooled perceptibly. It was time to get inside; night was coming on fast.

His shadow stretched grotesquely before him, and the shadow cast by the house was creeping closer across the snow. As he turned to go, something on the edge of the trees caught his eye, a tiny hump half covered with snow. He hadn't seen it before, but now the angle of the sun created a shadow that highlighted the lump against the darkness beyond. Like a partially hidden tree stump or rock, and nothing more, but he found himself drawn towards it almost against his will.

By the time he reached the lump, his nerves were singing again like high-tension wires. The part of the mound exposed looked like fur. He scraped at the snow with his hand. It was sticking to something hard and cold. He brushed back a bit more, and something stared up at him with cloudy eyes.

It was a cat.

He kneeled closer to it, fascinated in spite of himself, brushing back a little more snow until he uncovered the thin, ratty tail. This was the first animal he had seen since they arrived; there had been no birds, no mice, not even any tracks.

There were no marks on it anywhere, and he wondered what had happened. If this had been a family pet, had it been left behind? He dug a trench around it, taking off his glove and digging with his bare fingers. They brushed the fur, and the coldness of it filled him with disgust. Yet he continued to dig, unable to stop himself.

Up near the head on the side of the neck he uncovered a large, misshapen lump. It looked like a mutated gland, bulging out from under the animal's chin.

The conversation with Dan Flint, all but forgotten in the wake of Jessica's collapse, came flooding back to him. He grasped the animal firmly with both hands and yanked. It came free from the crust with a harsh ripping sound. He stood for a moment, sickened by the feel of the thing in his hands and unsure of what he planned to do. Then he found himself walking towards the porch, holding it out in front of him and hoping nobody had chosen that moment to watch for him out the window. *Look, there goes Daddy . . .*

He crouched and placed the animal behind a porch support post, scooping some snow over to hide it. He couldn't bring it inside, but his fascination and feeling of dread would not leave him. He wanted it analyzed, he wanted to know how the animal had died.

Do you really want to know?

He wasn't quite sure, but he knew he couldn't let it rest.

He threw one backward glance at the trees behind him; they remained silent and still, and shrouded in shadows. He decided to double lock the doors tonight. And maybe shove a chair under the handle.

Outside, a slight puff of wind rustled through the needles of the trees, moving branches and giving the dark and brooding woods the suggestion of life. It was deeply black with the coming night; the orange and red sunset had left the western sky and the stars exposed themselves to the world, one by one. The breeze spent itself on the solid and immovable tree trunks and died, and the needles once again swept down like a curtain, covering the figure in the shadows settling in to begin his long nightly vigil.

PART TWO

THE COMING STORM

CHAPTER EIGHTEEN

Now she was more than a little worried, Dr. Seigel admitted to herself; she was pissed off, and—yes—a bit frightened.

The latest results from the drug study that had occupied much of her time since last Wednesday were in a file on her desk, but Amanda was not studying them. Instead, she studied the wall, and then the fine line along the ceiling where the paint changed from eggshell white to antique white, or some such color. The line was faint because the colors were so similar, but if you stared hard, it was there.

Jonathan had not called. Not on Thursday, or Friday, or even Saturday. She had spent several hours yesterday in the office, catching up on her work, but the phone had remained silent. And now here she was on a freaking *Sunday*, of all days, supposedly working with the drug file but really waiting for him (and staring at the wall).

Actually, what she was doing was avoiding the decision she had become increasingly sure she would have to make. *Maybe if I wait, he'll check in. Maybe if I wait, things will turn out fine. Maybe if I wait, I won't have to get on a fucking plane and fly God-knows-where to find God-knows-what.*

It was that last thing that scared her the most.

Her mind went back to her patient, Ron King, the one who had thought he was being chased by the Mafia. He had spun out of control, run for his life, changed identities, stolen things. And finally, when he thought he couldn't take it any more, he had gone ahead and attacked someone. During delusions of persecution, patients sometimes showed signs of aggression. It became a last resort for them, the only way out as they saw it. Get rid of them before they get rid of you. The problem was, the patients were not living in the real world. *Jonathan is different*, she decided quickly. But things could change, people could change, and she was not as sure that the solitude he was enduring was such a good idea anymore. A job was good for him, yes, but maybe not *this* job.

Why do I feel so frightened? she asked herself. She lost track of former patients all the time, and nothing catastrophic ever happened. They always checked in eventually, or she heard from someone else close to them, or they ended up back in the hospital. Why was this one case upsetting her so much? The answer, she decided immediately, was right in front of her.

She picked up the file on the drug tests and opened to the first page, which contained a description of a junkie's "trip" on DMT. She had become interested in drugs and their effects in medical school when she was still thinking of becoming a surgeon, before the transfer to psychology. Now, the effects of drugs still interested her because they held possible answers to the causes of many psychological conditions, including paranoia.

DMT was also called "the businessman's high," because the drug's effects were both short and extremely vivid. People could find a quiet place and float in the clouds during a lunch break, then come down in time for the second shift at work. During the sixties, the drug was still legal, but it was outlawed eventually and fell out of use. In the last few years, Amanda had seen its popularity increase again, and it scared her. A trip with 5-Meo-DMT (the sister drug, and up to ten times more powerful) was one of the most intense you could find, and the most frightening. Upon taking it, there was an increase in blood pressure, and then an almost immediate onset of auditory and visual hallucinations that ranged from high-pitched whines and simple designs and patterns (caused by blood vessels in the eye and movements of the muscles of the ear), to complex memory recall; hallucinations of anything and everything in the memory circuits of the brain. These images and figures were as real to the tripper as his own hands (which, incidentally, danced and sang and bled bright colors when held in front of the eyes). And the trip could turn ugly at any time. Some people never fully recovered from the memory of that.

The really interesting thing was, scientists had discovered that DMT was a naturally occurring substance in the brain. Nobody knew quite why this was so (perhaps, in moments of extreme trauma, the body decides to "trip out" instead of face reality—tests had shown that an increase of the drug was released to the brain during stressful situations), but the fact was that DMT and its naturally occurring counterpart could be the key to mental diseases. If, as so many psychologists assumed, psychotic patients had an excess of natural DMT in their cerebral fluid, might that not account for their strange behavior and delusions? Might that discovery not hold the cure for some of these patients, the answer simply to turn off this cerebral light switch?

Of course, it was not quite as simple as all that, Amanda

reasoned, as she had many times before. If that turned out to be true, the question of *why* the excess was being produced still remained. It was a classic case of the chicken and the egg. Maybe the patients were hallucinating because of DMT, or maybe their thought processes were already screwed up in the first place, which led to increased chemical production. Or maybe the answer lay in some other part of the brain entirely, locked away until some brilliant scientist discovered it a year from now, or ten years, or fifty. Someone would find the answer, she knew—they always did, eventually.

But would they find the right one in time to help Jonathan?

Because in the back of her mind, something was whispering, and it had to do with what happens to the mind during solitary confinement, when thoughts wander and sensory inputs are eliminated. She decided to do a little refreshment research on the subject before she made the decision of whether or not to board that plane to God-knows-where.

But she knew somehow that he wouldn't call, that the problem would not go away, and that she would end up on that plane. Knew it with absolute certainty, the way she sometimes knew when she had failed a test or lost a bet. What would happen at the other end, when the plane landed? That was the real question. What would she find?

She wasn't sure if she wanted to know. The little voice in the back of her mind was whispering again.

CHAPTER NINETEEN

That night, David Pierce fluttered in and out of a dreamscape filled with creatures that stalked him through the blackness with a cold and persistent cunning. He slept very little, tossing and turning and twisting the sheets around his body like a death shroud. Several times he sat bolt upright in bed, certain that he had heard a noise in the house and that the creatures of his fitful dreams had arrived, but heard nothing more. He had gone around and checked every window and door before they had turned in; everything was secure.

About five thirty, before the long winter night had broken, he left Helen sleeping peacefully in bed and padded softly downstairs. He slipped through the darkness without much fear. The black shapes that chased him during the night had faded like an old photograph left in the sun, its edges yellowing and curled, the images pale and ghostlike. He hoped they were not chasing Helen and Jessie. He had told them as much as he could about what had happened in the woods. He had found a dead cat, and had gotten a bit rattled. He had seen the shed door. It did look strange. He thought it was some kind of animal that had done it. No, he didn't think there was anybody out there watching them.

The house was silent, the kind of quiet that envelops

a household in the early morning before people shuffle to the bathroom and the coffee smells waft up the stairs to coax the late risers out of bed. By the time he had reached the bottom step, sleep had left him completely, and he knew he was up for good. The rooms were dark, the stairs masked in shadow, the kitchen chairs vague shapes in the last of the moonlight shining through the windows.

He and Helen had decided last night before bed that they would get Jessie to a doctor as soon as possible. They did not otherwise discuss what had happened to her, refusing to face the doubts and fears that raced through their heads, refusing to give them validity by voicing them out loud. There was nothing more they could do, except wait and see what the doctor said. But that did not stop him from going over what had happened, again and again.

He realized that in his fear and concern he had forgotten to ask her why she had deliberately gone against his wishes and approached the woods. It was a temptation, he was sure, that was hard to ignore, especially after he had ordered her to stay away. But she had seemed so frightened of the woods before in the car that he had been quite positive she wouldn't want any part of them.

He opened the refrigerator and the light made him squint. There was some orange juice and a gallon of milk on the top shelf, along with a half-dozen beers, some cold cuts, a hunk of cheese, a few other items Helen had picked up in town. He paused for a long moment, then grabbed a beer. *What the hell*, he thought, swinging the door shut and popping the can's top.

The beer was cold and tasted surprisingly good, even at six A.M. He sat down in one of the kitchen chairs by the table and put his feet up, ready to watch the sunrise, propping the beer can on the arm of the chair. He could just make out the trees on the edge of the lawn outside the window. The night seemed especially still and clear; he imagined it was particularly cold. Someone moved upstairs, turned over in bed and mumbled something. He was beginning to realize just how much the openness of the house invited eavesdropping. The sound moved through the rooms and down the stairs, into the living room and back up over the second-floor railings.

The events of the past day came back to him again, tumbling lazily through his brain like a dark cloud. The phone call. What the hell was he going to do about *that*? Flint was serious, but that didn't change the fact that David didn't really know a damn thing. He was new on the scene, and newcomers wouldn't get much trust. Hell, they would probably figure he didn't deserve it yet. He could understand that. And he would prove them right.

Because, when it comes right down to it, you're scared shitless. Scared to go out on a limb and defend your job and the company you work for, because you think they might have really done something. You might be wrong.

Then again, he might be right.

That was the worst thing. Because if he was wrong and they were innocent, then he might be able to keep his job. *If* nobody thought his questions seemed a little too nosy, and *if* nobody found him snooping around files he shouldn't be snooping around. But if something serious was going on, then the plant would be shut down and he would lose the job, for sure. *Life's a bitch, isn't it? All those goddamned ifs.*

And after all that, after his decision to cooperate with Flint (and he had decided right away—was there any other way to go?), he had gone out to play the hero, and had ended up running in terror from nothing more than a shadow, and a dead cat.

Nothing more?

He sucked at the beer, and it softened his mind around the edges. He began to think more freely, images whirling and spinning across his sight. His daughter's collapse, the house in the light of the setting sun, his hand held aloft and the blood running wetly down his wrist.

He lifted his hand and studied it for a moment. It throbbed dully, the pain digging into his palm and up his arm. He unwrapped the tape, then the gauze that covered the wound, tossing it onto the table in front of him. His palm was swollen, the wound in the center an ugly, red mass. He touched it, and found the flesh wet with infection.

That was it. The wood had been dirty, and he hadn't washed the wound well enough.

But that was not exactly true. Helen had washed it for him thoroughly as soon as they unpacked that first day, and she had covered it with antibiotic ointment and clean gauze. It should have started healing by now.

He got up and made his way slowly to the bathroom where they kept the first aid kit, not bothering to turn on a light; the sunrise was softly lightening the windows. He put some new ointment on, wrapped his hand with new gauze and taped it securely. It continued to throb, pulsing against the bandage. The splinter must have gone much deeper than he had originally thought, and they had simply not gotten it clean. Still, it worried him. He didn't like doctors' offices, and this wound might send him to one if he wasn't careful.

Back in the kitchen, he realized the beer was almost empty. Grabbing another one was tempting, but he let it pass and poured himself some orange juice instead, wincing at the sour, acid taste. *You should have been wincing at that beer*, he thought. But he felt better now, more relaxed, his nightmares forgotten in the light of a new day. His decision to talk to Flint was the right one. If somebody was hiding something, they were the ones at fault, not him.

Some time later, he awoke to the sound of water running, and realized with a start that he must have dozed off. The sun shone brightly through the windows. He tossed the empty beer can in the trash, and walked up the stairs to the bathroom, where Helen was in the shower.

The door swung open at his touch. He could see the silhouette of her naked body through the curtain.

"Mind if I join you?"

She jumped, and peeked out around the edge of the curtain. "God, you scared me."

"It's been a rough couple of days." He stripped quickly out of his boxer shorts and T-shirt and climbed in. The water was scalding, steam rising in great clouds around them. "Are you feeling all right this morning?"

She sighed. "I guess. But still a little spooked."

He wrapped his arms around her and hugged her close, her body warm and soft against him. His wounded palm stung as the water softened his skin. "It'll get better," he whispered into the steam.

She turned around in his grasp, her full breasts now pressing against his chest, and leaned her head on his shoulder. "It's getting better already."

He rocked her like that, saying nothing for a long time, letting the heat of the water wash over them.

They took a long shower, touching each other softly and slowly. After they had toweled dry and while Helen was getting dressed and checking on Jessie, he went downstairs to make some calls. He wanted to get in touch with a doctor first. According to the phone book, there was only one in St. Boudin, a guy named Eustice Mudd. *Funny name for a doctor*, he thought with a grin. But he called and set up an appointment for Jessie later that afternoon.

Next, he called the police department. There was a long silence when he told them that his pet cat died and he wanted to know how to get an autopsy; then he was advised, in a voice crackling with laughter, to try the local vet. The local vet's name was James O'Leary. He was definitely Irish, which was a damned strange accent to hear after all the French and English of the past few weeks.

"Hello, my boy," he said, after David introduced himself. "What can I do for you?"

David told him about the cat.

"You better get him in fast, then," O'Leary said. "I can do it, but unless you keep him cold . . ."

David assured him he was quite cold.

"All right then, bring him by this afternoon, and I'll take a look."

David told him he would most certainly do that, and hung up, chuckling. It promised to be an interesting afternoon.

By the time Helen and Jessie came downstairs to join him, he had orange juice and some dry cereal in bowls on the table. Jessie was pale, and she had dark circles under her eyes. *Look like you've been in a fight, kiddo.* He supposed that in a way, she had.

He gave her a quick kiss on the forehead. "You hungry?"

"A little." She sat down and poured milk on her cereal

while Helen grabbed one of the glasses of orange juice. He glanced at her and she shrugged, walking back to the kitchen counter where she sipped the juice slowly.

"We're going to take a trip this afternoon and get you checked out, all right?" he said. Jessie froze, spoonful of cereal halfway to her lips.

"I'm okay, Daddy," she said in a small voice.

"Of course you are, pumpkin, but it would make us feel better. And maybe it will help your nightmares."

"They're not nightmares, they're real," she said calmly. "At least they will be, pretty soon."

He felt like the temperature in the kitchen had just dropped ten degrees. Helen looked at him, her face lined with worry, but he could not answer her. It was not what Jessie had said, it was the way she said it, as if it were God's honest truth and nothing at all could change that or stop it from happening.

Then the paralysis broke and he went to her. "I searched the woods a long time and *there is nobody out there*. This man that you see"—he paused and searched for a way to continue—"he's a scary man, but he's in your head and he can't hurt you. I won't let him."

She smiled distantly, and it chilled him to the bone. "He doesn't care about that, Daddy. He's crazy; he doesn't think right. When he thinks, it's all messed up."

"What do you mean, all messed up?" Helen had joined them at the table, and she looked as if she had seen a ghost; David saw a vein pulsing in her temple.

"He sees monsters and bad people everywhere, even if he's alone. His brain is like a scary movie."

"I think the best thing to do is tell the doctor about the man," he said, trying to keep his voice calm and even. "He'll be able to handle it better than any of us. You can trust the doctor, honey. And I'll tell you this right now"—he knelt and held her face in both of his hands—"I will never let anyone hurt you. I promise you that."

"Okay, Daddy." Her voice sounded so thin and fragile. He gathered her up in his arms and held her, and she grabbed on to him like she was drowning. He had the horrible feeling that he was losing her to something beyond his control, as if she was slipping away bit by bit and being replaced by a creature that looked like Jessica, sounded like Jessica, but wasn't really her at all.

CHAPTER TWENTY

Flint had lied over the phone, just a little.

More like a fib, an embellishment, really, to make things sound more serious. Although he had his suspicions, he had no way to prove the chemical in the water samples had come from the hydroelectric plant. And at the moment, though the lab tests *had* caused the deaths of several animals, the majority were still living. But the majority of those were seriously fucked up, so much so that even the lab techs, who were trained to understand these things, couldn't make heads or tails of it all. So the week he left open before he flew to St. Boudin was as much to give the lab time to run more tests as it was for Pierce to go hunting for answers.

Flint walked from the elevator to the stairs, flashed a clearance badge at the tired-looking guard on duty, who waved him by with a yawn, and descended the stairs to the first hallway in the area of the building most people never saw. Hell, most people didn't even know this place existed. It was a well-kept secret for several reasons: number one, because it kept the animal rights groups off their backs (there were a lot of pretty nasty things going on); number two, because it kept corporate spies from keeping one step ahead of them; and number three, because the government just had too much fucking money.

Why not burn some on a top secret, prisonlike facility with all the security of Fort Knox? It seemed that this was the only way to get things done these days—hide the tests so that the politicians wouldn't find out about them and yell foul. And he realized self-consciously that the more time he spent working here, the angrier he became about the whole thing.

He needed a vacation.

He slid a card into a slot on the wall, and a heavy door opened in front of him. Another hallway stretched out before him. Doors were spaced every five or ten feet on each side, all closed. Set into the center of each was a small window. The rooms looked like cells in a prison, and despite the glint of the metal walls and polished linoleum floor, the single row of fluorescent lights on the ceiling did nothing to lighten the atmosphere.

Flint's footsteps echoed a ghostly beat as he walked towards the very last door, the only one with a bright window. He felt a little like a player in a cheap horror flick, descending into the depths of the mad scientist's laboratory. *With all the money spent on the place, you'd figure they would have made it more pleasant*, he thought. He was glad that he was not one of the men who had to work down here all day. As he neared the door, it opened with a soft whooshing sound, and a man in a suit stepped out. He held the door, and nodded curtly as Flint went past him into the room.

Inside, it looked more like a zoo than anything else. The larger cages lined the back wall, and contained a variety of animals from cats and dogs to chimps. They leaped and paced about the confines of the cages, whining and scratching at the bars. Under and in front of these cages were several smaller ones containing guinea pigs and rats, and scattered in various places around these were the tools of the trade; microscopes, vials, scanning equipment.

Several people in white lab coats were huddled over a table in the center of the room, and he heard something snarling, though he couldn't yet see it. He paused for a moment and took a deep breath, trying to keep himself calm and detached from whatever was going on, and found that he couldn't. He wasn't sure if he wanted to see what was on that table anymore, to hell with Jackson Hydro. To hell with his job. He had a feeling that, once he looked at this, he wouldn't be able to turn back, wouldn't be able to stop whatever was building inside, even if he wanted to. Right now, he thought that maybe he should just turn away and walk out that door, just be a coward and do it. He didn't know why, but the feeling was there.

He was being a little melodramatic, he decided. This was his job, after all.

He walked up, pulled two of the white-coated techs aside, and peered in at the thing chained to the table.

The lab boys didn't say a word. They didn't have to.

CHAPTER TWENTY-ONE

After they finished some ice cream (a pint of Ben & Jerry's Coffee HEATH Bar Crunch from the local store), Helen dropped him off outside O'Leary's office, which happened to be in downtown St. Boudin, next to the police station.

Downtown, David thought. *What a joke.* The streets collided about a half mile back in an "L" formation, one continuing on to who knows where, the other stretching along this few-hundred-foot length of tiny buildings and concrete.

O'Leary's office was warm and cozy, a converted two-story house complete with screened-in front porch and second-floor balcony. Inside, there was a small waiting room that looked to be a converted front hallway, with several metal folding chairs and magazines on a table against the wall, and a closed door on the right-hand side. A stairway on the far right led upstairs, presumably to the vet's private rooms. David placed his cold bundle on the table and sat down to wait for the good doctor.

A minute later, the door opened and a man with a shock of orange-red hair entered, his face freckled and plump.

"Jim O'Leary," he said, extending his hand. The accent was not particularly strong, but certainly there.

David introduced himself and took the man's hand, and it was dry and felt recently powdered. He had a strong, solid grip.

"What can I do for you, David?"

He took a deep breath. *News travels fast in small towns.*

"I'm the guy who called about the cat."

O'Leary's face crinkled into a wide smile. "Right, you want to know why it died. I can't promise you anything, but I'll give it a look. Bring it on in."

David followed O'Leary through a doorway into a spacious, sterile room with a long metal table in the middle. Boxes lined the edges of a countertop and sink along the right wall. The air smelled of disinfectant.

"So the cat was a pet of yours?"

"We took it in when it was a kitten. Its mother was killed by a boy with an air gun."

"Those young boys are trouble," O'Leary said.

"I found it yesterday outside in the snow. Jessica—our little girl—doesn't usually let it roam around, but I guess this time it got out. We've been looking for it for a few days now."

The vet's face took on an appropriate look of remorse. "She must be heartbroken. If you leave the animal here, I'll get to work right away. If you want to come back . . ."

"I'll stay, if you don't mind." Helen and Jessie weren't due back from the doctor for another hour at least, and he wanted to get this done as soon as possible.

O'Leary nodded. "That's fine. You can wait in the other room. I'll do all I can here, but if I need some things analyzed, it'll take a day or two. Have to send it to Edmundston, you know."

"Right," David agreed, though he hoped it wouldn't come to that. He closed the door behind him, and sat down in one of the chairs to wait, flipping through the magazines. They were all several months old, and well perused. After a few minutes, he tossed the last of them onto the table and sat back in the chair, watching the door for O'Leary.

Eustice Mudd's office was situated about two miles down the road from O'Leary's. It was a fairly modern brick building with a large parking lot and a sign that read ST. BOUDIN MEDICAL CENTER, with the names of the four practitioners printed in large, gold letters.

Jessie hadn't said a word since David left the car. That in itself wasn't unusual. Whenever she became nervous or frightened, she clammed up, almost without exception. She got out on her side looking timid, and gripping Johnny Bear in her arms. At times like these, it was good for her to bring the bear along, though Helen occasionally felt pangs of irrational jealousy towards the thing. Jessie seemed to get more comfort from it than from her mother.

There were many times, she reminded herself, that Johnny Bear kept Jessie occupied when her parents had their hands full with something else. For that, she was thankful.

She took her daughter by the hand and walked through the cold winter air to the front doors. Inside, she slipped off her hat and gloves and held Johnny Bear while Jessie did the same. They were facing a carpeted staircase with a set of elevators to their right. A sign on the wall pointed upward to Dr. Mudd's office.

It looked like any other doctor's waiting room— magazines piled on end tables, prints in simple frames tacked to the wall. The receptionist sat behind a desk at the far end of the room, guarding the entrance to the doctor's chambers.

Helen went over to her and introduced herself. The receptionist, a young and overly made-up woman with frosted hair, nodded and smiled brightly. "He'll be right with you. You can wait over there."

Helen took a seat along the wall next to the magazines, but none of them interested her particularly. Jessie remained silent. *What's going on in your head?* she wondered. *What do you see in there when you go places nobody else can go?*

Jessie stared straight ahead, Johnny Bear held close in her arms. She looked like a little angel. Helen felt a great, unshakable sorrow well within her until tears threatened to spill down her cheeks. If they needed to leave Jackson to help her, well then they would do it, and to hell with the job. Ends would meet somehow; in any case, no job was worth their daughter's sanity.

"Dr. Mudd is ready for you," the receptionist said.

Helen wiped quickly at the tears that had welled up and took her daughter's hand once again.

"Come on, honey. Let's go see what the doctor has to say."

The examining room, complete with paper-covered table and stainless-steel sink, smelled of disinfectant, and it reminded her of her own visits to the doctor as a young child, and later those necessary but horrible appointments with the gynecologist, where she waited in rooms like this one to be poked and probed like a lab animal. She shuddered.

A kindly looking man with white hair and a round, soft face entered the room, and Jessie seemed to brighten almost immediately.

"I'm Dr. Mudd. At least I hope I am, or the sign on the door is all wrong," he said with a slight French accent, his eyes twinkling. "What can I do for you, young lady?"

Jessie smiled. "Ask my mommy."

"Well then," Dr. Mudd exclaimed. "What can I do for *you*? Helen, isn't it?"

"My daughter," Helen began, then stopped. She realized with embarrassment that she had no clear idea how to proceed. "Jessie's been having some trouble with bad dreams, haven't you, honey?"

"Night terrors?"

"Sometimes. But sometimes they happen during the day, when she's awake. It's almost like she slips into a trance. I'm not quite sure how to describe it."

"You're doing just fine. Just tell me anything you can think of about these episodes."

Helen told him about the last one. "And when we try to snap her out of it, she's unresponsive at first. Then it's almost as if she wakes up. And she talks about terrible visions, people hurting her or others, scary people. This 'blue man' who she says is watching her."

"I see. How long has this been going on?"

"She's had visions ever since she was a toddler. But they've been getting much worse lately."

Dr. Mudd turned to Jessie. "Are you feeling all right, Jessie?" he asked. She nodded. "Is there anything else you would like to tell me?" She shook her head. He performed a quick physical examination, looking in Jessie's eyes and nose and mouth, listening to her heart and breathing, taking her pulse. Then he looked from her to Helen. "Could I speak with you for a moment?"

Helen smiled thankfully, and he motioned for her to return to the outer room. "Stay here," he said to Jessie. "We'll be right back."

Just outside the examining room, Helen told him everything else she could think of, as quickly as she dared. She related Jessie's obsessive-compulsive tendencies, the clarity and strength of her visions, the physical symptoms when she entered one of her trances. When she had finished, he nodded thoughtfully. "You've just moved to the area?"

"Just last week."

"Hmmm. I think that it would be best if I discussed this with your daughter for a while alone. Perhaps she will open up to me in some way, and say something she has trouble talking about around you. Sometimes children feel it is necessary to protect their parents from their problems. They're really quite sophisticated, you know."

"Maybe you're right."

"I'll be out in just a few minutes."

Jessica waited patiently on the white paper lining of the table, her legs dangling over the side. They didn't make these tables in her size. She was nervous, but not as much as before in the car. Dr. Mudd (it was a funny name, she thought) was a nice man; she could tell just by looking at him. He *felt* right. But just in case, she kept Johnny Bear close to her side.

Her mommy was scared, she could tell. But she wasn't scared like Jessie, she wasn't afraid of the blue man, she was afraid that Jessie was going CRAZY. It was a funny word, but she didn't want to practice saying this one. This word gave her bad pictures of big white rooms and funny suits with no arms and straps that hung down like tentacles. She didn't think that she was going CRAZY, at least she hoped not. Daddy sometimes thought the word too; not all the time, though. That made her feel better.

As they drove here in the car she had been thinking about her PERCEPTIONS, not about what happened in them but the things themselves. They were getting stronger. She noticed this the very first day they got to the house; the pictures in her head were brighter and more real than ever. Now when they came, she saw everything clearly.

Like yesterday in the front yard. That picture had been the brightest and strongest she had ever gotten. Afterward her head felt clear and sunny, like all the cobwebs had been cleaned out. Now she knew exactly what the man looked like, and she never wanted to see him again. He was huge and horrible looking, and dark red stuff dripped from his nose.

The door opened and Dr. Mudd came in. Again she was struck by the goodness of him, and she began to feel even better.

"Hello, Jessica," he said. "I'd like to talk with you about your bad dreams, if that's okay."

She studied him, and found he was telling the truth. That was another thing about him. When he thought something, he said it. No hiding.

"Okay," she said.

"Tell me all about them."

When she had finished with the last one, about how she saw the man and fell down in the snow, Dr. Mudd was silent for a long moment. He looked like he was thinking hard.

"Jessica, I'm going to try something, and I want you to go along with me," he said finally. "Will you do that?"

"Okay," she said, trusting him.

"It's a game. I'm going to think of something, and I want you to tell me what it is."

"Sometimes I can't do it," she said cautiously. Nobody had ever played this game with her before. In fact, she had never actually tried to see what people were thinking; when it happened, it just came to her and she saw it in her head like a picture on TV.

"That's fine, Jessica. Just try it, and whatever happens, happens. It's not a test. I believe everything you've told me."

"So if I can't tell you the right thing, you'll still believe me?"

"Of course. I'm curious, that's all."

"Okay."

Dr. Mudd smiled at her and closed his eyes. Jessie was suddenly afraid; she wasn't sure if she liked reading people's thoughts. It made her feel yucky and a little dizzy sometimes.

But he's waiting for me. I have to do it. She poked at him a tiny bit with her mind, unsure of exactly how to *make* it happen. There was nothing there, and it felt all wrong. Usually, she was thinking of something else, or nothing at all. She tried to make her mind go clear, imagined an eraser working on a chalkboard.

It floated up from far away, an image spinning in a black background. The colors were reversed; it reminded her of once when her daddy had held up a strip of NEGATIVES, where pictures came from. The thing floated closer, and she recognized the shape, it was familiar to her, a fuzzy creature with shiny eyes . . .

"Johnny Bear," she said. "You want me to hug my bear."

Dr. Mudd opened his eyes and stared at her for a long time. "You're absolutely right. Of course, it could have been a coincidence . . ." His voice trailed off, and he wasn't looking at her anymore; he was watching something else far away.

Finally, he looked at her again. "Let's try another one."

They tried four more times, and she got all four right. The last one came to her without warning. He hadn't even closed his eyes yet.

"You want to kiss the lady who sits behind the desk," she said. "You think about that a lot."

Dr. Mudd looked surprised. He leaned back, then let out a hearty laugh. "I suppose I do, don't I? You have a gift, young lady. I've had the strangest feeling ever since you walked through that door, almost as if I knew you were coming." He smiled at her, and again she felt reassured by his presence. He was someone she could trust; she knew that without anyone having to say it.

"I'm a doctor, and doctors don't usually believe in this sort of thing. We like to think that everything can be explained. But sometimes, they can't."

Jessie decided that Dr. Mudd was the smartest doctor she had ever met.

"We're going to have to be very careful with what we say to your mother. Something like this can have a very bad effect on parents. And I'm not sure if she'll believe me, anyway. Sometimes you have to experience it yourself." He smiled and winked at her. "I'm not suggesting you try this with her, either. You can if you want, that's up to you. But it could change the way your mother thinks about you and the way she treats you. You know that, am I right?"

Jessie nodded. She did know, though it was hard to tell if she had gotten the idea from Dr. Mudd or from somewhere else.

"I'll talk to her, if you like." He leaned forward and looked at her seriously. "Now, the important thing.

This man you see—you're sure that he has been watching you?"

"Yes."

"Well then." Dr. Mudd sat back again, and Jessie could tell he was thinking hard. "We'll have to do something about that. In the meantime, I think it's best if I warned your mother about this, as gently as I can."

Jessie felt much better already. If anybody could help her, Dr. Mudd could.

"Go get your mother and send her in here, all right?" He stood up and opened the door. "I'll see you soon."

As she walked out with Johnny Bear, Jessie glanced back and saw Dr. Mudd sitting on the edge of the table, chin in his hands. He looked confused, and a little worried.

She didn't feel quite as good anymore.

James O'Leary walked back through the door from the examining room half an hour later, rubbing at his temples, a sour look on his freckled face. David had given in and started glancing through the September issue of *Time Magazine*; he tossed it on the table and stood up quickly.

"Mr. Pierce," O'Leary said, "this cat was definitely not a pet. It's thin and malnourished. Also, its coat is very unhealthy and there's a lot of scarring, which leads me to believe it's been in a few pretty serious fights. All of this is not as important as the time of death, of course."

"Which was . . ."

"Well, I'm not equipped to give you an exact time, and the fact that the animal was partially frozen slows down the process of decay a great deal, but I would say it's been dead a long time. At least a month."

"A month?"

"An educated guess. It is a little unusual, since you would think another scavenger of some sort would have found it by that point and had it for supper." O'Leary smiled. "I hope you aren't offended by my callousness, but I'm assuming the animal was a stray."

"I'm sorry. I found him in my backyard yesterday, and I was afraid you wouldn't take a look right away if I didn't make up a story. I noticed that lump on his neck and I was curious."

O'Leary was silent for a long moment. Finally, he said, "Are you bothered by the sight of blood, Mr. Pierce?"

"Not particularly."

"Follow me. I'd like to show you something."

O'Leary led him back into the examining room, where the cat lay in the center of the metal table, illuminated by the bright spotlights that dangled from above. The cat's skin had been sliced cleanly and peeled back from its head and stomach, exposing the muscle and bone. A large, purplish lump covered in a thin membrane bulged from the animal's neck.

"He's already begun to thaw out," O'Leary said. "That will help us get a better view of things." The vet picked up a long, thin metal probe from a tray beside the table. "I want you to look at this." He poked at the lump in several places. It reminded David of how a kneecap slips around under the skin.

"What is it?" he asked, clamping down on the sickness that churned in his stomach.

"A tumor of some sort. It grew enough to cut off the cat's windpipe. I'm going to send a piece of it to Edmundston for lab work. But there's a pretty good chance this is what killed him."

"Is this common in a wild animal?"

"Not particularly, especially around here. I want you to look at something else."

O'Leary grabbed a long pair of tweezers from the tray. He slipped on a white rubber glove and grasped the animal firmly by the neck just under the lump, using the other hand to slide the tweezers slowly into the opening in the animal's stomach. Something gave inside, and thick red blood oozed out.

"Come have a look."

David forced himself to bend over the cat, and O'Leary spread the handles of the tweezers, opening up the slit in the stomach.

"We really should be calling it a she," he said, peering into the opening. "What you're looking at are the structures surrounding her ovaries."

O'Leary moved the cat slightly, and David could see two little lumps inside nestled among a web of veins and muscle tissue. They were covered in tiny white dots, and the end of one was black and stunted.

"The white spots are mostly scarring, the markings of some sort of disease or injury. The black area is a place where the disease is more advanced."

David turned away and studied the wall, trying to keep his nausea under control. "What does this mean?"

"It means," O'Leary said, placing the instrument back on the tray, "that she was sterile."

"And you think this has something to do with the tumor on her neck?"

"Almost certainly. I would say that the scars on her ovaries were caused by a similar condition, perhaps cancer. A tumor this size doesn't normally grow overnight."

"Does this happen a lot, with cats?"

"Not really. A tumor like this is relatively rare, and

it's usually caused by something harmful in the animal's environment. You see it more frequently in strays that hang around manufacturing plants, areas where heavy spraying is going on, that sort of thing."

"Jesus. Should I be worried?"

"I wouldn't jump to any conclusions just yet," O'Leary said. "Look, I don't know why you chose to tell me that story about the cat being a pet. I guess you had your reasons. But I wouldn't panic. I'll send the sample in to be examined. If there's something to find, they'll find it."

Helen walked back through the door and into the doctor's examining room, leaving Jessie with the receptionist. She seemed happier, and had begun talking again, which was good. But even so, Helen felt her palms begin to sweat and her neck tense up with nervous energy. It didn't really matter how Jessie looked to her; it was Dr. Mudd's opinion that really counted, and she was afraid of what he might say.

The man sat on the edge of the examining table, and looked up when she walked in.

"Hello, Mrs. Pierce," Dr. Mudd said. "Please, sit down."

Helen took a chair in the corner. He got up and closed the door, then turned to face her.

"I'm not sure exactly what to say to you about Jessica," he said, walking up and down the tiny space between the sink and door in front of her. "I will begin by saying that I don't believe she's lying about these dreams."

"Of course not," Helen said. "Why would she?"

"I'm sorry. I mean, I don't think there is a problem with Jessica herself. Most young children are extremely imaginative, and it often worries the parents. Imaginary friends, for example. At Jessica's age, most children make up imaginary companions, and a lot of them carry it to your daughter's extreme or even further. It's good for them, good for the mind and developing normal human relationships." He paused. "The problem is in how these encounters or dreams are taking shape. Now, I'm not a psychiatrist, but I can make a pretty educated guess at why she is having these nightmares. You and your husband have been having some sort of trouble, am I right?"

"Yes," she said slowly. "He was out of work for about a year, until he got the job at Jackson Hydro. We moved here about a week ago."

"So Jessica had to leave the only place she's known, the place she has grown up in. Naturally, she's feeling a lot of stress. She could be vocalizing her fear of the move, transferring her anxiety into something she can handle."

"Or?" Helen asked.

"The other possibility is that she's really seen something that's frightened her."

"Are you actually suggesting we have some kind of stalker?"

"I'm not saying that. But children's active imaginations don't always measure up to their ability to process information, to reason things out. To them, a shadow moving across a window really *is* a monster waiting to jump at them in the dark. An argument overheard late at night—"

"We don't argue in front of Jessie," she said. "We're very careful about that."

Dr. Mudd smiled. "I'm sure you are. My point is, children don't know how to process things that frighten them, and so they make up their own answers. In Jessica's case, she's imagined the bogeyman."

"And you're sure it's nothing physical?"

"I want to examine the records from her pediatrician," Mudd said. "But I don't see anything that would lead me to believe there is anything physically wrong with her, no. You'll need to keep a careful eye out for other symptoms—if she begins to report odd smells, for example, or persistent headaches. If anything like that happens, I want you to call me immediately."

"Of course."

"Mrs. Pierce, I'm really quite sure everything is fine. Just to be on the safe side, I'm going to recommend a therapist to you." He drew a piece of paper from his front pocket, scribbled something and handed it to her. She stuffed it in her purse without looking at it.

"I'm also going to ask the police department here if they can check out the area around your home, just to be safe."

"You don't *really* think there could be somebody . . ."

"I want to reassure your daughter," Mudd said, "that I did everything I could. There's no harm in having a car drive out there."

"If you say so." Helen stood up and offered him her hand. "Thank you for all your help, Doctor. I know you cheered Jessica up a great deal."

"I hope I can do more than that. I want you to keep me posted on how things are going, all right?"

"Okay." She turned to go.

"One other thing, Mrs. Pierce. Be very patient with your daughter. She is a remarkably intelligent girl; sometimes I don't think any of us give children enough credit."

Helen smiled and nodded. "You're probably right.

Thanks again." She left him standing in the center of the examining room.

Helen picked David up at O'Leary's minutes after he finished his conversation with the vet. She explained the doctor's opinion to him briefly as they walked back to the car, Jessie waiting for them in the backseat. Helen seemed relatively calm, though uncertain of exactly what to believe. He sympathized. She had always had a phobia of psychiatrists.

It was tough to face the thought that their little girl needed professional help. On the other hand, the thought of some stalker out there in the woods was ridiculous. What proof did they have for that? A little girl's dreams and a shed door that had probably been pawed at by some cold and hungry dog? He logically sided with the psychological explanation, yet something nagged at him.

The woods were empty, remember?

They stopped at the general store to buy groceries, the same one that had supplied them with the ice cream earlier. Helen shopped methodically, buying only the most necessary things as she had been trained to do these past few months: milk, bread, cereal, a few others. He watched her carefully for any sign of strain or collapse, but saw nothing other than the exhausted way her shoulders drooped, and reminded himself that the doctor had not recommended a psychiatrist because Jessie was crazy, only because she was having trouble adjusting to the move. Perhaps Helen needed to be reminded of that as well.

As they drove back to the house in relative silence, the wind picked up, rocking the little car with periodic gusts that quickly faded away, only to return, stronger the next time. It was four thirty, and the sun hovered just above the horizon. The sky remained clear.

We'll lock the house up. I'll check the place out and we'll lock it up tight.

Somehow, he could not find comfort in the thought.

The hilltops looked close in the late afternoon sunlight as David pulled the car up to the porch about twenty minutes later. As he got out, he scanned the woods in a long, slow circle, but nothing moved except the tips of the branches swaying in the wind. He opened the trunk of the car and gathered the groceries in his arms.

"Let's get inside," he said.

Helen nodded, taking Jessie's hand and leading her up the steps to the front door, where she waited for him.

He shifted the bags in his arms and slipped the key in the lock, swinging open the door. The house was fairly dark, as the sun had moved down in the west, and so he reached around and hit the light switch on the inside wall. The living room flooded with light.

He kicked the door shut against the wind, muffling the sound. It swirled and spun about the eaves of the house, as if searching for a way in. *Screw you*, he thought bitterly as he put the bags on the floor and stripped off his jacket and gloves. Winter was getting to him. It was March now, and they had yet to see any sign of spring.

While Helen sat with Jessie on the living room couch, he began an extensive search of the house, carrying a heavy piece of wood from the fireplace for security. It was important, he decided, to show Jessie that they were taking her seriously. He moved cautiously from room to room, checking every shadow and closet, under every bed, feeling a little silly. It reminded him of when he was a little boy and frightened of monsters. His father would come in every night before he went to sleep and check his closet for him. David could never quite leave it at that, though. He always ended up checking it himself, more afraid of not knowing than he was of the monsters themselves.

The closets were empty, the space under the beds populated solely by dust balls.

Finally, after ten minutes of searching, he returned to the living room where his wife and daughter waited patiently.

"I've checked and locked every window and door, looked in everyone's room," he said. "Everything's okay."

Jessie remained silent, staring up at him with eyes as large as saucers.

"Let's unpack the groceries," he said. "And maybe try to eat something."

As they put the supply of food into the refrigerator, the sun sank below the horizon. David started the fire, which had gone out while they were in town. He was quickly becoming an expert at it, building on balls of newspaper, kindling, then small logs with the skill and delicacy of an artist. They had hot dogs and salad for supper, but nobody ate much. Afterward, they all went into the living room and sat where it was warm.

"Are you okay?" he asked Jessie finally, unable to stand her silence any longer.

"I'm okay, Daddy. The doctor is going to help us. He's a good man."

"How do you know that?"

"I don't know," she said, shrugging. "I just do."

I just do. It was funny, but somehow he believed her. The night outside the windows darkened until the woods were no longer visible. They continued to sit in the living room, comforted by each other's company. Eventually, Helen picked up the copy of *Grimm's Fairy Tales* from the coffee table and started to read to Jessie. The wind continued to gust and moan around the roof of the house, rattling the large panes of glass on the south side. He looked at his wife and daughter, huddled close together on the couch. They seemed fragile, and far too vulnerable to hold up under the pressure that was building around them like a giant, helium-filled balloon. He couldn't wait for O'Leary to call him. It was time to do some checking up on Hydro Development, so he would know exactly who or what he was up against, if anyone. And before bed, he would inspect the house again. Just to be safe. The phone call from Flint, the cat, the doctor's advice—it had all gotten him rattled. And he didn't like the feeling.

He listened to Helen's voice, calm and sweet in the warmth of the fire, and the wind.

CHAPTER TWENTY-TWO

Nothing had prepared him for this.

The creature (what had been a dog, but what was now some sort of slobbering, half-crazed beast) lay on its belly on the table, sweat-flecked sides heaving, bloodshot eyes rolling wildly in their sockets. Wires ran from electrodes on the creature's skull to a machine on the floor. Though it was pretty obviously dying, it was still trying desperately to get at any of the various humans watching the spectacle; jaws speckled with yellowish foam and bits of blood snapped and snarled, and lips curled upward, exposing long rows of teeth. Blood ran freely from its nose and spattered in tiny dots on the surface of the table.

If the creature hadn't been securely chained to a bolt on the tabletop, Flint might have left the room then and there; as it was, he took a single, involuntary step back.

"Jesus, Jimmy. What the hell is going on?"

"What, did you think I was lying to you?" a man in white at the head of the table said. "I love having you down here, Danny, but really."

"Yeah, well, I just didn't expect *this*." Flint wasn't sure what he had expected, but no amount of description over a phone line could prepare you for a real live Cujo, right here on a laboratory table.

"He's the last one." Jimmy gestured towards the animal's head, and earned a fresh snarl and a loud snap of the jaws. Jimmy seemed unconcerned.

Flint couldn't keep his eyes off the dog. It seemed that once this had been a German shepherd, but now . . .

"How many have died?"

"Seven, four of them today. Hemorrhaging from every orifice. Five mice, a cat, and a guinea pig. The cat was the latest one to go. The bigger they are, the longer they survive."

The dog watched them through bloodshot eyes that still held a glint of intelligence. Flint shivered. *This thing may be ready to die, but it knows what's happening, and it's going to fight us to the end.*

"The hound from hell, eh?" Jimmy said, and Flint felt a momentary disgust at the man's callousness. "He'd kill you if he could, in a second. Damn near took Theresa's face off earlier today."

"Just give me the facts."

Jimmy walked over to the machine on the floor, and Flint followed him around the table. Closer to the screen, the man's face took on a slightly greenish hue as he bent to study the spiking lines.

"Brain activity shows some unusual patterns closer to REM sleep than a conscious state. Brain waves are jumping all over the spectrum. Normally, we see high points here and here"—he gestured to blank spots on the readout—"but now they're much higher, as you can see. What this probably means," he said, pausing for emphasis, "is that our little friend is hallucinating."

"Hallucinating?"

"You got it." Jimmy let the computer printout fall,

and turned back to the dog. "Dancing dots, tunnels, smells, the works."

Flint watched as the dog fell into a momentary period of quiet. Its sides still heaved, but the snapping jaws were still.

"This is some pretty nasty stuff. It's different from anything I've seen before. It's similar to 2,4-dichlorophenoxyacetic acid, or 2,4-D, a common enough herbicide—mixtures of that and 2,4,5-T, another one, was used in Vietnam. Nasty little gem called Agent Orange. But I've never seen this exact structure in my life."

When Flint nodded, Jimmy continued. "As we all know now, dioxins turned out to be pretty toxic, but not at low levels. It was used for a long time in commercial herbicides here at home, even while they were spraying it over there."

"But . . ."

"But, this stuff is different. Agent Orange was pretty short-lived in the topsoil, maybe a few weeks at the most. Picloram was another, and that stayed around a while longer, maybe a couple of months. This stuff we have, I don't know when it will ever break down. We've only had it a few days, but who knows how long it's been in the water out there, and it's still going strong."

"So this could just keep building up to higher and higher levels, like some sort of chemical landfill?"

"Something like that." The technician pointed to the computer screen, which was filled with scientific formulas. "This is what we have so far. This is the part"—he pointed to the end of a long line of numbers—"I can't yet figure out."

"And you isolated it from the samples taken near the plant."

"Mmmhmmm. So far, we haven't found heavy concentrations in the water supply ten miles below the plant. Looks like it's being contained to some degree, at least."

"And the dog . . ."

"He got a major dose of it. Most of what we had left."

"What exactly has it done to him?"

"Fucked him royally," Jimmy said. "He's bleeding all over the place, inside and out, which makes some kind of sense if you think about it. A lot of Vietnam soldiers complained of nosebleeds during the spray runs over there. His brain's higher than a kite. And if he lived long enough, he'd probably be sterile and die of cancer."

"Jesus."

"Even Jesus couldn't help the poor bastard now," Jimmy said. He had put out his hand slowly towards the dog's head, almost comfortingly.

"Jimmy—"

The animal leapt at him, jaws open and dripping in a sudden snarl. Jimmy jerked his arm back, but only the tight line of chain around the dog's neck kept him from losing a finger.

"See what I mean," Jimmy said, and his voice seemed to shake a little. "He'd kill you if he could. And then he'd tear your pieces to pieces."

Flint turned away from the spectacle, feeling the sick spot deepen and twist at his insides. There were people up there, hundreds of them, who could be eating drinking, breathing this stuff. He had to start making some calls, inform the EPA, FBI, get a containment team organized. And find out exactly what the hell was going on.

Tighten the screws.

"Quarantine every man and woman who went near that place," he said. "Test them for anything and everything; I don't want this to happen to them. And keep that shit bottled."

CHAPTER TWENTY-THREE

On the morning of March 5th, Bobby Babcock received a mighty strange phone call from the doctor.

Joe's funeral had gone as well as a funeral can go (much better than Bobby had expected), and he ended up staying through to the end, after all. Nobody blamed him for what had happened. People were too busy grieving, or dealing with their own shock and guilt. Almost everyone who had been involved in the search was there; even Hank had shown up. Hank had been uncharacteristically silent through the whole thing, even during the brief gathering in the church reception room afterward—though that was to be expected. It was, after all, a funeral. Later, after it was over, Bobby got out of that goddamned jacket and tie, and over the past few days he'd been able to forget some of the guilt that had been haunting him since Joe's disappearance.

The phone call from Dr. Mudd changed all that.

Bobby was busy with a magazine, feet up on the desk, feeling pretty good about himself, when the doctor called. Marie answered (she was not only his wife, but the receptionist at the office as well), and yelled at him to pick up line one. He cursed, set the magazine down, and pushed the button.

"Robert? Eustice Mudd here."

Bobby knew the doctor, but not particularly well. He couldn't imagine what the phone call would be about. "What can I do you for?" This was Bobby's standard question upon receiving phone calls from anyone other than a close friend. It made him sound friendly, but not too much so, not so much that the caller would expect anything right away. Bobby liked to keep his options open.

"Well, I have a rather strange request," the doctor continued. "I'm not really sure how to say it."

Uh-oh, Bobby thought. "Go ahead, Doc."

"It's about the new family that moved in over in Jackson, on the old Kennedy land."

Bobby took his feet off the desk. "What about them?"

"Well, I had a visit in my office from the mother and the girl, Jessie is her name, and I'm afraid that something funny might be going on out there."

"Why would they come talk to you?"

"They're worried about their daughter. She's been having these . . . nightmares, and she thinks she saw someone out in the woods, watching her." The doctor's voice seemed to waver a little saying this, but Bobby would never have any idea exactly how hard it was for him to do.

"And you'd like me to check it out." Bobby was pissed off now, not really at the doctor, just that someone had to bring up this crap again. Just when he was feeling good.

"Would you?" The relief in the doctor's voice was clear. "I don't know, I just have a bad feeling. I think the girl's telling the truth."

"I'll send somebody over."

"Thanks a lot, Bobby, really. It's a load off my mind.

With the recent . . . problems and everything, and that being the same house and all, I just got to thinking . . ."

He called me Bobby, Bobby thought, even more pissed off now. *I hardly know the guy.*

"Yeah, okay, sure."

"Thanks. Listen, let me know how it turns out, will you?"

"Will do."

Bobby hung up with a bang. "Fuck," he said softly, and picked up his magazine again. He would get to it later. But goddamn it if he didn't feel like hell again. Leave it to that doctor to bring everything up, and ruin a perfectly good day.

CHAPTER TWENTY-FOUR

Jonathan Newman, though he might have been once, was not human anymore.

Only the extensive canned supplies he had stocked earlier that winter had kept him alive. Dr. Seigel would hardly have recognized him; he had lost over thirty pounds, though he still tipped the scales at 230 and retained most of his strength through pure, crazed adrenaline. The weight loss had added to his horrific appearance. The skin of his head was pressed and stretched tightly around his skull, the thin scars on his lips and cheeks purple-white.

A few weeks ago, the auditory hallucinations had begun, high-pitched screaming and loud pops, snapping like broken bones. The normal movements of the muscle and tissue of his inner ear had become a nightmare of sound, and as he slipped deeper into his own private hell, the poppings and whines became whispers. He saw long, black robes of eyes, flowing holes that twisted and spun, the eyes opening and shutting in an obscene wink. The eyes of the Devil lost in shifting faces. And glimpses of a blade, silver and twinkling in the blackness, laced with red, something barely remembered, something from long ago. The blade scared him more than anything, more than the eyes or the whispers, though why that was, he didn't know. He only knew how it filled him with a deep, despairing fear, the kind that used to grip him while he snuck through jungle shadows and waited for the guns of the enemy to cut him down.

He barely remembered to eat. Sleep, when it came, held no escape. He spent most of his time watching from the woods, wanting desperately to know where THEY were at all times, so THEY could never sneak up on him. Once, after he saw the dog-creature in the pink jacket (when David had searched the woods), he actually climbed a tree and waited like a vulture, knife clenched in his teeth, for one of the Dark Eyes to walk underneath. It had been close, so close, and he was going to pounce, and then it had moved off, running in fear; it had *smelled* him somehow. He would have to be more careful.

Inside his body, the deadly march of the toxin had already begun; his nose ran blood, his kidneys swelled with pus, his testicles shriveled. But he had time left, time before these things ended his life.

So he waited patiently for his chance, wanting to move on them before they could move against him, something dimly remembered from the war days. Kill or be killed.

The time would come soon.

CHAPTER TWENTY-FIVE

The small, twin-engine Cessna touched down at the one-strip airport in Edmundston, "the Land of the Porcupines," at ten past three Thursday afternoon. The ride from Boston had been rough, and now Amanda Seigel felt the queasiness in her stomach kick up a notch. She was scared, no doubt about that, though the reason for that fear refused to come to the surface. Jonathan hadn't called, that was true, and when she tried the police in St. Boudin, they couldn't help her, either—nobody that she talked to had ever seen or heard from a tall, bulky man with a scarred face (though when she mentioned that he was her patient and might have become, well, *sick*, she could have sworn there was an unusually long silence at the other end of the line). But still, there was no reason for her to get on a *plane* and fly up here, really. She was only a doctor, after all, and there were plenty of other, more qualified people to deal with problems like these. She didn't need to make it her own personal crusade.

Except for that feeling she had, the feeling that something had gone terribly, terribly wrong, and that she was at least partially to blame for allowing him to go in the first place. Amanda Seigel did not allow herself to blame the hospital board and its cutbacks, or the government and their disappearing funds—she was not the type to set the blame on others.

She had spent most of yesterday looking up descriptions of sensory deprivation experiments. She had found plenty of descriptions, and they all pointed in the same direction. One had been a study done by a well-known scientist with a sensory deprivation tank, a tank filled with water in which the subject floats for hours without light or sound. She recalled studying the experiment in school. The scientist had found that without sufficient input and stimulus from the outside environment, the mind tends to wander. After an hour in the tank, during which the subject can't see, hear, or smell, he begins to hallucinate, have lengthy conversations with beings only he can see, and experience flashbacks to childhood memories.

That set her heart pounding because, though she realized that Jonathan should have work to keep him busy, the deepest reaches of the Canadian woods in winter were just a little bit like a sensory deprivation tank. All that snow, the silence, the loneliness. He *would* be isolated, and he *was* still a little bit unstable.

He's more than just a little bit unstable, she corrected herself grimly, *as much as I tried to dismiss it. He shouldn't have left the hospital. It's as simple as that.*

And then, as she was getting ready to leave the library, she had come across the last study, the one that had proved to be the final stone to tip the scales and send her rushing to the airport. Even now, thinking of it tightened the hand that had seemed to wrap itself around her heart.

It was a lengthy and important study on the combat veterans of the Vietnam War, and concentrated on veterans especially haunted by nightmares and those who had spent periods in mental hospitals. The study found that most of the veterans had gone through periods of intense trauma, usually in prison camps or under heavy enemy fire for long periods of time, and most of them had spent long periods in isolation. Many of the veterans admitted to strong hallucinations, sometimes even "inventing" a friend who provided comfort and strength, and helped them through their ordeal. Often, after the soldiers escaped or were rescued, they were surprised to discover that they had been alone the entire time.

The door to the plane opened, and she saw that someone had wheeled one of those moving platforms of steps across the runway to the plane. The wind through the door was bitterly cold, and she pulled her thin sweater around her shoulders for warmth. She hadn't packed much, hadn't been prepared for such weather. That had been foolish, she knew, but she had been busy with other things.

The study had gone on to describe the present state of mind of the veterans, and almost all of them described vivid flashbacks, during which they felt as if they were back in the middle of the war again. Some of them even admitted to having new hallucinations, though in those cases the hallucinations almost always had a trigger that set them off, some sort of catalyst. Many of the veterans who turned to drugs as a possible answer to the constant nightmares simply found another door to more vivid and terrifying horrors. Some of these patients had turned violent.

And none of them, not a single one, had the added burden of an existing paranoid personality.

She waited until most of the other twelve passengers had left, and then grabbed her bag from the overhead shelf. The pilot's mechanical "Have a good stay," and "Come fly with us again" went all but unnoticed at the door; the wind cut into her thin outfit and she gasped, ducking her head to descend the steps and get out of the cold as fast as she could. Once at the bottom, she noticed that the sky had gone a deep gray-black, and she hurried across the stretch of tar and concrete to the terminal. It was another two hours to St. Boudin, and she wanted to get there quickly.

And once you do? she asked herself for the first time. *What then?*

If she found Jonathan living happily and doing his job, she would feel a bit foolish, but that would be okay; that would be just fine with her. She could stand to feel a little bit foolish.

By the time she had found the rental place, it was four o'clock, and the day was turning quickly towards night. She got what she hoped were rock-solid directions to St. Boudin from the front desk, as well as the name of a possible place to stay in town. Apparently, there weren't any real hotels there, but a bed-and-breakfast could be found if you knew where to look. And as she got into the car and began her drive, an idea formulated loosely in her head. *There must be someone in town associated with the plant*, she thought. She could get in touch with them. They might know something about Jonathan.

That was how Amanda Seigel ended up calling David Pierce early Friday morning.

CHAPTER TWENTY-SIX

He woke up in utter blackness to the sound of the phone ringing in a distant part of the house. The clock by the bed said six thirty-five. They didn't have an extension for the bedroom yet, and he stumbled through the hallway to the top of the stairs, hitting the light switch and swearing at whoever it was calling this early. They had been in bed by ten, but he had only fallen asleep a few hours ago, the thoughts that revolved around in his head finally silenced by utter exhaustion.

He reached the phone downstairs on the seventh ring.

"Mr. Pierce, my name is Amanda Seigel," the voice said. "I'm a psychiatrist from Boston. I'm sorry for calling so early, but I spoke with someone in Hydro's Quebec offices who gave me your name and number. We need to discuss something, and it's urgent."

He was tired and pissed off and about to refuse, but something in the woman's voice stopped him. Was it desperation? He wasn't quite sure.

"I hope you don't think I'm a flake," she said, rushing on as if afraid that he might suddenly change his mind and hang up on her. "But I'm worried about one of my patients. He was employed by Hydro Development this winter, at the Jackson plant, and he was supposed to check in with me, and I haven't heard from him—"

"Look, isn't this a job for the police or something? Missing persons?" David's tolerance was fading quickly, and he thought about how tired he would be when nine thirty finally rolled around.

"I realize this sounds crazy," she said. "But the police can't help me." Her voice had toughened, and David realized that she (whoever she was) would not be put off so easily.

"A patient, you said?"

"Jonathan Newman. He was hired to look after the place through the winter."

"I don't know a thing about that."

"Maybe we could talk in person? I flew up here last night—I'm not far from you."

"Jesus, you must be one hell of a doctor," he said. "Look, I really don't know anything that could help you, but I'm meeting with someone today in town, and maybe I could see you after that."

"I'd be grateful. I'm in St. Boudin now. I thought maybe you could show me the plant—"

"It's snowed in, lady. Nobody's getting out there without a snowmobile."

"Just give me ten minutes. Please."

"You must be desperate. I guess you deserve whatever help I can give."

"Thanks so much. You don't know how much I appreciate it."

"I'll be at the Railway Cafe in St. Boudin at around nine thirty. If you came around ten thirty or eleven—"

"That would be fine. Thanks again."

She hung up, and David realized he never found out exactly what she wanted to know. He put the phone down, wondering why he had agreed to meet with her in the first place. He doubted that Dan Flint would take kindly to him talking with strangers about the plant.

The hell with Dan Flint, he thought suddenly. *That woman is in trouble; I could feel it. If I can help her, I will. I only hope she'd do the same for me.*

Helen was awake as he reentered the bedroom. "Who was it?" she asked, sitting up and pulling the blankets close around her breasts.

"A shrink from Boston." He laughed. "Don't ask."

"Why—"

"I've got a meeting in St. Boudin with one of the FERC guys this morning, and she wants to meet me later to discuss something."

"Are you going soon?"

"I think I'd better." He sat down on the bed next to her. "Listen, if you want me to stay—"

"No, we'll be fine," she said. "Besides, I want to call the doctor about Jessie. This meeting, it won't take long, right?"

"I'll make sure of that." He smiled and touched her hand. It was ice-cold. "Listen, I'll stock the fire, okay? And I'll try to be home before lunchtime."

She nodded, and he dressed quickly, not bothering to shower. He wanted to be there and back as soon as possible.

Once downstairs, he checked the fire. It had burned down to coals, and he stirred them until they glowed red, then packed the stove with more wood. The supply in the house was running low, and he made a mental note to restock it from the pile outside. After he had finished, he got his jacket and gloves on quickly and stepped through the door, locking it behind him.

The sky was a dull gray in the early morning light, and the wind continued to gust, dancing along the top of the porch and stirring the snow across the driveway. He ducked into it and pulled the collar of his jacket up to cover his ears, walking quickly to the car.

Once he hit the main road, he switched on his head-lights, trying to cut into the gloom that blanketed the ground. The car's dashboard clock read seven thirty-two. The sun was up by now, but it was difficult to tell through the cloud cover. He would be early, but that was okay. He needed some time alone, and maybe a cup of coffee.

By the time he hit the outskirts of the town forty min-utes later, the sky had begun to spit snow, hard little granules that bounced off the windshield and hood of the car, and the wind had picked up even more. The roads were clear of traffic, and he drove down the long hill, taking the left towards downtown, without seeing anyone. It was eerie, almost as if there wasn't a soul left in St. Boudin. The clock on the dash read ten past eight.

As he pulled into the parking lot of the Railway Cafe (parking in very nearly the same spot where his wife had parked several days before), he noticed that the windows glowed cheerily, and was relieved that the place was open for business this early. *A good, warm cup of coffee*, he thought. *And maybe a donut or two.*

And after settling down in one of the corner booths (he and a large waitress with gray hair were the only people there), he ordered just that. Soon enough, both Flint and then Amanda Seigel would arrive, and they would have plenty to talk about. He hoped he could help her find who she was looking for, or at least point her onto the right track.

As it turned out, her track and his were one and the same.

CHAPTER TWENTY-SEVEN

David Pierce sat in the Railway Cafe for a good long time, not moving much. The corner booth was enough for him, along with the occasional refills of coffee that the waitress brought (Angela was her name, as he saw by her name tag). He was doing some heavy thinking about the sudden move, his wife's happy face during that snowball fight just a few short days ago, Jessie as she explored the magic of the castle in Quebec City, and his own feeling of relief when he began work again. These things mixed with thoughts of the first meeting with Flint and Thompson, and Jessie's nightmares, and that tumor that slid about under the cat's skin like a kneecap.

He felt an unexplained anxiety well up within him, and with it came a flood of nostalgia for the house in New York. The house on the dead-end street, with the little green park at one end, overlooking the highway. They had only lived there a few months, but it was there that he wanted to be right now; back there with the unemployment and the blessed ignorance of all this crap he had found himself buried in, back to the old life. He felt out of place here and in over his head.

And then someone spoke up in his head. *Enough with this crap, Davey old boy*, the voice said, and it sounded like Chuckie Howard again. *You've got a chance to set things in the right direction here. Now go on and do it. Do whatever you can.*

It was good advice, he decided, even if it did come from a snot-nosed little brat like Chuckie. He laughed out loud. It was almost funny if you thought about it. Here it was, barely a week since they left the Château Frontenac, and already that place seemed years away. Meanwhile, some poor slob from the FERC was coming here today to ask him questions as if he actually knew something.

This was how Dan Flint found him when he finally arrived twenty minutes later, and dropped the bombshell that would change their lives forever.

"Mr. Pierce," Flint said when he approached the table As David started to stand, he waved him back into his seat. "Listen, thanks for coming. I wasn't sure you would, after our phone call. I hope I didn't seem too forceful."

"I try not to hold a grudge."

"That's a good policy. May I?" Flint gestured to the plastic seat across from him, and David nodded.

Angela sauntered over and Flint ordered some coffee, eggs and bacon and a side of toast. "What I have to tell you," he said, when she had gone, "stays between us for now. I don't know how long it's going to take to get a team up here, and I don't want to tip anyone off."

"Tip them off to what? What the hell is going on?"

Instead of answering, Flint sat back and waited for Angela to pour his coffee. When she stepped away, he leaned forward again and lowered his voice. "Do you know why Hydro Development hired you?"

"They liked my pretty smile."

"Could be. Or maybe they liked your track record? You left quite a trail at EPC."

"That's a cheap shot. You've been checking up on me?"

"Enough to know you weren't exactly in great demand at the time they brought you on board."

David sipped his coffee and tried to remain calm. "I don't understand where this is going."

Flint dug into his jacket pocket, took out an envelope and spread its contents out on the table. David picked up the top photo; it showed some kind of animal in full restraints, lying on a steel examination table. Even in the photo, the animal's aggression was evident, muscles straining, its bloodshot eyes staring into the camera, foam-flecked jaws snapping at someone just out of the shot.

"Is that a dog?"

"It is. The poor thing died about an hour after that photo was taken, bleeding from every orifice, still trying to tear anything within reach to pieces." Flint put the photos back into the envelope. "That dog wasn't just antisocial. It was dosed up with a chemical we pulled out of the river near the Jackson project. This chemical is similar to the dioxin found in Agent Orange, but it's been reengineered on the molecular level. Our technicians tell me it's really quite clever."

"You mentioned some sort of contamination before. What makes you think it has anything to do with the Jackson project?"

"Agent Orange was a herbicide, a pretty nasty one. This new compound is far deadlier to many types of plants, but what it seems to have been built for is algae.

It's stable in water, has a very long killing cycle, and builds up over time. In fact, we saw no reduction in its effectiveness over a period of two weeks."

Algae. David felt a trickle of sweat run down his back. He had seen several references to algae build-up within the underground storage reservoirs in early document files. Early pumped storage projects had trouble with it clogging the lines running underground. Flint seemed to notice his hesitation. "Something you want to tell me?"

"No, nothing."

Flint studied his face for a long time. Then he shrugged. "Listen, I'm going to tell you what I think, and then you can make up your own mind. I believe they knew they had a problem with their facility here in Jackson. Maybe they wanted to test something out, and it got away from them a bit. Instead of asking for help, they tried to cover it up. When that didn't work, they went out and hired you as a backup plan. Maybe they even forged a few documents so that when things thawed out and the shit really hit the fan, it would look like you were the one responsible. With your history, when you fought back, who would believe you?"

"That's crazy."

"Really? How about the way they treated you at the meeting in Quebec City? And sending you out here in the middle of winter. Hell, the project's snowed in; nobody can even get to it for the next couple of months. Why put you here now? And let's face it, they've got the money to hire anyone they want. You're not exactly a shining star in the industry. I'm not telling you anything you don't know."

Angela arrived with Flint's breakfast. When she'd arranged the plates, refilled the coffee cups and left,

Flint leaned in again. "Seems to me you have a choice. Either stand with them and go down with the ship, or work with me on the inside for the next few weeks to help me build a case. If you can't uncover anything incriminating, we'll know I'm wrong. If you do, I can make sure your name stays out of everything. You get out with our highest recommendation. I can even help you relocate."

David's mind was reeling. He didn't want to believe it, but everything Flint said held the ring of truth. Hydro Development had to know he'd take the job, and they knew his history. He was the perfect scapegoat, if that was what they wanted.

"Hell, those forged documents might already be floating around with your name on them," Flint said, as if reading his mind. "You ever think of that?"

That was when Amanda Seigel walked through the door.

"That storm has really turned ugly," she said, shaking off the snow. "I'm sorry I'm a little early, but I couldn't wait. I hope I'm not intruding?"

Flint just stared at her, and David shrugged. The day couldn't get much worse, right?

He was wrong.

The storm had gotten ugly indeed, and it had taken Amanda over fifteen minutes to drive the three miles or so from the simple bed-and-breakfast where she had spent the night to the Railway Cafe. Even so, she got there half an hour ahead of time, hoping to have a cup of coffee and settle her nerves.

From the moment she got into the rental car, she realized just how nervous she really was about this meeting, and how much it meant to her. She wasn't sure if she would be welcome there; after all, she didn't even know the man. But what made her even more concerned was the simple fact that if she didn't learn what she wanted to know about Jonathan from Mr. Pierce, she had nowhere else to turn. The only other thing to do would be to drive out to the plant herself, and she had heard from the nice silver-haired lady who ran the bed-and-breakfast that the roads out to the plant were "simply impossible." She believed it, judging by the amount of snow on the ground, and the threat of more to come.

And if I did make it out there, what would I find? She tried not to think too much about that, but it *was* important to consider. What if Jonathan was gone? Or worse. How would she feel then? Everything was on her shoulders. She had been responsible for him, and she had let him go. Her instincts had been flat wrong.

She had dreamed about him last night. Even thinking about it now sent shivers down her spine. She'd been standing outside a house in the country, and she and Jonathan were about to go somewhere together, but she had forgotten something inside. *Could you go get it for me, Jonathan?* she asked. *There are spiders over there on the lawn, and I don't like spiders.* There was a little pond between them, and she had to throw him the keys so he could get in the front door, but she didn't want them to fall in the pond, so she threw them high into the air. But the keys landed in the water and sank out of sight. *Oh no,* she thought, *we'll never find them now; they're lost forever.*

Don't worry, Jonathan said, his scarred mouth moving in slow-motion dream-speech, the lips curving into a smile. *I can get in.*

She stepped around the pond and into the higher

grass. The spiders were closer to her now. The sky had turned black and cold, and as she looked down, the grass at her feet became brambles and bushes. A spiderweb had become stuck to her, and a fat gray spider crawled up her arm. She shook it off in disgust and turned to leave, but the bushes had grown up behind her, and webs were all around her now, the spiders crawling up her legs.

Jonathan, she cried, *help me!* But he only stood above her on the hill, grinning. *Don't worry*, he said again. *I can get in.*

A rustling noise made her whirl around. Something was pushing through the bushes. Her horror and revulsion grew towards panic as thick and coal black, hairy legs felt their way through the branches. The thing kept coming, more long, hairy legs—a gigantic black spider with Jonathan's head on its body, his face dripping with dark blood.

She awoke bathed in sweat, her heart leaping in her chest. She didn't know what the dream meant but it had shaken her up badly. There was something evil about the way he looked on that hill—the grin, as if he understood something she did not, and the way those scars on his cheeks and lips had turned white. And the spiders—she hated spiders. In the dream, they had been everywhere, everywhere she turned, covering her with their long, hairy legs and fat, slippery underbellies, and then that *thing* . . .

It was a lousy beginning to the morning. After she got up and went downstairs, she gave herself a nasty slice on the ring finger of her left hand with a knife during breakfast. When she got outside and in the car, the roads were filled with blowing snow and covered with drifts, and her windshield wipers didn't do a thing against the snow that was already falling thickly. She had never been in such a bad storm, and it was only supposed to get worse. "A real doozy," the silver-haired woman, her landlady, had said. "You really shouldn't leave the house."

But she had, of course. It had been no real trouble to come, just as long as she was careful. *No trouble yet*, she thought, but soon the roads would be impassable.

After she arrived, both men had been civil enough. But she noticed the tension between them. There were a few exchanges of pleasantries; she ordered a cup of coffee. David Pierce sat ramrod straight, his lips pressed together in a thin, white line. He was angry; she could feel it. And there was something else coming from him, the same almost palpable smell that had filled her bed-clothes last night; the smell of fear.

"I *am* interrupting," she said finally, after her coffee had arrived. "I'm sorry, but I need some answers, and I'm not sure where to turn."

"What exactly are you looking for, Ms. Seigel?" asked Flint. His fingers drummed on the table, as if he were anxious to be somewhere else. She found it more than a little distracting.

She explained herself again to both men, and as she went on, she imagined they both sat up a little straighter, paid a little more attention. She was no storyteller, but what she had to say clearly had them interested. "And you flew all the way here from Boston," Flint said. "This guy must be pretty important."

"He's an unusual case. Medications never seemed to work very well for him, but therapy worked wonders. I can't say I've had anyone quite like him before. I've always diagnosed him to be harmless, but physically, he's . . . intimidating. And he's been through a lot of trauma in his life. I can't say now where that might take him, and whether he might become dangerous to others. I can say that any suspicion that someone might be watching him, or anything that might make him feel threatened, could send him down a very bad path."

"Now why would Hydro Development put a guy like that at their plant?" Flint said. Then he looked across the table at David Pierce, who had suddenly gone white as a sheet. He was staring at something over Flint's shoulder. "Hey, you okay—"

Abruptly Pierce leapt to his feet and ran for the door. Flint stood and shouted at him to wait, but he never even looked back. Flint went to the window, but by the time he looked out, Pierce's car was already accelerating, wheels throwing plumes of slush and snow high into the air as he fishtailed out onto the road.

When he returned to the table, Flint turned to see what Pierce had been staring at. On the wall, pinned to a bulletin board, was a "Missing" flyer, with the photo of a little girl in pigtails and a big, gap-toothed smile.

CHAPTER TWENTY-EIGHT

Helen slept comfortably for the first time in a long while. Her dreams melted into each other; she floated through a white bedroom with many skylights, then into another place that looked like a gigantic version of their old home in New York, the walls receding until she could no longer see any boundaries at all. It calmed her until eventually she did not dream of anything but floating naked through a clear blue sea.

When she finally awoke and left the dream world, the lazy feeling remained. She did not immediately think of the past week's events, or the doctor's words; in fact, she hovered for several long minutes in that state between sleep and full awareness. When she finally opened her eyes, she did it with a deep sense of regret.

The clock beside the bed read nine thirty-two.

She had the profound and irrefutable idea that someone was watching her.

Feeling her heart pound heavily in her chest, she sat straight up in bed, pulling the sheets close around her body.

Jessica stood in the doorway, holding Johnny Bear loosely with one hand. She looked tiny and lost, dwarfed by the doorframe. Helen let out a great sigh of relief.

"You scared me, honey." She smiled, and began to climb out of bed. Her daughter's words stopped her short.

"He's coming for us, Mommy," she said. "The bad man is here."

PART THREE

THE DECAPITATOR

CHAPTER TWENTY-NINE

For Bobby Babcock, the trouble really began with the storm, but it didn't end there. As hard as it was to believe, the day only got worse.

He had been answering the phone all morning, calming down all the people without power, without water, as well as those people who were just lonely and wanted company. There were lots of those. It never occurred to them, he supposed, that he might be a tad bit *busy*, that he might not have the time to sit there and chat about the new disco in Edmundston, or Aunt Judith's dentures, for Christ's sake. Quite a few of them reported seeing strange things in their houses, flashing lights, dead relatives, the works. One had even suggested that they were under attack from a bunch of UFOs. If he had thought about it a little more, Bobby would have realized that even the crazy people seemed to be hallucinating a bit more than usual today. But he spent the time trying to calm them all down because he supposed that in some way it was his job to do so. Besides, he wanted to keep the job for a while longer, and people remembered things like this for years to come.

So while the storm caused Bobby some trouble, it kept his mind off those other funny phone calls he had been getting lately. The one from the doc, then yesterday one from some whacked-out psychiatrist from Boston who wanted to know if he had run into a patient of hers. When she told him the guy could be a few rungs short of a ladder, he had felt a momentary unease, and had the chance to think that maybe he should ponder the possibilities a while longer, and then she was going on again about how worried she was and how she was going to fly on up there to look for him. He told her they hadn't seen heads or tails of him around St. Boudin, and that was the truth, as far as he knew.

Now he supposed she was in town rooting around for clues like some second-rate Sherlock Holmes. It sure as hell wouldn't make *his* life any easier. She'd probably get it in her fool head to go hiking out in the woods somewhere during the storm and get lost, and he would have another missing person on his hands. And the power was bound to go out soon, then probably the phones.

A great big mess, and he would have to clean it up.

But he refused to let that old guilt come slinking in again, no sirree. He'd licked that for good.

Until the door burst open at a little past ten that morning, that is.

What followed was something right out of a *Three Stooges* video. Two people came rushing in, a man and a woman, babbling on about some kind of "real trouble" down at the hydro plant, and that sent the rest of the station into an uproar, people running about like a bunch of chickens with their heads cut off. It took a full five minutes for Bobby to calm them all down and find out exactly what the hell was going on, and it seemed like hours. It turned out that one of them was that psychiatrist, Dr. Amanda Seigel (and a pretty little thing she was too), but goddamn it if he didn't wish she had just stayed in Boston where she belonged. There was trouble all right, at least according to them, and some idiot had gone rushing off into the storm to try and do something about it. *That* was foolish; there was nothing any of them could do until the roads were cleared, and that wouldn't happen for a while. Andrew Richeleau, who plowed the roads (and owned the only landscaping business in town, to boot), well, he didn't get up all that early. And besides, the snow was just going to keep on piling up. The radio said they were due to get close to a foot.

He sat them both down, gave them a cup of coffee (decaf, of course), and made them tell him exactly what was going on, slowly this time. And after they had finished, goddamn it if that guilt didn't come rushing in like the tide. Maybe something was up after all, but it might just be too late to do a thing about it.

And the snow kept falling.

CHAPTER THIRTY

David sped along the narrow roadway towards Jackson, Flint's words coming back to him: *When that didn't work, they went out and hired you as a backup plan. Maybe they even forged a few documents so that when things thawed out and the shit really hit the fan, it would look like you were the one responsible.* How could he have been so stupid? Olmstead's eagerness to hire him and get him up there, then that strange initial meeting with the FERC and Hydro's willingness to let him do his thing, with little or no direction—he would have denied it in the end but who would have believed him? Desperate times require desperate measures, as they say.

The snow had thickened while he was inside, falling steadily now in an almost solid sheet. The speedometer read seventy-two; it was as fast as the little car would go over the hills, and it seemed faster than was humanly possible in these conditions. There was a good two inches in most places where the wind hadn't swept it away, and no sign of a plow truck yet.

He had tried to reach Helen by phone, but the house line was busy and he knew she didn't have her cell on. *Think, you son of a bitch. Think.* Had he left the phone off the hook after the conversation with Amanda Seigel this morning?

For the life of him, he couldn't remember.

About halfway to Jackson, he finally had to slow down. The car was fishtailing wildly around the corners, its skinny tires slipping in the snow that blanketed the road. The driving was getting worse. He switched on the radio, hoping to take his mind off things a little, take the edge off the silence, maybe catch a weather report. The radio was playing a country song, "Take This Job and Shove It." *Appropriate*, he thought. *Except I'm going to do a lot more than shove when this is all over.* He thought of Mike Olmstead, and their friendly first meeting; it made him feel sick inside, like someone had thrust a knife into his stomach and twisted.

The song ended and the announcer came on. "Looks like an ugly one out there," he crackled, fading in and out. "Hope you're inside, wherever you are. It's the ninth of March and it's snowing, folks! It's been forecast as the largest spring storm since the one that dumped over sixty centimeters on us in eighty-six. Keep warm, people."

He switched off the radio, feeling even more anxious than before. The wipers slipped across the windshield, scraping softly, and he turned them up a notch. Outside, the snow came down even harder, if that was possible. He stepped gingerly on the brakes, slowing the car down to fifty-five, which was still breakneck speed. *Thank God there's no traffic*, he thought. A car had passed by him on the way out of town, but he had yet to come up on one traveling the same direction; apparently, nobody else was stupid enough to drive in one of the worst storms in recent history.

The clock on the dashboard read ten fifteen. He was only about twenty minutes from the house, but he fought the urge to press the accelerator to the floor again, knowing that if he did, he might never make it to the house at all.

They're fine, Davey, just fine. Take it easy.

But there remained the very real possibility that he was dealing with a madman here, a man who had been under the influence of some sort of chemical hallucinogen for God knows how long, and the last thing he wanted to do was run off the road and into a tree. His family needed him. He prayed he had not already let them down. *Why did I leave them this morning? Why didn't I take them with me?*

By the time he saw the beginning of their driveway through the heavy snow, he almost missed it and slid past into the drifts. It was visible only as a vague opening in the trees that huddled like ghosts along the road's edge, and when he saw it he automatically hit the brakes, putting the little car into a skid. Swearing, he fought for control, the back threatening to fishtail and swap ends with the front.

When it ended, he was sideways in the wrong lane. Feeling a little shaky, he swung the car gingerly around and into the driveway, thankful again for the lack of traffic and the guardian angel that had gotten him this far. The gusting winds had blown the snow into drifts here and there close to a foot high already, and he had to constantly gun the engine and then feather the brakes to maneuver in it, knowing he was pushing the edges of the envelope but equally sure that he could not stop or he would never get the car going again.

About halfway down the driveway, the tires caught a frozen rut hidden under the new snow's surface and the wheel was yanked out of his hands with incredible force. He felt the car begin to slide and then the wheel shuddered again and the front tires leapt the shoulder into the deeper drifts. The car came to an abrupt stop, tilted forward and stalled. It was suddenly nearly silent, nothing to hear but the sound of the wipers scraping the glass and the thin hum of the heater fan.

He turned the key, jamming the car into reverse and flooring the gas pedal. The tires spun uselessly, buried in the drifts.

Looks like you walk from here.

He opened the door and the storm attacked him, whipping hard granules of snow at his face and neck. He pulled the collar of his jacket up as far as it would go, jammed his hat over his ears, and stepped out into the wind. The front of the car was almost completely buried in the drifts that lined the road's edge. He looked down the driveway in the direction of the house, but the storm blotted everything out farther than twenty or thirty feet. *It can't be more than a quarter mile. No sweat.*

It was hard going on foot. The new snow evened out the ruts and potholes in the road until they were almost invisible, and his feet kept slipping off the hard edges and into the deeper pockets. Several times he stumbled and fell to his knees, the shock of the hard, cold ground rushing up through his legs and palms of his hands. The pain in his injured hand was dulled somewhat by the frigid air, but it was there, a constant ache, and he could feel the wetness inside his mittens. *Still bleeding.* Something was working at him. Was it possible that whatever might be in the water at Jackson Hydro had spread this far? If so, he wondered what else it had done to him, to *them*, that he didn't even know about yet.

He could see no farther than ten or fifteen feet, and even that was pushing it; the trees alongside of him were nothing more than humps of indistinct white and green. The world was swiftly reduced to the small square section of road in front of him, and he concentrated on that with all his strength, refusing to think about the car in the ditch or worse, his family and what might have happened. It seemed he could see shapes coming at him out of the pines, broad-shouldered men dressed in blue. He ignored them all and concentrated on the road.

Minutes later, the house loomed up out of the mass of blowing white snow, and he sighed with relief. His nose and cheeks were numb, and the tips of his fingers ached with cold. But he stopped in front of the porch, suddenly laced with fear for what he might see inside.

They'll be sleeping peacefully. There's nothing to worry about. We'll go get the car out and drive until we see some sunshine.

They would have to go a very, very long way; in fact, standing out there in the wind and snow, he wasn't sure if he even remembered what the sun looked like.

He could see the front door clearly from here; it looked solid and closed up tight. The sight calmed him, and he walked up the steps and tried the handle. It would not turn. Locked.

That was when he realized that he had left his key ring dangling from the ignition of the car a quarter mile back.

He pounded on the door and shouted Helen's name, the wind tearing the words from his mouth and carrying it away faster than he could draw another breath. His lips and cheeks were now completely numb. There was no answer from inside to his repeated shouts, and he struggled around the corner of the deck and into the full force of the wind, hunching his shoulders and leaning into it.

Something was wrong with the kitchen window. *Oh God the glass is shattered . . .*

Holding in the fear that threatened to overpower him, he peered in through the shards of glass that lined the window's edge. A pile of snow had formed on the kitchen table and along the wall, and more was blowing in every second.

In the center of the drift on the floor was a footprint of a man's boot.

He thrust himself over the window sill and into the room, ignoring the sharp pain in his hands as he landed with a heavy thud on the hardwood floor. It was almost as cold inside as it was out in the storm. He stood and looked around frantically for a weapon, finally settling on the few lonely pieces of firewood next to the stove. He grabbed a heavy piece, holding it with both hands out in front of him, his whole body shaking with adrenaline. The kitchen and living room were empty, and there was no sound except for the wind whipping through the broken window.

Chuckie Howard spoke up in his head again. *The man's an Army veteran*, the voice said. *He's been trained for this kind of stuff. The most you've done is taken three classes of karate when you were twelve, and I remember those. You got your ass kicked, as I recall.*

He moved forward as quietly as possible and climbed the stairs. The door to their bedroom was slightly ajar, and he pushed it open the rest of the way with the end of the log, every nerve in his body alive and screaming. Several boxes from the move still sat against the far wall, and the bedsheets were crumpled at the end of the mattress.

The room was empty.

He stepped into it cautiously, holding the wood out

like a baseball bat, and moved quickly over to the walk-in closet. The door was battered and cracked, as if someone had beaten on it with a heavy instrument. He felt the pulse pounding in his temples, and the shake in his arms, and he pushed open that door too with the log and saw the smeared handprint on the wall and the deep red pool of blood on the floor.

They had fought it out in here.

A broom handle lay broken on the floor, one end of it stained red and sprouting bits of thick, coarse hair. The bastard had suffered at least one good blow before he took them.

Feeling sick and frantic, David Pierce called 911 from his cell. The dispatcher told him to sit tight and they would be out there as soon as they could make it through the snow. He screamed at them to hurry. Then he searched the rest of the house as quickly as he could. The rooms were empty and there were no other signs of a struggle.

He knew in some inexplicable way that they were still alive, felt it deep within him as if when they died he would feel it as a death inside himself. Help was coming, right? Surely Flint and the psychiatrist would get someone. But what if they hadn't? He tried desperately to think. They had been taken to the hydro plant, of that he was sure. *Because he wants me to come after him. It's a war game and Helen and Jessica are the bait.*

Hank knew the woods, and he had a snowmobile. David prayed it was out of the shop by now. He would call Hank.

And then he would go after them himself.

CHAPTER THIRTY-ONE

Hank Babcock peered out the windshield into the fiercely driving snow, every fiber in him concentrating on the task at hand. The old Cherokee plodded valiantly on, and he blessed its soul again as he had fifty times in the last few minutes. He had chains on the tires, but by this point the storm had dumped at least five inches of new powder on top of a road already laced with ice. It was definitely not a Sunday drive.

He wondered briefly why he had decided to come at all. He got the call from Pierce just as the Celtics-Lakers game hit the air, and he was settling into the La-Z-Boy to catch as much of it as he could before they lost power. *Goddamn phone's more trouble than it's worth*, he thought. But he was glad of it, all the same. Because no matter how hard he tried to deny it, he did feel a sense of responsibility towards the Pierces; after all, he had set up the house deal, and maybe they wouldn't be in this pack of trouble if it weren't for that.

But going out into a blizzard to help track down some crazy killer? Well, that maybe went just a little too far. Yet here he was. *Never could turn down somebody who needs help*, he thought, not without a sense of regret. It was a flaw he could live with, he supposed. *Hopefully I can live with it through the next couple of hours.*

He did believe Pierce's story, as crazy as it seemed. It could have happened like this: Olmstead, maybe that little bastard Thompson too, find a lonely spot and a lonely guy and they leave him there with a bucketful of death, just to see what might happen. They're probably a little nuts, but they do it. And after they lose contact with the caretaker and people start getting lost out there, they come up with the plan of hiring David and pinning the whole mess on him.

Things hadn't been the same in Jackson since the plant construction started. There was the disappearance of the Kennedy girl, and, of course, Joe Thibideau, but it was more than that. People were acting crazy all over town.

Towing the trailer and snowmobile, the Cherokee tended to weave more than usual, and with the heavy gusts of wind, Hank had to fight to keep it under control. He was only about three miles from the house now, thank God. Another hour of this snow and nobody was going anywhere. Even on the snowmobile it was going to be a rough ride, especially through those woods, if that was the way they decided to go. He knew them by heart, had cut trails most everywhere by now, but when the visibility was less than thirty feet, it didn't matter if you were psychic. Every place looked the same, and those big drifts could do a hell of a lot of damage when you hit them at fifty miles an hour. Turn that drift into a tree, and you were in a pack of trouble.

A hard gust of wind almost spun him around, and he jerked the wheel back to center, feeling a tingle of fear run its fingers down the nape of his neck. He wasn't going more than thirty-five, nowhere near fast enough to get really hurt in a crash, but it wasn't the crash he was worried about. If he got stuck out in this, there was a good chance he would freeze to death before anybody came along to rescue him. He'd been on the road now for close to an hour, and he hadn't seen one car, not one.

He slowed it down to thirty.

Five minutes later, he pulled into the Pierces' driveway, feeling the weight of the trailer holding the Cherokee back a little. It was rough, but he was handling it just fine.

Then, ahead of him through the white sheet of snow, a form loomed out like a demon, red eyes glowing with fire . . .

It was a car, front end deep in the drifts just off the road. He swerved and hit the brakes, and still the ruts almost pulled him directly into it; he barely managed to yank the wheels out of them with a bump and thud. He felt the weight of the trailer behind him threatening to tip over, and maybe take the Cherokee with it.

Then he was past it, the front fender just scraping by the other car's bumper by a hair. *Christ but wasn't that close.* He swiped at the beads of sweat running down his forehead, his fingers shaking so badly he could hardly control them. *Just a goddamn car. I gotta lighten up a little. A demon, Jesus.* But he slowed down even more, and blessed that Cherokee's soul one more time.

David Pierce stood in the middle of his daughter's room, looking down at her bed.

He hadn't bothered to take off his hat or jacket, even though it was warmer up here where the heat tended to linger. *If you hurt my little girl . . .*

The sounds of the storm were muffled through the walls, but he knew it still raged fiercely. Wincing in sudden pain, he glanced down at his hand. He had been squeezing it tightly into a fist, the nails digging into the tender palm through the gloves. He pulled them off carefully. The center of the gauze wrapping was soaked with blood. The wound seemed to be getting worse, and he wondered if he would have to go to the hospital for it. *Imagine that: Hey, Doc, I seem to have picked up a splinter here, and damn if it isn't a nasty old slice, could be fatal . . .*

What was he thinking about his palm for? For a moment, he fancied he heard the house itself whispering about him, the very walls engaged in a secret finger-pointing session exposing his guilt, *Yes, really, Mr. Pierce, you should have seen it coming. The job was a bad idea with Jessica's problems, you know, and we tried to warn you, didn't we, yes we did, but you wouldn't listen, no you wouldn't. Money was more important than your family, you chickenshit . . .*

The whispering voices turned into the wind, which turned into the faint growl of an approaching engine.

He realized he had been sobbing out loud, and shook off the steely grip of his conscience. It would not do to lose control, not now. As he made his way downstairs, the wind hit him through the broken window. The pile of snow in the kitchen had grown considerably while he searched the house, and the footprint had vanished completely, almost as if it had never been there. But the jagged pieces of glass that clung to the window frame above where the footprint had been would not let him forget about the hard reality of the attack. *He was here. He was in my house and I was not around to help defend it.*

There was only the wind, and the snowflakes skittering across the boards outside like ghosts.

A car door slammed, and David ran to the front of the house to pull back the bolt. A moment later, Hank ducked inside, followed by the blowing snowflakes.

"Thanks for coming," David said simply, when Hank had shaken off the snow from his hat. "I don't know what I would have done if you hadn't answered the phone."

"You'd do the same for me, I hope." Hank smiled, and stuck out his hand. David took it gratefully. They stood there like that for a moment.

"We don't have long," he said finally. "Snow's gettin' worse."

David nodded. "Listen, you don't have to—"

"Forget it. Figure I know my way around these woods better than anybody, and I couldn't let you go out there alone. It'd be suicide. Besides, got to keep track of my snowmobile. My bread and butter, you know." He winked.

"We've got to be careful. This guy's a trained killer."

"I brought a few surprises for him. They're out in the Cherokee. Don't worry, we'll get him."

If he doesn't get us first. But if he did, Helen and Jessica would die. David would not, could not let that happen.

They bundled back up as best they could and stepped out into the storm.

CHAPTER THIRTY-TWO

It was so very, very cold.

It ate into her fingertips, her bare shoulders, numbing them until the feeling turned into a bone-deep ache that made her moan with the pain. She kept her eyes closed for a long while, hoping that everything would just float away and leave her in peace. But it only got stronger, more vivid, until she could feel the hard floor beneath her and smell the heady bite of oil and gasoline (from where? She didn't know) surrounding her in this prison.

Helen Pierce opened her eyes to a nightmare. She lay in almost complete blackness, clothed only in a pair of white lace underpants and bra, her arms aching from the cold and the hard floor. For a long moment she was disoriented, dizzy, and then she raised a hand to her head and felt the sticky warm blood and it all came flooding back. She had to choke back a scream of terror at the memory that forced itself down upon her like a wave.

She remembered bits and pieces of the attack: the sound of breaking glass from downstairs, and Jessie's unnerving calm, trancelike state; the mad rush for the closet, trying to barricade the door against someone or something that threw itself against it with brute force;

the sound of cracking, snapping wood; and finally, a glimpse of his eyes as she swung the broom handle with all her strength at his shape in the doorframe. Those eyes were empty, glazed, the eyes of a madman. She remembered nothing else.

Jessica.

What had happened to her daughter?

Helen sat up, fighting back a wave of nausea and ignoring the pain in her shoulders. She reached around blindly, searching for Jessie's form in the blackness, but found nothing but bare floor. She fought herself to keep calm, fought the urge to leap up and run screaming through the dark until she found something, anything that could tell her where she had been taken to and how she could get out.

He could be right next to her.

Realizing this, she froze in renewed terror, eyes and ears straining to pick up any movement, any noise that might give away his position. All she heard was the sound of the wind, moaning and whispering around her prison walls.

Where was she?

She stood up, choking back a sob, her knees and lower back screaming in pain. She wrapped her arms around her breasts and squeezed, partly to reassure herself and partly to keep whatever warmth she had left from escaping into the frigid air. Her nipples were hard little points thrusting out from the thin lace of the bra, the gooseflesh along her arms like a rash.

She saw something. Not much, just little slits of gray, dull light like prison bars. She strained harder, keeping her breathing as soft and regular as she could. Yes, there was some light ahead of her, and she could feel the air moving as the wind gusted outside. She stepped towards the light, her hands outstretched in front of her face, shuffling forward with her heart in her throat.

Something brushed against her forehead and slipped off through her hair. She let out a yelp of fear and swatted at it instinctually, feeling it slide across her hand.

It was a cord. She grabbed it and pulled.

The room flooded with light from an overhead bulb. Momentarily blinded, she blinked furiously to clear away the tiny red dots in front of her eyes. She stood in a small, square room, the walls made of coarse wood. Shelves lined the wall opposite her, mostly bare, one corner stained a deep brown, which was probably the source of the gasoline fumes.

There was nobody else in there with her. The room was empty.

She began to shiver and shake uncontrollably. The cold was unbearable, and her hands and feet felt as if they had gone to sleep. *Got to keep moving, keep warm.* Her mind had become curiously sharp all at once, as if her senses had been turned up a notch, and she no longer cared where she was or where her attacker had gone. The need for warmth obsessed her, overpowered her. She shuffled over towards the wall, moving her arms and legs as quickly as she could. The effort awakened them and they tingled as if stuck by a million tiny pins.

Air puffed against her skin and she put her eye to a crack. Helen saw what she thought was the house across the lawn, a dark presence among the blowing snowflakes. She was in the tool shed near the edge of the woods. She was close enough to the house, and David would be home soon, he had to be.

She remembered a course she had taken in college on human adaptation to physical and psychological stress.

Soon it wouldn't matter when he returned, because the cold would lower her body temperature until she went into shock, slowly freeze each and every cell as hypothermia set in. If she didn't die, she would lose her hands and ears, maybe her feet.

It was time to fight for her life.

She scanned the shed carefully for any way out. The door was to her right, and she grasped the handle firmly and yanked and pushed. It held solid, either locked or snowed in. *Think.* It couldn't be snowed in yet, because he had to have gotten her in here somehow, and if she had been unconscious more than a few hours in the cold air, she would have never opened her eyes again. *So it must be locked.* Yes, she heard the padlock rattling against the wood when she shook the handle.

It was a fairly heavy door made from large boards and braced with crosspieces. She searched the tiny room frantically for anything that could help her, feeling the cold creep up her legs, numbing them past the calf. Then she heard what sounded like an engine growling through the howling wind. She hobbled back to the crack again and peered out, and this time she saw something moving up near the house, close to the ghostly, snow-covered shape of the U-Haul. It looked like a truck. She was about to scream out for help and then held it back, biting her tongue. *It could be the man who put you here. Don't let him know you're awake.*

A figure got out (it was some sort of Jeep, she saw now) and ran up to the front door. A moment later, it opened and the figure moved inside. She studied the vehicle carefully. It was towing something, but she couldn't make out what it was through the snow.

Then the door opened again and two people ran out into the storm to the Jeep, and she saw David's red jacket and blue gloves, *it was him*, and she screamed with all her strength. The figures didn't come running over to rescue her. They didn't even stop. They hadn't heard her at all. The wind was too strong. Still, she screamed again and again until her throat was raw and her voice hoarse with fatigue, rattled and shook the door, kicked at the walls until her legs gave out.

She crawled back to the crack and watched them unload a snowmobile and heard it start up. Then they climbed on and sped away down the driveway.

They had been less than fifty yards away.

She slumped against the wall, tears freezing against her eyelids. The reality of what had happened forced itself on her like a rape. Her daughter was gone, and she was locked inside a frozen coffin.

She was going to die here.

CHAPTER THIRTY-THREE

Amanda Seigel, Doctor of Psychiatry and an expert in the study of paranoid disorders, found herself shaking like a baby. They were out of the wind and the snow now, but the cold refused to leave her bones, and she sipped eagerly at the coffee Babcock had given her from a paper cup, welcoming its heat. The coffee was bitter and had probably been sitting around for a while, but she didn't care as long as it was warm. And though the warmth did nothing to calm her shaking hands, she didn't really expect it to anyway. The shakes didn't have much to do with the temperature, really.

On their mad dash through the storm to the station, the spiders had returned. This time, she had hardly been able to tell the difference between what was real and what wasn't.

It took them only a moment after David Pierce's mad dash out of the diner to figure things out. Angie, the waitress, told them about the murder of the local farmer and the disappearances of the little girl and the deputy who had gone looking for her. Clearly, Pierce had decided his own family was in danger. When Flint had explained more about the suspected chemical leak and its effects, Amanda felt the pieces click into place. If Jonathan had been exposed to something like that, there was no telling what he might do. They had to act fast.

She followed Dan Flint out into the wind and blowing snow, thinking that it was lucky the police were practically next door. It was hard not to think about Jonathan and David, but it was important for her to keep her head, and if she started thinking about them, she was afraid she would lose whatever cool she had left. The wind was fierce, and the snowflakes thick. She could hardly see Flint's back, even as he stumbled along five feet ahead. He looked more like a troll than a real human being, hunched over with his jacket pulled up around his ears. She remembered a cartoon she had seen as a young girl, based on *The Hobbit* by J. R. R. Tolkien: Bilbo the Hobbit and his gang of treasure hunters sneaking through the forests of Mirkwood, where unspeakable creatures lurked in the blackness, ready to pounce. The group had stopped to camp in the middle of the forest. *Don't go to sleep!* she had screamed at the screen. But they had, of course, and when they awoke, something horrible had happened.

The spiders had come.

It came back to her all at once. Those terrible creatures that didn't look like cartoons at all; giant, hairy legs, black bristles and huge fangs, their faces with their insect eyes and yet so horribly human. Their hissing language, and fat, black underbellies. And most of all, their thick, sticky webs.

As she watched Flint's back through the swirling snow, the ground disappearing around him in a pattern of shifting white flakes, she saw shapes there, moving, twisting like little dancing dots of light. The snowflakes turned into white, hairy legs, the drifts became fat, juicy abdomens, the quick flashes of ground huge, dark fangs. And for a second, *just a second*, she was sure the spiders of Mirkwood had turned white like chameleons to hide in the depths of the snow, waiting to sink their fangs into her stomach and lap the blood as it poured from her like a crimson fountain.

She had fought the urge to scream. And then they were gone, and the snow was just snow. A minute later, the station house had loomed up out of the blowing flakes.

Now she was inside, drinking this shitty coffee and wondering why she couldn't stop shaking. No, that wasn't quite true. She knew why she couldn't stop shaking. *Everyone has some kind of irrational fear, whether it be closets or dark rooms or dentist's offices or whatever, the kind of fear that visits them when they're alone and lonely. I think I found mine.*

Still, they had been so real.

Flint was over at Babcock's desk, and she studied him from across the room. He was a handsome man in his early forties, but he looked exhausted, and she wondered how deeply he was involved with all that had been happening. *I wonder what his private nightmare is*, she thought. *And I wonder if he's found it yet.*

As she watched him, he turned, gave her a look that seemed to say, *these people are driving me nuts*, and shrugged. She smiled and froze as she saw something move on his left shoulder. Just a glimpse of something, feeling its way along. Then it was gone.

She shook her head as if to clear it. Flint had come over to her, looking puzzled at her reaction. "What's wrong?"

She brushed a hand across his shoulder. Nothing there. *Of course not*, she thought. *I'm tired, worn out. That's all.*

She remembered cutting herself that morning with the bagel knife, and washing the wound in what was probably river water from the sink. *My God*, she realized, *I opened right up and took it in*.

Somehow, even up to this very moment, she had been hoping they were wrong, and that things were all being blown out of proportion. But the *scope* of the thing was unbelievable. If it had gotten to her miles away from the plant . . .

She looked down at her finger. It was an angry red, and still bleeding slightly. "I think we'd better do something," she whispered, and Flint looked at her strangely.

"We're doing all we can," he said.

And in that moment, she realized that it was the same for him, and that he really didn't want to believe it was true either. *We're not doing all we can*, she thought. *We're sitting here on our big fat behinds and bitching about some storm when there are people out there dying*.

The phone rang. A moment later, the dispatcher yelled something about an emergency call from a man who said his wife and daughter had been kidnapped by some psychopath out at the hydro plant. "It's them," Amanda said to Flint. "David was right. Jonathan has them!"

"Jesus," Flint said. He rubbed at his face.

"I'm going," she said, suddenly sure of what she wanted to do. "I don't care about the storm. I'm going to convince that cop to take me. You can come, or stay."

And that was how the three of them ended up in a police cruiser in the middle of one of the worst storms in recent memory.

CHAPTER THIRTY-FOUR

David swung the front door shut and followed Hank to the Cherokee, keeping his face low inside the collar of his parka. It was good to be moving again. The long wait (at least it seemed long to him) in Jessie's bedroom had worn his nerves thin, his own sanity hanging by a thread. The police weren't coming, at least not until it was too late, and he knew it was up to him. He no longer felt fear, at least not like he had those first few minutes inside the house. That had been like nothing else he had ever experienced. *And I hope I never have to experience it again.*

Something told him that he would.

The snow was steady but the wind seemed to have calmed just a little. *Maybe we'll have a chance at this after all*, he thought. It didn't reassure him. His guilt at what had happened was overpowering, and the only way he could silence those insistent voices in the back of his mind was to bring his wife and daughter back safe and sound. There had to be more than a chance. He was counting on it.

They were at the trailer. "Give me a hand with the ropes," Hank shouted. "The knots get mighty tight and my joints ain't what they used to be."

David nodded, taking off his gloves. His hands became

numb almost immediately, but he worked the frozen knots furiously with his fingernails, yanking with all his strength. They wouldn't budge. He pulled his pocketknife from his jacket pocket and sawed through both ropes.

Hank tipped the trailer, and they grabbed onto the runners of the machine, yanking with everything they had. The snowmobile slid off into the five inches of fresh powder that now lined the ground.

"You ever ridden one of these before?"

David shook his head. Hank leaned over and spoke into his ear. "This here's an older model, but she's dependable. One of the best they ever made. You got a throttle and a brake, here and here." He pointed them out, twisting and squeezing each in turn. "It's like a bike. You turn the handlebars to steer, and when you do, watch out 'cause she'll want to go over. Just follow my lead." He straddled the long black seat, and started the engine with a yank on the cord. "Didn't have electric start when this baby was made!"

The engine coughed and roared to life, sputtering for a few moments until Hank pushed in the choke located in the center of the console. "She'll hold both of us," he shouted. "Stay put, I got to get some things from the Jeep!"

He returned a moment later with a couple of flashlights, neck warmers and two firearms. He handed one of the guns to David. It felt heavy and smelled of oil.

"What is it?"

"That there is a genuine .357 Magnum revolver. It'll blow a hole right through a brick wall. Be careful, it's loaded."

David felt as if he were holding a rattler. *What do I know about guns?*

Christ, you've seen Dirty Harry, *now stop whining and get moving!*

He nodded at Hank and took one of the neck warmers. It was made of thick, fuzzy wool.

"My wife made that," Hank shouted. "It'll itch the hell out of your face, but you'll be glad you got it when we get crankin'!"

David slipped it down over his head. It fit nicely, covering his face up to his eyes. When he pulled his hat down, only a thin slit of flesh was exposed. He looked over at the machine, where Hank was sitting, nursing the controls.

"Okay," he said, voice muffled by the thick wool. "Let's go." He didn't know if the man heard him, but he climbed on behind.

"Hold on," Hank yelled, turning back to him. "It's gonna be a hell of a rough ride!"

As the throttle revved and the heavy track caught the new snow, he thought he heard something above the noise of the wind—a thin, high-pitched scream.

Then they were moving, and he forgot about everything but the ride.

CHAPTER THIRTY-FIVE

Jessica was in the bad place.

It was all here. The smell of old wood, the darkness and the shadows that crept across the floor, even the cold feeling she remembered that climbed deep within her and settled, digging its claws into her bones. In reality, it was more horrible than her nightmares, but she didn't feel frightened, at least not like she had on the way here. Then she had been paralyzed with fear, not even able to kick and scratch the bad man like she wanted to, unable to do anything but hold still as he dragged her into the woods. She was so cold. Mommy had put a sweater and pants on her before the man had come, but she didn't have her mittens or her hat, not even her pink jacket. And it was snowing hard. The bad man didn't seem to care about that. He knew exactly where he was going, even when the tree branches closed in around them like giant fingers. And she got the strangest pictures from his head, as if she wasn't a little girl at all to him. She was one of THEM.

She didn't know what that meant. All she knew was that she could feel what the man felt, and see what he saw. It had been getting stronger every minute. When he left her here, in this cold, dark room, she knew that he had gone to meet Daddy, and the man wanted to hurt him. He was out in the snow now, stomping around the buildings where she was hidden.

When Daddy came, she would scream. But she wouldn't scream the way the bad man wanted her to, no, she wouldn't lead her daddy into a TRAP. She would give him a picture, and he would know what to do. She thought she could do it now; her head felt funny, like it was on fire, all hot and tingling.

The man had taken Johnny Bear. She tried not to think about that, but Johnny was in trouble and she didn't know what to do. She wanted him near her, because he was her friend, and he could help her be less afraid when the time came to warn Daddy. But the bad man had taken him when he left her here in this cold room because he wanted her to be alone and afraid.

She looked the room over. It was made out of old, rotten boards, and there was a window above her head, too high for her to see out. There were things hanging on the walls, things she didn't want (HEADS there are HEADS) to think about. She squeezed her eyes tight and tried to scrub away the things she had seen, but the dark color of blood would not go away.

The door to the room was down at the far end, but she knew it was locked, knew he had locked it when he left. The wind tried to get through the boards, whipping the snow at the window and moaning around the corners, and she sat huddled against the wall, as far away from the shadows as she could get. The floor was ice-cold, and she shivered. Her feet were numb too. It was all just like her dreams.

But she didn't need the dreams to scare her anymore. This was real.

* * *

Jonathan Newman was a walking, grinning skeleton, a horribly disfigured demon. He was bleeding heavily through the nose, and it weakened him to the point of collapse. If he hadn't become completely and hopelessly insane, he would have been finished long ago. But the mind is capable of curious things, and Jonathan's mind was screaming.

He worked silently, beating a confusing mixture of footprints into the fresh snow, ignoring the cold that deadened his fingers and slowed his feet. The footprints would be vague depressions in a few minutes with the wind and snow, which was good; he wanted to confuse the Dark Eyes when they came. Jonathan had been through worse than this, much worse, and they weren't going to bring him down this way, not if he could help it. He had their scout creature locked up back at camp and their woman hidden right under their noses. He felt a great contempt and hatred towards the woman. Later, he would return and take care of them. Right now, the important thing was to conceal his prints and confuse the enemy.

Then he could hunt them down.

He felt the blood coursing down his upper lip and tasted the saltiness of it in his mouth. He was getting weaker, but he couldn't stop the blood flow. The Dark Eyes were behind it, he knew that, just as they had been behind everything that had happened to him since the day he was born.

Is it not enough that you own the world and everything in it, the sea the skies the jungle, why do you send these birds of prey to kill me hunt me down like an animal just want to be left alone LEFT ALONE . . .

He was catapulted back into the war. He was under

friendly fire. Hueys chattered overhead, searching for him through the clouds. He hunched and ran for cover. He needed a gun, any gun. All he had was the knife, and soon they would be stripping the jungle and blowing up anything in their path, anything that dared challenge them. His knife was small, puny compared to that.

Still, he raised it high in the air and shook it in defiance of them, screaming until blood sprayed from his mouth like spittle.

The sound of the engines faded, and the jungle dissolved around him, thick, green leaves turning into deep green needles, the patter of a jungle rain slipping into the howling of a winter storm. He stood still, confused, as the images faded and joined, then faded again.

The bear sat against a tree, grinning at him. It looked like a Vietcong. The little bastard was taunting him.

"Aren't you afraid of me?" Jonathan said. He was confused. Everything hurt—his head, his arms, legs aching until he wanted to scream with the pain.

"Afraid? Of you? That's really fucking funny." The thing waved its stubby brown arm. "I'd tear you apart without even thinking about it."

Jonathan stood still for a long moment, blood beating in his ears. Then he screamed and leapt for it, grabbing it by the head and holding it up in the blowing snow. Its eyes were a glassy brown.

But still it stared at him. He had to stop the staring.

He took it by its ear and sawed at the throat with his knife, thirsty for the blood that would surely spurt out of it, gush all over him as the veins and arteries severed. He ripped the last bit of its head clear and held it up, to show them what he had done.

"I am not afraid of you!" he screamed. Thin white

bits of stuffing floated down, were caught by the wind and whirled away from him and into the storm. He probed into the neck cavity with the point of his knife, but met no resistance at all.

There were no bones.

Moaning, he tossed it aside. *No bones.* His trophy case would have to wait for a new addition.

He knew it would not wait long.

CHAPTER THIRTY-SIX

Helen paced the tiny room, trying desperately to keep warm. Her head ached terribly and the ends of her toes were blocks of ice. She wondered if she had lost them already.

Don't think about it. Just get out before you lose anything more. Get out before you lose your life.

She had watched the snowmobile disappear with renewed terror, unable to believe that help had been so close and yet it had slipped through her outstretched fingers. The snow outside showed no signs of stopping, and the wind still whipped around the walls of her prison. If anything, the temperature was dropping. She could not wait until they returned. She had to get out now.

How, that was the question. She leaned on the door and pushed with all her strength. It did not budge. Soon, she would not only be working against the padlock, but the weight of the swiftly accumulating snow in front of the door. She slammed herself against it, again and again, until the throbbing pain cut through even the numbness of the cold. It rattled, but would not give. She turned her back to it and slid down to the cold floor, exhausted.

Who was this man, and why had he put her here? It

didn't make sense. He didn't take her with him, but he didn't kill her either. Yet he had to know that she would die soon from the cold, that unless someone rescued her within a few hours, it would be all over. Why would he want to kill her? What had she done to make anyone want to kill her?

He's insane. There doesn't have to be a reason, not one that anyone normal would understand. He has his own fears to deal with, things that must seem pretty logical to him. Jessie had been right, dreaming about the bogeyman.

And Dr. Mudd too. Thinking of him, she felt a new hope. He had promised to call the police, hadn't he? Maybe they were on their way right now; maybe they would drive up to the house any minute and hear her screams for help.

She felt very sleepy, her limbs unbearably heavy and sluggish, as if someone had tied heavy weights to her hands and ankles. It was so easy to just lie here, her back resting against the wall, her legs stretched out in front of her. She felt like they didn't belong to her, as if they were somebody else's legs, a pair of rubber ones that had been plopped down in front of her as a joke. *Very funny*, she thought, trying to smile. Her mouth didn't seem to want to move. *That's very, very funny.*

It had gotten warmer, it seemed. In fact, it was more than comfortable in here, it was downright hot. She felt as if she were snuggling down among some thick, soft blankets, drifting off to sleep. Her thoughts began to wander—the warmth of a wood fire, the Château Frontenac with its high turrets and beautiful rooms, her father taking her to town for a soda at the end of a long day in the fields.

I'm dying. The thought struggled to come through the haze that was swiftly overpowering her mind.

This is how it feels to freeze to death. Don't give in. Fight.

She opened her eyes and struggled to her feet, trying to stop her swaying, shaking legs. The wind through the cracks in the wall helped to clear her head. She bit down on the inside of her cheek, and tasted blood. *God, that was close,* she thought. *Don't you ever let that happen.* She remembered something her father used to say. *If you have to go, go down swinging.*

She felt each board along the wall, testing them for weaknesses. The shed was made of new wood and it all felt solid. There were several loose knotholes, one down along the floor in a corner, and one next to the door. She worked at both of them, ripping at the wood until her fingernails were cracked and bleeding, but they would not come free. *Not that freeing them would do any good anyway—I couldn't very well squeeze through a two-inch opening. You might have lost a few pounds since yesterday, honey, but that just ain't gonna cut it.*

The boards were nailed to two-by-four framing. She pounded them with her fist where they were nailed together, hoping to loosen something. But they held tight, even after her fists were bruised and stinging. She needed something stronger to hit them with, a rock or piece of wood.

Finally, she turned to study the shelves on the far wall. There were four of them running the length of the small room, and three were bare. The fourth was just above her head, and she stood on tiptoe, trying to feel along it with her fingertips. They were numb, the ends dead and clumsy, and she fumbled through the search hardly able to feel the rough wood under her hands.

Her fingers felt some resistance along the wall on the left-hand side. She shoved at it, unable to tell what it might be, then jerked her hand back, suddenly afraid it was something that might cut her.

But it didn't really matter, did it? In another few minutes she would be dead herself. She forced herself to reach back there, feel for the thing. In a second, she had it again, and tried to pick it up, but her fingers were too numb, like her hand had fallen asleep. She pushed at it, sliding it along the wood to the end where the shelf met the wall, then dragged it forward. It reached the edge, and fell with a thud to the ground.

It was a piece of heavy plastic, broken off of some garden tool. Maybe the handle of a spade.

Discouraged, she kicked at it, sent it spinning away from her underneath the bottom shelf. It was about as useful right now as a bottle of sunscreen. She felt tears stinging her eyes, threatening to overflow the lids. *Don't give up now, not yet.*

What about the shelves themselves? Maybe she could use them to batter down the door, or break the boards. She grasped the top shelf as firmly as the nerves in her deadened fingers allowed, and yanked. There was a loud cracking sound, but the wood held. Desperately, she hung all her weight on it, bouncing, jerking down as hard as she could. She felt something give and then it came down with a sickening screech as the nails pulled from the wall. She landed hard, smashing her knees into the floor, but didn't feel much of anything through the numbing cold.

The broken wood of the shelf hung down above her head, and a stinging pain ran along her forearms. Blood dripped slowly from her elbows, and she held her arms up to look at the two long, ugly scrapes that ran the length of each forearm where they had caught the edge of the next shelf on the way down. Most of the skin was gone, and yet she felt nothing more than a slight, irritating pain—bothersome, but not unbearable. Even the bleeding was slowed by the frigid air.

She got to her feet and yanked one of the broken pieces of shelving from its brace. It was about six feet long, one end jagged and splintered, and it felt heavy and awkward in her clumsy hands. She felt sleepy again, as if someone had slipped her a drug. Time was running out.

She flipped the piece of wood over, straight end pointing at the opposite wall. Taking a deep breath, she gathered it under her arm, bracing with both hands as tightly as she could, and stumbled towards the door, falling into it as hard as she could. The broken shelf scraped backward under her armpit, and she could feel the splinters digging into her tender flesh.

The door shuddered, and held strong.

Blood now ran freely down her side. *Oh Jesus*, she thought, *please help me*. It was getting harder and harder to stand. Her legs shook uncontrollably, and she felt nothing in them at all now to her waist. Her arms refused to obey what her mind told them to do. She had dropped the piece of wood after ramming the door, and now she stared down at it dumbly. Why had she ever thought that would work? It was a waste of precious time. There had to be some other way.

She turned and studied the wall, forcing her fuzzy mind to focus. There were funny metal things there, she saw now. Funny little pieces of metal, like hooks. The shelf braces. One of them hung down from the wall, dangling by a single nail, and she yanked it loose. It was L-shaped, made of a sturdy, lightweight metal, and flat on both ends. Not strong enough to beat the door down, but it had to be good for something. Her mind felt sluggish and confused, whirling ideas and thoughts around in random ways, somehow missing the piece of the puzzle that could help her escape. *Come on, Helen, think, you can do it, one more time.*

The words came as if from a ghost, as clear as if someone had spoken beside her. *Crowbar. Use the brace to pry the boards apart.*

She turned, and somebody stood there, a tall, broadbacked man dressed for the fields. Helen felt no fear. In fact, she felt a great, soothing calm wash over her body, warming her legs until she could stand without shaking.

Go ahead, the man said, his voice soft and yet curiously steady. *It's simple, really. Go ahead and try.*

Helen staggered to the wall and fell to her knees in front of it, slipping the flat end of the brace in between the wall boards and the frame they were nailed into that ran along the floor. It slid in a fraction of an inch, and she tried to pry them apart, but the metal end of the brace slipped out before she could put any weight on it. She tried again, with the same result.

Then she thought of the piece of plastic under the bottom shelf. With a growing sense of desperation and panic, she crawled over to the shelf and thrust her arm under it. Blood dripped from the scrape along her forearm and spattered upon the floor. Her hand felt like a slab of meat flopping around on the end of her arm, and she was about to give up when she felt something move against her fingers. The dark piece of plastic rolled out from the darkness towards her, its tapered sides making a soft clicking noise on the wood floor.

She grabbed it in her clumsy grip as best she could, and crawled back to where the brace stuck out from the base of the wall. Holding the plastic with both hands, she hammered it down on the end of the brace, again and again, until the metal was dented by the blows and wedged in as far as it would go. *Please, God,* she thought, and pushed on the end of the brace with all her strength.

The metal began to bend, and then the board jerked and separated from the crosspiece with a groan of protest, the nails sticking out sharp and bright against the brown of the wood. Helen felt the frigid air against her cheeks as the storm rushed into the tiny room, whipping and dumping great white flakes of snow all around her. She struggled to her feet and kicked at the loose board as best she could. It jerked out still farther from the top crosspiece, and then fell with a thump to the ground outside.

The wind beat at her nearly naked body as she pressed herself desperately into the thin opening, the rough wood tearing at her breasts and tender stomach. There was no more than ten inches of space, and for a moment she thought it was not enough, that fate would tempt and then yank the rug out from under her ruthlessly. Then her hips were through and she fell out into the soft, cold depths of new snow outside the shed, into the screaming face of the storm.

There was no time to rest. With the full fury of the wind upon her, she struggled to her feet, ignoring the dull pain in her side and forearms, trying to ignore the frightening sensation in her feet *(like there's nothing THERE but bloody stumps)* and calves. It was so hard now to keep focused on what to do; so many different things descending upon her head like flies, buzzing about the confines of her mind, confusing her thoughts. The house was in front of her, a misty shape that she knew meant safety, real safety. That was where she could lie down, only there.

She lurched towards it, keeping her eyes focused on its shape through the snow. It seemed to be the only thing that kept the flies away. She still heard them buzzing, throwing themselves against her skull, but they weren't able to get in, not yet. Gusts of wind buffeted her body with terrific force, and several times she almost fell, but she knew somehow that if she allowed herself to do that, it would be all over. The snow would claim her like a long-lost lover coming home to bed. Even now it sucked at her feet, pulling at them, trying to trip her and send her tumbling down into the emptiness that waited just out of reach.

The house was closer now. She could make out the deck, even the front steps. The Jeep sat at the foot of them, its white sides spotted with brown rust like dried blood. She was bleeding still, she knew. It dripped down her arms, a warm, sticky mess. *My life, dripping away.* She felt it leaving her, and the flies were buzzing louder and louder around her head. She began whispering softly. "Still screaming . . ." Her lips were numb and clumsy forming the words. Why was that? It was hard to remember.

At the steps, she stumbled and came down hard on her shins, feeling an odd sort of pressure below the knee. She went up the rest of the steps on all fours, her cracked fingernails digging into the wood. Something down near her feet didn't work right, but she didn't know what it was. Her legs wouldn't support her weight anymore, and the steps were cold, so cold. She couldn't move any more, not now, not ever again. *It's over,* she thought numbly, and the thought came easily. She would welcome the darkness when it came.

Helen.

She forced her head up and saw the man again, floating before the door, his brown slacks twisting around his legs as the wind blew. He held out one muscled arm and long finger, and pointed at the door handle. *So close, honey*, he said, and in that one moment, Helen realized with a shock that the man was her father, young and healthy and so different from the man who had been broken and hunchbacked at fifty-three, but her father, nonetheless.

Oh God, Daddy, she thought, *I can't*.

Yes, you can, her father said, smiling gently. *I didn't raise a quitter, and neither did your mother. So go on*.

The door handle was above her head, and she had to strain to reach it. The metal was slippery and almost impossible to hold onto with her hand feeling so numb and clumsy. *This is my nightmare*, she thought with a sudden burst of clarity. *Don't let it win*.

The knob turned, and she fell through the door into the living room. Somehow she managed to push the door shut against the howling wind, but the flies still buzzed. It was impossible to shut them out.

I made it, Daddy, she thought. *I didn't quit*. She managed to pull the edge of the little rug they kept by the door over her ice-cold body. It helped a little, and she didn't try to fight the flies any longer.

What about Jessica?

And then there was nothing but blackness.

CHAPTER THIRTY-SEVEN

They sped along the shoulder of the road at breakneck speed, the tiny headlight of the snowmobile cutting a faltering swath of light through the thick snowfall. The wind was a howling demon at his neck, and he had to squint to see anything at all. What he saw was the back of Hank's head, covered with the dark blue of his ski mask, and the headlight glowing in front of them. That was all. It seemed to be getting darker by the second.

The fastest way to the plant, Hank had said as they sped off, was to get to the river and ride it right down to the heart of the place. What they might find there, well, that was anybody's guess. David prayed they would find his wife and daughter. Of course, that also meant they would have a run-in with a raving lunatic who probably thought he was still buried in the depths of the Vietnam jungle. The last few hours had forced him to think about many things. It would be hard to keep himself together long enough to face the man. By that time, maybe he'd just join the guy and together they'd lock arms and skip straight to the loony farm.

No. I won't let that happen. I'll kill him.

He suddenly saw his daughter in a dark and hideous place filled with damp wood and looming shadows. The image was only there a fraction of a second, and then it floated away. He tried to grasp it again, his mind feeling about in the darkness, but it was gone.

It had been clearer than anything he had ever imagined. In fact, it had been more than imagination—it was as if someone had opened his skull and painted it on the inside, then erased it with a flip of the brush. *Black paint on a dark canvas.* He wasn't sure what it all meant, but he knew something: he could recognize that place. And his daughter was there.

How the hell do I know that?

He struggled with this new possibility. *Does it really matter? If it leads me to her, does it really matter?*

Hank slowed the snowmobile down, the engine idling to a choking growl. David saw the river to his right, a faint opening in the woods through the swirling snow. It would be easy to reach the level of the ice; the shoulder sloped gently down for about twenty feet to the river's edge, and the fresh powder looked soft and smooth. There was a wide-open path between the beginning of the bridge and the trees. The wind had died a little, though he couldn't tell for sure if that was due to their reduced speed or the storm losing strength.

Hank angled the machine onto the shoulder and down through the deeper snow. They hadn't seen a single vehicle on the road, not even a snowplow, but the wind had more or less swept the tar clean, with the exception of a few heavy drifts. Now, David felt the snowmobile bogging down in the deeper snow, its track spitting out a geyser of white flakes behind them. The engine produced a deeper, louder growl with the increased stress. *Might as well broadcast our arrival through a loudspeaker,* he thought grimly. But then again, they were still close to a mile away from the plant, and there was no way they had been heard yet. Right now, speed was the most important thing. *Every second gives that bastard another chance to hurt them. Or do something worse. He wants me to come after him. That's true too, isn't it? I'm the one he wants, the one he sees in his twisted dreams, the one he wants to kill.*

He didn't know why he knew that either, but he did. It was not a reassuring thought.

The going was a little rougher than he expected, and he had to grip tightly to the plastic handgrips down below the seat to keep from being thrown off. The machine dipped, rose, and then Hank gunned the engine, shooting them forward and into the air. David saw the ground a few inches beneath them for a quick second, then they hit hard and he was thrown into Hank's solid back. They had leapt the edge of the bank and were on the ice. Right now, there was at least six inches of new powder on top, and he was startled at how much had fallen in such a short time. The storm had been raging for the better part of two hours now, and if it kept up at this pace for another two, they might not make it back.

Out on the frozen riverbed, there was more room to maneuver, and Hank gunned the engine, shooting the machine forward to its limit. David wondered at the courage of this man—someone who was risking his life to help a family he hardly knew. He had to be in his fifties, seemed content with the life he led, had no reason to offer anything more than some advice and perhaps a little good luck. And yet he had. *Why didn't you stay at home and keep the couch warm, drink some beer, feel sorry for us and maybe fall asleep with the TV on? Isn't that what you were supposed to do?*

Maybe it was, but David was damn glad he had decided to lend a hand.

Hank was slowing the machine down. "We're about a quarter mile from the place," he shouted over the wind. "We oughta buck off 'round here somewhere so he doesn't hear us, go the rest of the way on foot!"

David gave him the thumbs-up sign, and felt the machine slow down a bit more. Hank headed them towards the riverbank and the woods. The trees were thick, monstrous shapes with waving arms in the darkness, a line of giants determined to keep them out. It was like some nightmare from which he couldn't wake up, his legs churning and going nowhere while something huge and hideous with gnashing teeth and dripping jaws chased him down.

The snowmobile stopped along the edge of the bank about ten feet from the trees. From here they looked even thicker. It discouraged him not just because it would be so hard to get through them, but also because the man they hunted had slipped through the trees on foot for a mile or more. Probably carrying a screaming child, and forcing an unwilling partner ahead of him. He had to know these woods backward and forward. *How can we possibly stop a man like that?* Yet they had an advantage, though David could only guess how much it really counted. The chemical had been working on the man's mind for a long time. Maybe he would make a mistake. It was not much, but it would have to be enough.

"You just follow me, and keep your head down," Hank said as he hit the kill button on the handlebars and slid off the smooth, plastic seat. The air was calmer here by the trees, and they could speak without shouting. "I was cuttin' trails round these parts just a month ago, and I still remember it pretty well. Once you get into it a little, the trees are spread out."

With the throaty growl of the machine gone, David had a sudden, eerie feeling of unreality, as if he were watching the events on a movie screen. They stood in a semicircle of trees, where the riverbank jutted out to a point and formed a cove. It was strangely quiet with the storm all around them. He pulled the gun from his pocket.

"All you gotta do is pull the trigger," Hank said. "Be careful, she's got one hell of a kick to her." He unzipped his jacket and took out the old, pump-action shotgun he had kept for himself. "Me, I like this one. It's seen a few years, but that's only seasoning. It ain't real accurate neither, but what the hell, it don't have to be if you're close enough." He pumped the barrel once and then zipped his coat back up. "You ready?"

David nodded. "I've never shot anything before, Hank."

Hank put a hand on his shoulder. "Nobody ever said it was easy. But the way I see it, your choices are looking pretty grim. If it comes to him or me, you know who I'm gonna choose to go out. And I'll think you'll feel the same."

Hank grabbed the keys to the snowmobile and shoved them into the rear section of the machine's rubber track. "If you get back here without me, you'll know where they are," he explained. "Don't wait for me. I know my way around."

Without waiting for a reply, he turned and headed for the trees. David followed him cautiously, holding the gun at his side. There was no more time to think. Now there was only their harsh breathing, the storm, and the shadows that leapt and slithered about within the depths of the woods.

And whoever or whatever waited for them in his own silent world of terror and twisted dreams.

CHAPTER THIRTY-EIGHT

Amanda Seigel peered out through the windshield as the wipers tried to clear a sight line through the storm. The interior of the car was deadly silent; everyone was concentrating on the task at hand. Once they hit the main road, the snow had gotten worse, and Amanda now wondered if they had made the right decision to come out into it. Then she thought about the spiders again, and shivered. Anything was better than sitting in that office and waiting.

Flint was in the backseat, checking and rechecking the two guns Bobby Babcock had thrown in with them. She had a feeling that he didn't know much about guns, but at least it gave him something to do. Everyone needed something to take their minds off what was to come.

"How long?" she whispered finally. Bobby just shrugged, and so she turned back to the windshield again, determined to keep silent and out of the way. They could be very close now. They had been on the road for what seemed like hours.

Sure enough, in another five minutes Bobby was turning into a snow-covered driveway and cursing at the impossibly high drifts that faced them. "Shit," he said, and glanced back at Flint. "Hold on to those guns."

Amanda felt the cruiser surge forward, and then they hit the snow and she was thrown forward against the dashboard. The car lurched and bounced, and for a moment she thought they might get through, but then it ground to a stop just a few feet in. She groaned.

"Looks like a hike from here," Flint said from the back. "Anyone know how far?"

Bobby grunted. "Probably about a quarter mile, maybe less."

They all sat in silence for a long moment. The wipers hummed and squealed against the glass.

"Well," Flint said finally. "We can't just sit here."

That decided it. All three of them bundled themselves up as best they could, and got out of the car. The wind was fierce, and the snow actually hurt her cheeks as Amanda bent her head into the collar of her coat. "Doesn't look too bad," she shouted, pointing at the front wheels. They were buried in about a foot of loose snow.

Bobby came over to where she was standing. "We could get it out," he said, "but we can't go any farther up this road in the car."

She nodded. Flint came around the back carrying the guns. "Do you know how to use this?" he asked, holding one out to her. She shook her head and shrank from it, all the while thinking *Don't be such a baby, it's just a gun.* Her voice sounded like one of those stupid slogans in her head. *Guns don't kill, people do.* Flint just smiled grimly and handed it to Bobby.

"Let's go."

All through the hike to the house, Amanda kept expecting to see the spiders again, but mercifully they didn't come. She thanked God for that. But the snow didn't let up either, and by the time she finally heard a shout from Bobby, who was in the lead, her ears and nose were numb from the wind and frost lined her eyelashes. They were passing a car, all but buried in the drifts.

A few minutes later, she saw the house herself. She thought that nothing had ever looked so warm and comfortable. That feeling was gone a second later when she watched Bobby and Dan sneak off with their guns cocked and ready, and she realized that Jonathan could be anywhere. She struggled with her emotions; here was a patient of hers who was in serious trouble. All her training told her to find him and help as much as she could. But her instincts were screaming at her to be careful, because God only knew how dangerous he had become. She knew that she was the only doctor there, and that she would be expected to anticipate his every move, and that filled her with dread. Because if she guessed wrong, someone could die.

In another second, she realized that she was alone in the storm. Flint and Bobby had disappeared. Feeling her heart leap to her throat, she began to walk carefully towards the house, her arms half out like a blind woman. And she did feel blind, with the snow blowing in her eyes and the wind drowning out all sound. She took several steps and could make out the porch about twenty feet away, its wooden boards now covered by close to a foot of snow, and with drifts up against the house that must be two or three feet deep.

Feeling that something horrible was about to happen, Amanda took a deep breath in the frigid air and walked towards the steps.

Something was happening to Jessica Pierce. She felt it invading her, soaking into her skin as if her body were a dry sponge. It moved up through her feet to her legs, then up towards her head, numbing the skin and insides.

It was not the cold. That was there too, but it was not what she felt. This was something much different, and it was not just being soaked up, it was changing her somehow. She felt calmer, more sure of herself, like somebody had just told her every little secret she ever wanted to know about anything. She felt the fear that had immobilized her earlier fading away.

But that was not exactly right. The fear was not gone, it just had a different effect. Now it only served to heighten every one of her senses, sending tingles running like tiny insects up and down her arms and legs. She felt as if she could smell every scent, hear things from all over the world, see things that weren't even there, at least not on the surface. She could see through the very walls if she wanted to, see the large expanse of white surrounding the building where she was imprisoned, the snow falling across the dark green of the pine trees and the white and gray branches of the others.

See her daddy coming for her through the woods.

But that was only there for a moment, and then it was gone. It was a PERCEPTION, but it was more than that. It had been a clear picture, almost as if she were really viewing it. Every detail was sharp-edged and vivid, down to their white clouds of breath that were quickly snatched away by the wind. She tried to get it back but could not, and it frustrated her immensely.

Earlier she had tried sending Daddy a picture of where she was, the dark and scary place with cold floors and whispering shadows. It had been much easier than what she had done with Dr. Mudd, but she wasn't sure if he had gotten it. She did it by imagining an empty chalkboard like the one her parents had given her last year. They had put it up in the attic (her attic) and that had been one of her most favorite things to do on rainy days, draw pictures with the many pieces of colored chalk and then erase them and start over. This time she drew on it in her head, and she colored it with pieces of chalk that were not real. Somehow this picture had not turned out like the others she used to draw, with the funny stick arms and legs and misshapen fingers. The chalkboard in her head was magic, because when she drew a funny, crooked line it came out straight and thick, and her figures looked like the real thing.

And then she thought about her father, and the picture went flipping away from her, getting smaller and smaller until she couldn't see it at all. She didn't know if it went to him or not.

The room was getting colder. She knew it was darker outside, partially because the window did not let in as much light now and partially because she just *knew*.

Just like she knew that the man was coming. He was frightened of her, and that seemed strange; why he should be frightened when she was the one locked up in a dark scary room, she wasn't quite sure. It seemed to have something to do with the funny way his mind worked. She had to be approached cautiously. She was one of THEM.

She stood up and faced the door, curling her hands up into tiny fists, waiting for him. He would come soon. The strange foreign thing continued working on her mind, tuning it to a different frequency. It felt like tiny fingers pushing at her skull, working their way deeper the way worms move through the soil. It came at her through the wood floor, through the walls, through the very air. She felt sick to her stomach and a little light-headed.

As she stared at the door, the wall around it began to evaporate, the wood becoming lighter and lighter until she could see through it like a sheet of water. It began from the farthest corners, the ceiling and floor, and worked its way inward until the wall melted away to the edges of the door. She saw all this from the corners of her eyes, never looking away from the door handle. The door itself remained solid wood, and now it stood strangely alone in the middle of the storm, standing without support, its hinges swung wide and dangling naked screws like fingers of bone. She stood in a three-walled, open room, but the wind did not enter it, and the snow swirled about and around the door as if against a gigantic pane of glass.

She knew that what she saw wasn't real, but in a way that didn't matter. To her it was very real. It existed within this different part of her mind where the fingers squirmed and dug like worms; it came from her dreams.

The doorknob was turning. She knew that she didn't want to see what was behind that door, that whatever it was could be more terrifying than anything she had ever experienced, and then the door was swinging open, and though the snow swirled all around it, that rectangular section was a deep black shadow, a strange chunk of coexisting space that did not fit with the rest.

The man stood within it. Rather, he floated; she sensed he did not really exist there at all, that this was another part of her mind creating and blending two things together. He was really still several hundred feet away, moving towards the room through the storm. But this was where he existed inside her head. His face was concealed by shadows, only the bridge of his nose clearly visible. His arms were long and muscled, hanging close to his knees.

There was something wrong with him; she could sense that without really seeing it. It emanated from him like a palpable smell, the smell of disease. He was bleeding from the nose, had been for some time, and his insides were terribly bloated and misshapen. It was the foreign thing that had done this to him.

And suddenly she knew what her mind was about to do, and screamed, recoiling from it as if struck by some unseen hand. It was as if she had no control over her own thoughts and actions, as if she, Jessie, lived a prisoner within herself and was powerless against another part that had taken over. She flew towards him at an incredible speed without moving, as if someone had shoved a telescope in front of her eyes and was zooming in until his face filled the lens. Then it was as if another doorknob turned, like the first, only this one was inside his mind, *she was opening his mind*, and the nightmares waited there crouching like beasts to spring upon her.

Part of her went black, the little Jessie part, but another part of her watched curiously. This was the part that was in control now, and wanted the answers to it all. This part was much older and felt little fear.

At first there was nothing, only blackness. Then the blackness was split by flashing images, bright lights that illuminated the space like a strobe. She saw whirling shapes and figures during the flashes, dancing dots of light, checkerboards and spinning tunnels. She smelled burning things, horrible things. The space was gigantic. It made her feel small and helpless. She knew that she was reacting to her own feelings mixed with his, and that together each deepened the other until everything was doubly intense.

Gradually she realized that these flashes were not strobe lights at all, but some kind of explosions that rocked the ground, sending up bright tendrils of smoke like fireworks into the night sky. There were things around her now, shapes that moved and slithered along, leaving slimy paths of wetness behind. And there were many smells in the air, smells of death and fear. She began to hear noises, softly at first, then louder, whisperings that turned into shouts of warning, then screams of pain, as the noises became human voices.

She was surrounded by the horrors of war. Vines and huge, flat leaves hung like death shrouds over bodies dangling from the trees, the explosions of shells that rocked the ground around her, the screams of pain from the soldiers as they went down. The horrible slithering things around her were *people*, mutilated bodies dragging themselves through the dirt, faces contorted with pain. Some were almost unharmed, while others were missing arms and legs. One man pulled himself forward with his fingernails, his face blank with shock, his entrails dragging behind him like huge twisting snakes. Another man thrust his hand up towards her in a pleading sign for help, and as she reached for him he fell face forward in the dirt, his lungs expelling a huge burst of dark blood at her feet.

Soldiers ran about in total confusion, firing machine guns at anything and everything. The bullets passed smoothly through her body. The shouts became louder, and then louder as the planes screamed overhead. She pressed her palms to her ears but still it was louder until it seemed her very eardrums would split under the pressure, exploding inward with two tiny pops entirely unnoticed by anyone except herself.

Then it was completely silent, and she knew she had left that world as suddenly as she had been thrust into it. She stood in a vacuum of silence so complete she could hear the beating of her own heart. There was blackness around her again, swallowing her every move, every thought. She knew that the little Jessie side of her was still missing, and that this new part of her was the only thing that kept her sane. In the world she had just left, nothing was as it seemed except the smell of death. That world had helped to shape the man. But that was not the beginning.

She found herself in a gigantic room, well lit from the ceiling. Everything was huge, even to her, as if she were a mouse looking at a giant's house. Someone was moving around, and she knew it was the man's mother, knew it just as she knew her own mother. She struggled to find the shape of the woman (it was fuzzy and unclear, like looking through unfocused binoculars) and suddenly the image sharpened.

Mother stood in front of her. Flesh hung from her in rolls, bunching around her chin, sagging from her arms. There was something wrong with her. She swayed slowly, from one side to the other, and Jessie could smell the sweet-sour stench of old booze. Her hair was long and knotted, and her clothes did not quite fit together right, as if her shirt was buttoned in the wrong holes and her pants were on backward. It was not only the booze, Jessie could tell. There was something else wrong with her, something inside her head.

She bent towards an object and picked it up from the floor. It was a baby's bottle, with a fitted rubber nipple on the end and a plastic body filled with milk. *Don't you do that*, she said, waving the bottle like a shaking finger. *Don't you do that, you brat, or I'll kill you.*

She thrust the bottle towards something sitting in a chair by the table. All these things materialized, beginning as vague transparent forms that got stronger and stronger until it was difficult to remember that they had not been there all along. When the room first appeared, it had been spotted with blank areas that were now full. The whole thing reminded Jessie of once when she had watched a Polaroid picture slowly come to life.

The thing sitting in the chair in front of Mother was a baby. It was crying softly, the dull, steady cry of something that did not expect to be helped. Blood dripped from the corners of its baby mouth and ran down its chin. It was starving to death, but Jessie sensed, all the same, a hysterical aversion towards the bottle that the mother held, as if it contained something more horrible than even the crippling pangs of hunger. It was an ENEMY, something that could give the baby great pain, and Jessie knew that somehow the bottle was the cause of the bloody cuts in the baby's lips and cheeks.

Mother held the bottle out in her huge, doughlike hands. *Take it!* she screamed. *Take it, you ungrateful brat, and if you drop it again I'll shove it down your throat.*

As the child wept harder and reached for it Jessie saw something glint in the nipple. A razor blade. She was pulled closer against her will and saw the blade sticking out both sides. *Don't take oh please don't take it*, she thought but he did, because the hunger was too great to refuse with the mother's milk in front of his eyes. He raised it to his lips.

There, Mother said, when the blades dug cruelly into the sliced and tender flesh. *You suck at me like a parasite each and every day and now you'll pay for it, won't you. You've driven away everything that I love and I won't stand for it! I won't!*

The child continued to suck at the nipple. Fresh blood ran down its chin and neck.

Get it while you can, Mother taunted, circling the chair in a horrible dizzying pattern. *That's what your father always used to say!* She slapped at the end of the bottle and it twisted in the child's mouth, slicing fresh paths along its gums. The baby screamed and dropped it, and it fell with a thud to the floor, rolling away under the table.

Now look what you did! Mother shouted. *I told you not to do that anymore.* She picked up the bottle again and advanced on the child, holding it out in front of her. Jessie closed her eyes tight as the child screamed again, squeezed her eyes shut as hard as she could on the horror in front of her that went on and on, louder and louder until she couldn't bear any more.

Suddenly it all stopped. It was utterly silent for a long moment, and then she heard voices whispering softly. She kept her eyes screwed shut for a long time, and then finally opened them, but it was completely dark, so black she couldn't tell when her eyes were open or shut. It was as if she were blind, and she felt panic rising within her until it threatened to take over completely. The voices became louder and she could make out snatches of what they were saying. She realized the voices were really all one voice speaking many different things. . . . *sensitivity to the thoughts and feelings of others . . . aloof and suspicious, resentful . . .*

Jessie didn't understand what the words meant, but she knew that they came from the man's memory of a place he had been. The walls were cream colored, there were hanging plants and nice furniture, and a woman sat in the room with her long legs crossed and her hands in her lap. It was her voice Jessie heard, and she was a doctor.

Something has happened to you, Jonathan, the woman said, *that has made you so afraid. What is it?*

(A sudden picture of Mother lying in a pool of her own blood and the razor the bottle and the cold steel blade.)

Jonathan listened to the woman with a wary sense of what surrounded him, the way a dog sniffs out unfamiliar territory. He liked the woman, but what she wanted to know (*the razor the RAZOR*, Jessie tried to shout) was locked away deep inside, where even his own conscious mind could not go.

The image spun away into blackness, and just before the last of it disappeared she thought she saw something else: long, thick arms covered with hair, and fangs red with blood. Then it was gone, and Jessie found herself again in the three-walled room. Her heart beat a crazy thumping pattern in her breast. The little Jessie part of her was awake now, and it was scared to death.

She watched as the wall around the door slowly materialized, wood forming out of thin air, building itself from the inside out to the farthest corners. As the last bit fell into place, she felt her mind do a quick flip and then everything was real again—the dampness, the flickering shadows, the smell of rotting wood. It was no longer her nightmare world. This one could hurt her.

She slid down the wall to the floor, a sob in her throat. The man was at the door.

She felt herself falling down again, down into a deep black hole of unconsciousness.

CHAPTER THIRTY-NINE

The branches tore at their bulky jackets when they entered the woods. David followed Hank's shadowy form closely, trying to avoid the worst of it by slipping through before the gaps closed. Among the branches, the wind was almost nonexistent. The snow was no more than a few inches deep in most places because of the shelter provided by the thick growth, and they broke through the first layer of trees in a few seconds, thanks to Hank's lead.

Inside the woods, the trees opened up and spread out, and that allowed them to move along fairly quickly. David wasn't sure how Hank knew where he was going, but he never faltered in choosing their path. The snow fell thicker here, but the fury of the storm was blunted by the tall pines. It was darkening fast.

They walked for what seemed like a long time, the fresh snow deadening their footsteps, their breath coming in great white clouds of moisture. If the madman chose any part of that path for his attack, they would go down easily. But he did not.

Finally, Hank stopped and leaned his back against a tree. "It's just through those pines," he said, pointing ahead and to the right. "We better have a plan."

Good point. David struggled with what they were

about to do. He felt a debilitating fear creeping up on him, prickling the hairs on the back of his neck. They were facing a killer who lived with a completely different set of rules and would not stop until his twisted thoughts were satisfied. And he may have already killed David's wife and daughter.

But how did they know they were headed to the right place? He could be anywhere. They'd had to make a choice, and David prayed it was the right one.

He's got my family, and he will do anything to stop me. This is your best shot. Don't lose it now.

It was then that they heard the scream.

Jessica stood rooted to the floor in the center of the three-walled, wooden room. The far wall where the madman peered through the open doorway had once again dissolved into that sparkling sheet of glass, and the doorway itself was shrouded in shadow that seemed to swallow all light. From the center of the blackness protruded a hairy, muscled arm that seemed cut off just before the shoulder, and in the hand . . .

She tried to peel herself away from it, but her eyes refused to leave the head in his grasp. Slowly, more of the man began to appear as he moved forward out of the shadow. Another scream caught in her throat as she saw his legs and torso, then his other arm. He wore blue overalls. *The blue man.* It was as if the darkness was giving birth to his form, vomiting it up from the depths.

It was his face that she saw last, as he had his head bowed against his chest, and when he lifted it to stare at her with icy gray eyes she saw with horror the remnants of his mother's cruelty. His lips and cheeks were twisted and traced with ugly white scars, one eyebrow pink and hairless where it had been neatly sliced off many years ago by the razor.

He grinned at her.

Then he tossed the head in his grasp into the room and it hit with a soft thump, rolling over and over until it came to rest at her feet. For a second she could swear she saw blood on Johnny Bear's neck. *Oh Johnny not you not you oh please.*

She whimpered and pressed herself back against the wall as hard as she could, feeling the rough splintered wood through the numbing cold. The bad man stepped back outside and closed the door softly behind him, and then the wall around it was whole again. She knew he had gone to meet Daddy. She had done enough, all that the bad man wanted.

She had screamed and brought him running.

The foreign thing was probing at her again, kneading with its claws like a cat. It sank deeper now, through the last barrier of her mind and into her very soul, claiming her as its own and at the same time showing her everything.

She sent one last message to her father, and it went tearing through her head like a thunderbolt:

WATCH OUT DADDY HE'S COMING.

David Pierce ignored Hank's hoarse shout. *That sounded like Jessie. Dear God, that sounded like my daughter.* He heard Hank's muffled patter of footsteps behind him, and knew with a blooming gratitude that the man was following him even now.

He stumbled through another layer of pines and then the ground opened up before him, and he had to slide to his knees to keep from going headfirst over the bank and onto the frozen riverbed. There it was beneath him, and beyond it the dark, unfinished compound that had come to haunt his dreams, though this was the first time he had laid eyes upon it. The thing was gigantic, acre upon acre of cleared trees like the ruins of an ancient city. The river had doubled back, and though they had come a more direct route through the trees, they had met it again at this place. Now he faced a wide, empty stretch of snow and ice that offered no cover whatsoever. But what was more important, what was infinitely more terrifying and yet somehow reassuring, was that he recognized it. He had not to this day seen the plant, or pictures of the plant, nothing other than the technical drawings and descriptions in the briefs he had read. Yet one darkened building across the empty ice caught his eye, made him stop and stare in dumb astonishment. He recognized it because he had seen it in his head, not twenty minutes ago. Jessie was there, he was sure of it.

He threw himself over the steep bank, using the heels of his heavy boots to slow his progress down as much as he could, sliding along the snow and frozen ground until he reached the bottom. He glanced back and saw Hank's dark form at the top of the riverbank, arms raised and holding the shotgun out. David gave the thumbs-up sign, and turned to look across the ice.

The wind was stronger out here in the open and the snow continued to fall, but the storm had died some, he was sure of it. The simple fact that he could make out the buildings across the ice testified to that. He knew that whatever happened next, he would remember the look of the half-finished power plant, like some disease growing in the depths of the forest, a scab on the face of untamed wilderness.

He started running and his boots sank into the fresh

snow, cold flakes touching his mouth and cheeks and the wind pulling at his jacket. He heard nothing more from the building, and he held the gun at his side, feeling the awkward weight of it bouncing against his upper thigh with every running step.

When he heard something behind him, he glanced back and saw Hank had made it down the incline to the river. He reached the other side and scrambled up the short bank on his hands and knees, ignoring the dull ache in his palm. The building was no more than twenty feet from him now, and next to it was the opening to the old mine shafts, a small, dark square built into a rise in the ground. He watched for movement, and saw a mass of footprints all around the walls and leading off in different directions. There was no sound other than the soft moan of the wind around the corners of the building.

David's throat tightened and the adrenaline surge turned his stomach. He stood out in the open and felt incredibly vulnerable and helpless. The gun shook in his hand as he held it out against the shadows that slipped around the building's strange angles and windows. Thoughts ran in fragments around in his head, images melting and blending into one. *Me standing on the driveway in the cold next to the pile of snow, little Chuckie Howard perched on the roof and taunting in his high, singsong voice . . .*

In the end, it was the thought of his wife and daughter that drove him forward through the icy fog of terror that threatened to overpower his rational mind—that and his stubborn refusal to let Chuckie Howard win this one last time. He stood up to his full height, cocked the gun in his hand and went for the door of the rotted, old mine building. As he did, he had a nagging feeling he was ignoring something important.

And then it hit him like a bulldozer, this shouted warning inside his head, *WATCH OUT DADDY HE'S COMING*, and he wasn't sure if he went down through the reaction of pure reflex or through the simple weight of the thing leaving a bruised and bleeding trail through his mind.

Something swished through the air and he felt a dull pain in his shoulder. The knife sliced past an inch in front of his left eye. He threw himself backward and rolled over and over on the snow, struggled to find his feet and realized he had dropped the gun. He glanced upward to see a huge, looming figure reaching out for him with monstrously long, misshapen arms and hands and a face that was creased with ugly white scars. The glint of the knife flashed again, and he knew he was a dead man.

A cracking sound split the silence, then another, and the man's right elbow exploded outward in a gory mass of blood and tissue, flinging him back against the wall of the building and throwing quarter-sized droplets of blood against the grimy window.

Hank stood on the frozen riverbed, both barrels of the shotgun still smoking in his hands. He shouted a warning and fumbled in his pockets. David scrambled backward and got to his feet but the man was already past him and headed for the ice, stumbling down the gentle bank, his ruined arm hanging limply at his side.

It all happened incredibly fast: Hank struggling frantically with his heavy gloves, finally stripping them off and throwing them to the snow; the man lurching towards him, leaving a bright red trail behind; Hank dropping the new shells clumsily to the ground at his feet. David's terror broke all at once and he scrambled for the gun that lay several feet away. As he reached it, he heard a horrible shriek.

They stood on the center of the barren, frozen river bed like a puppet and his master, the killer still holding the handle of the knife embedded in Hank's throat as the man jerked and writhed on his knees.

"No." David shook his head from side to side as the killer twisted the knife in Hank's throat and ripped down, sending an arterial spray across the white snow. David raised the gun and squeezed the trigger, feeling it recoil against him as the shock ran up his arm and through his chest. David pulled the trigger again and this one sent up a fine plume of snow from the ground just to the left of the two figures. The killer slid the knife out of his victim's throat, and Hank's body collapsed onto the snow.

David pulled the trigger again, something in the back of his mind shouting at him to stop before the bullets were spent, and this one went too high into the air and took down a pine branch, heavy with snow. The branch fell with a thump against the riverbank.

The figure on the ice spun around and ran across the snow to the far side of the river, his wounded arm jerking and flapping against him like a slab of dead meat, the elbow broken and useless. David aimed the gun once more, but didn't shoot. If he couldn't hit anything standing still, he sure as hell couldn't hit a moving target already more than fifty yards away through a snowfall. The killer disappeared into the woods above the far bank.

David ran down to where Hank had collapsed. A stain spread outward from the body in all directions, coloring the snow a deep red, and a fine, rust-colored bubble of blood sat upon the open wound in his throat. It only took a second to see the man was dead.

Rage pooled deep within his stomach and ate away at him like acid, an anger that this man had to die, a man who had shown him nothing but kindness since the day they met, a man who had risked his life and died to help a family he hardly knew. The thought of Hank's wife and boy brought tears to his eyes, and they were hot and bitter on his cheeks. Then he thought of his own wife and daughter and turned to the old mine building with his heart in his throat.

The door swung open with a long, slow, creaking sound. What he saw as the dying light hit the far wall made him freeze in horror.

The wall was covered with bones.

Skulls in various stages of decay hung from wooden pegs. Raccoons, deer, dogs and a black bear. Other bones, stripped clean of flesh, had been nailed below the ragged heads.

Three of the skulls were human.

Jessie lay on the floor underneath them. He thought she was dead until he saw the slight puff of breath in the frigid air and ran to her. *Thank God, oh, thank God.* Then he saw the stuffed bear's head in front of her.

Jesus, what did he do to you?

"Jessie?" he whispered, crouching beside her still body. "Please, baby, wake up." He touched her with trembling fingers. She didn't respond, and he kissed her eyes and nose and turned her gently, looking for blood. *Please, be okay.* Her limbs seemed intact, and she was breathing evenly and peacefully. He checked her pupils, and both looked normal.

He shuddered and wiped tears from his face. The fresh wound in his shoulder stung angrily, and he was reminded of the danger all around them. *He could come back any time. What's to stop him from finishing the job?* Surely not some frightened man with a gun who couldn't hit the broad side of a barn if his life depended on it.

He scooped up his daughter's limp form in his arms and held her close, his shoulder singing out in pain, and went back outside. Hank's bloodstained body on the center of the frozen riverbed was the only reminder of how close he himself had come to death. There was no one else in sight.

Where is Helen? What has he done with my wife?

"Jessie," he whispered again, this time shaking her gently. "Please, I need you to tell me what happened to Mommy."

It was like talking to a rag doll. Jessie's eyes opened slightly, but they showed nothing but thin slits of white. He shook her harder, praying for some reaction. She did not stir.

Outside the open door of the mill building, early evening drew closer to night, and the snow still fell, already beginning to cover the bloodstained figure on the ground. David ran from building to building, carrying his daughter in his arms and shouting Helen's name. He got no response; the huge and ghostlike compound was silent except for the wind. Finally, after what seemed like hours of searching, he felt the tears come again, and they burned hot tracks down his cheeks like furrows in frozen ground. He had searched everywhere and could not find her, not a single mark or sign. Jessie stayed limp in his embrace, but he held her tightly to him like a child might hold a favorite doll.

The only thing they could do was return to the house, or freeze to death.

David walked past the bloodied corpse on the ice as quickly as he could, refusing it even one glance, knowing what could happen if he allowed himself to feel anything for the man. *Quick dark path out of my mind, the men in white suits coming to take me away.* He concentrated on following the footprints back to the snowmobile before they were covered by the snowfall or blown away. They were fading so fast.

Once he entered the thicker trees, it became harder and harder to see, and the tree trunks loomed out of the dark like floating ghouls. Their footprints were faint shadows against the deeper snow that lined the ground, and several times he lost the trail only to find it again a moment later, his heart pounding in his chest. He heard many things, whisperings that ran along the tree branches and down around his head, moanings of pain and fear. He tried to dismiss them all as the wind.

As the trees became thicker and closer together, he felt the familiar disorientation that had attacked him in the woods around the yard. Shadows leapt out at him and then sank back to disappear in the false twilight. As he rounded a thick trunk, something stood in front of them—a dark, huge form with vacant black holes for eyes, and a long, pale face that grinned hugely among the moving shadows. A creature holding a giant silver knife that shone with slick, red blood.

And then it was gone, and he realized that it had been a trick of the fading light and the swaying branches. *Nothing but a trick of the mind.* Where the creature had stood, he now saw a gap in the trees opening out to the river, and he struggled towards it as quickly as he could, sweeping the final heavy branches aside. The snowmobile sat before them, its plastic seat already covered with half an inch of new snow. He wiped it off awkwardly with his left arm while holding Jessie with his right, then set her down on it and searched for the keys in the rubber track.

When he'd found the keys, Jessie still sat in the same position, staring out into space. He straddled the seat and put her in front of him, and she leaned against him limply. It was difficult to pull the cord in that position, but he managed several quick jerks. Nothing happened. *Jesus, please start*, he thought, and yanked the cord again. The engine coughed, and then nothing.

Finally, he remembered the choke.

He pulled up on the little knob in the center of the dash, took a deep breath, and grabbed the cord. *Come on, you son of a bitch.*

The engine roared to life, and he grabbed Jessie tight. He had to get help.

They sped out of the sheltered cove and into the weakening storm.

CHAPTER FORTY

Helen came to, one slow piece at a time.

Her first thought was pain. Deep, throbbing pain lighting up and down every nerve in her body from her head to the tips of her toes. No, not quite the tips; those still felt as dead and numb as the piece of plastic that had provided her ultimate salvation. And her fingers too. She tried to wiggle them one at a time and found she couldn't tell whether they were moving or not.

It was dark in the front hall near the living room, and for several moments she was not sure where she was, or what had happened. Then it all came flooding back—the attack and waking up in her prison cell. And her father, yes, her father had come for her. She looked around quickly, but saw no one. *Just a dream*, she thought, *nothing more than that.*

And the shelves. She remembered them as her salvation as well as the thin, otherwise useless piece of garden tool she had used as a hammer. More specifically, the shelf braces. *Whoever decided to use metal instead of wood deserves a big, sloppy kiss*, she thought, and smiled thinly. Yes, there was still pain, a lot of it, but at least her head was clear again. She felt as soldiers must feel coming home from a long battle. Exhausted but whole, more or less. She wondered what time it was, and judged by the faint light coming through the living room windows that it was late afternoon, though the storm made it hard to tell. *How long was I out? One, maybe two hours?*

Then she thought of Jessie and felt panic tighten the back of her throat. Her daughter was still out there somewhere.

She tried to move from underneath the thick rug and felt a dizzying pain shoot out below her left knee. Only then did she remember the fall she had taken on the deck steps outside. *Oh, please don't let it be broken, please.*

But it was. She could feel the bones moving under the skin of her leg and the pain made her bite her lip so hard she tasted blood. She managed to throw the rug aside, favoring her stinging arms. They were covered with deep, ugly scrapes. She ached all over, and felt the beginnings of bruises on her elbows, hips and knees, as well as in some places she could hardly remember hurting.

But the thought of her daughter drove her to fight her way over into the living room and to the couch, using her numb fingers and bloody nails to pull herself along in a kind of jerky, out-of-water, sidestroke. Finally, after what seemed like an eternity, she reached the first cushion. It was still very cold in the house, and she realized that the window in the kitchen was broken (yes, she remembered the sound of breaking glass from downstairs when HE came) and the storm continued to lace snow against the walls. Some of it was surely getting inside, along with the wind she heard whipping through the broken window.

And what else was inside? *Who else?* The house seemed darker, and around every corner, within the depths of every shadow, she could hear the creaks and groans of wood settling as the wind pushed at the walls.

Her father was gone now, and there was nobody else here to help her fight.

Movement in the hallway next to the door. The rug she had used as a blanket was piled up in the corner, and next to it . . .

She blinked and the figure was gone. A moment before, she had been ready to scream, frozen in terror by the figure crouched in the darkness, and now she could clearly see there was nothing there at all.

Get a hold of yourself, girl. She had always been a little embarrassed by the stereotype of the screaming, hysterical female in the movies, and now here she was joining them.

She struggled to a sitting position, then forced her body upward onto the couch, her leg protesting every second. Something scraped its way along the side of the house like long, skeleton fingers. "A branch, only a branch," she whispered. Her voice sounded hoarse and unnatural to her in the dark. She had to get dressed before the cold got to her again.

The fire poker stood against the wall a few feet away, and she dragged herself over to it, using the wall for support. The poker only came halfway up her thigh, but it would have to do. *And it's heavy enough if it comes to that*, she thought. A renewed rush of adrenaline dampened the pain in her leg, and she was able to half stand with her back to the wall. She leaned against the poker carefully, pound by pound until it supported most of her weight.

Moving like that, it took her over two minutes to reach the phone in the kitchen. It was dead. *But you really didn't expect anything else, did you?* The storm was still raging, and the lines were surely down somewhere. Or perhaps he'd cut the line. Her cell was somewhere in the house, but chances were it wasn't charged. She rarely used the damn thing; David was always telling her to be more careful. What if she broke down on the highway and needed help? She never listened. *I'm sorry, baby*, she thought, and moaned. She blinked back tears. Not now. She couldn't break down now.

It took her another five minutes to climb the stairs, step by agonizing step. But they had no clothes downstairs, and she needed something warm if she was to go outside.

Outside? Are you nuts?

But it was the only way to find her daughter and get the hell out of Dodge, wasn't it? And that was what she planned to do. She wondered what had happened to her husband and that man he was with, the one driving the old Cherokee. She had to assume they were off looking for her. It gave her a quick, warm feeling inside, and she increased her pace, ignoring the pain from her leg as best she could. The rush of adrenaline worked like a fine narcotic, dulling the pain enough for it to be bearable.

In the bedroom, she struggled into a loose-fitting top and sweater, and then a pair of David's big, warm corduroy pants, gritting her teeth at the pain when her foot twisted in the pant leg. Fine droplets of sweat clung to her forehead and nose, and ran down the back of her neck as her numb fingers fumbled at the snap on the corduroys. She slid a belt through the pant loops and cinched it tight.

Not much of a fashion statement, she thought as she glanced in the mirror on her slow trip back to the stairs. A bloodied, terrified woman stared back at her, dark hair hanging in heavy clumps over her face, but she was alive and moving, and that was something close to a miracle, even if she did look like death warmed over.

I'm certainly not going to win any beauty contests, anyway.

She heard a noise. Just a soft thump, hardly discernible above the wind. Yet it stood out from the noise of the storm and the house settling. This was the heavy sound of something being dropped.

Or someone leaping quietly from the windowsill to the floor.

She looked around the little bedroom frantically for a place to hide, a weapon, anything. The closet was there, but the door was shattered from the last attack, and besides, it would be the first place he'd look. Fighting panic, she limped back to the open doorway, praying that *if it was him, God, please keep him downstairs, just a little longer.* The dim light from the bedroom skylight fell in a thin rectangle on the floor of the hallway, not quite reaching the stairs. The hall itself was deeply shrouded in shadows as it led off on one side to the bathroom and on the other to Jessica's bedroom. It was empty. Still, her heart beat a heavy, constant pulse in her ears, and she felt a wave of dizziness and nausea.

She took one faltering step out into the empty hallway. Her breathing was harsh and ragged, and she tried to gulp it back inside and silence the noise it made. There was a shadow at the bottom of the stairs. She saw it clearly, even from her position, looking down into the darkness. It slipped along the wall among the other vague night forms, a deeper shade of black within the grays. She sucked in her breath and it made a harsh hissing sound through her clenched teeth.

She froze. The shadow had stopped. Now she wasn't sure if it had been there at all, it was so difficult to see . . .

She took a step to the left as gently as she could, trying

desperately to keep that damned poker from ringing against the wood floor, grateful for the noise of the wind. Off to her right past the stairs, the hallway ended abruptly at the bathroom door, but to her left it stretched out into the darkness, past Jessica's room and around the corner, where it opened up and looked out over the two-story living room. She shuffled ever so slowly down that way, glancing back and forth from the top of the stairs to the hallway in front of her. As she neared Jessica's room, she heard another noise, this time much closer.

. . . Oh God, he's there he's on the stairs . . .

She turned and limped as fast as she could around the corner, the poker scraping softly against the floor, her leg dragging behind like unwanted baggage. As she reached the railing, she clearly heard the sound of a footstep on the wood floor behind her. She whirled around, her back to the opening over the living room.

He was just behind that bend in the wall. The light from the bedroom skylight glowed dimly around the corner, and she could see his shadow moving on the floorboards. Her pulse pounded in her ears, the pain in her leg forgotten. She gripped the poker in a death grip and pressed herself into the bend where the wall met the railing, praying he couldn't see her in this dim light, *because if I can't see him then he can't see me, right, oh God, don't let him know I'm here, please.*

She waited, the poker cocked and trembling, watching the entrance to the hall beside her where he would first appear. There was only darkness and shadows and the thin, high creaking of the floorboards. *This is insane, this is not happening.* She squeezed her eyes shut tight and then opened them, trying to wish it all away, straining to hold herself together, concentrating so hard that when Amanda Seigel finally did come through the archway, Helen had to hold herself back from swinging that poker as hard as she could.

"Jesus," the woman said. "What happened to you?"

Helen collapsed to the floor, sobbing. She heard the poker ring faintly as it fell beside her legs. The woman crouched beside her.

"You're going to be all right, but you have to listen to me," the woman said. "I've lost track of everyone. Where is Jonathan? Do you know?"

Jonathan? Helen thought, confused. She looked up to see a shiny, flat, silver blade poking out of the hallway shadows like some obscene phallic symbol, and then he took another step and she was staring straight into the huge man's eyes, not two feet behind them, his face running with blood, lips and cheeks lined with white scars. A demon straight out of her deepest, darkest nightmares.

She screamed. The woman next to her turned on her haunches and was struck in the side of her face by his fist. Helen saw blood and a broken tooth, and she grabbed for the poker, pushing up with her one good leg and swinging it with all her strength. It connected with a soft, satisfying thud in his midsection, and he doubled over with a *woof* of air, dropping the knife. Helen let the poker slip from her grasp to the floor as she stood, frozen in terror, the man right in front of her. The other woman lay against the wall, several feet away, silent and still.

Until now, as frightened as she had been, it hadn't been *real*, not this part about a killer hunting for her in her *own house*, and now that she was faced with the proof of him, she stood rooted to the floor like a wild animal caught in the headlights.

Something spoke up from the depths of her brain, breaking her paralysis as he sank to the floor, left hand against his midsection. Something was wrong with his right arm; blood dripped onto the floor from his dangling fingers. *Run, damn it!* But she couldn't run; he blocked the hallway and her only way out. She let out an involuntary cry, and limped backward until her body was pressed against the railing. Time seemed to slow down to a series of freeze-frame pictures as she watched him rock back and forth, holding his stomach with his left hand, eyes squeezed tightly shut, until nothing existed except her harsh gasps of breath and the movements of the man.

Finally, she turned and looked over into the living room, because *he was getting up*, and she had to do something. The couch lay directly below her, and she swung one leg over the edge before she knew what she was doing, twisting her body until her raw and tender stomach pressed against the railing and her feet dangled down over the drop. She let herself slip down the rough wood, feeling the wall with her legs and knees, refusing to look down because to do that would surely cause her to lose her nerve, even though she could see the man reaching for his knife now, even though he was turning to stare at her with something more than hatred in his eyes.

She took a deep breath, and let go as he lunged for her.

For a second, she fell and then her feet hit the couch and she buckled and shrieked from the pain, her broken ankle twisting among the cushions as she fell sideways and off the edge of the couch to the floor. Her head hit hard and she saw nothing but blackness for a long moment before retching in great, gasping heaves. Her leg was on fire.

Then she heard him coming for her and she pulled herself to her feet somehow, her ankle screaming under the pressure. The door seemed to be a mile away. She heard him thudding back through the hall upstairs, and knew she only had a few precious seconds.

The Jeep, get to the Jeep, her mind screamed. She tried to take a step and her broken leg buckled again underneath her, sending her tumbling to the floor. "Get up," she heard herself whisper in a cracked and trembling voice, and wondered if she were finally losing her mind. *After all this, it comes down to right here right now. Do you have what it takes or are you just going to give up? Come on, move!*

She turned her head and saw him come off the last step not more than twenty feet away. Somehow, she found her feet again and limped to the doorway, shooting pains making her scream with every step. She felt a moment of pure panic *(what if it doesn't open, what if I can't get out)* before the door swung open and she stumbled out into the wind, hearing the woman shout from the railing above as she did.

It was still snowing but she could see the Jeep sitting just beyond the steps, half-buried in the snowdrifts. The brutally cold air cleared her head, and she slammed the door closed behind her just as he reached the front hall. She got to the steps and heard the door open behind her. In a spurt of pure adrenaline, she stumbled and hopped down them to the ground and limped frantically towards the Jeep, her breath coming in gasps, the back of her neck prickling in anticipation of the hand that would surely come crashing down at any second, her gasps turning to half sobs in her throat.

As she reached the door, she risked one look back and he was leaping down the porch steps. *Only have a second now, grab the handle, pull . . .*

The door would not open. *Oh my God, it's locked or stuck and I don't have a prayer anymore.*

She spun around and he grabbed her by the throat with his left hand, throwing her up against the Jeep with brutal force. He held the knife in his mouth. Her legs buckled beneath her and she sagged downward, his strong grip holding her up and cutting off her air. She made a harsh choking sound, and then he spoke, his words coming to her muffled around the blade of the knife.

"Gonna cut you, Mother," he said, leaning forward, drops of spittle and blood flying from his mouth to land on her cheeks and forehead. His eyes were vacant and stared through her, as if focusing on something far away.

Mother? she thought, and then everything disappeared in a thin, gray fog of unconsciousness.

Death, so close he can taste it. Death that tastes like smoke—bitter and dusty. Filling his mouth, his throat like a wriggling snake. It is their deaths he tastes, and his own for what he has done. He knows the Dark Eyes will not stop until they end his life, and it does not matter to them if he has his revenge on her or not. But it matters to him, oh yes. It matters to him.

And he may smile, and triumph in the sacrifice, because the Decapitator has come. It came in the black of night, a shape taking form from the darkness as his prayers were finally answered. It is impossible to look at; it is like the sun in its brilliance—no, the opposite of the sun, a darkness so black it hurts the eyes. It is a desperate time, but his Savior has arrived, and it is pleased with the boncs on display for it. He has become one with the Savior, and the Savior directs his course. "You may not live," it whispers, "but you will make one more sacrifice to me."

Death is no longer bitter; it is sweet and juicy, and it makes him whole in the Savior's eyes. They will truly be one through the bite of the knife.

He feels his limbs itch and turn black, and knows that soon he will be holding their heads in his hands, and the Eyes will search for him, but it will be too late. He will dig them out until their sockets are empty and blood-drenched, and he then will add them to his factory of bones.

Amanda came to and realized all at once what had happened. The left side of her face stung, and she felt the warm flow of blood from the cut on her cheek. She probed the hole in her gums with her tongue where a tooth had been, and winced. Then she stood up and looked around.

The room was empty.

She heard someone moving heavily through the hallway to the stairs, and she ran to the railing just in time to see Jonathan Newman lumbering to the door. *Dear Lord*, she thought. *He hardly seems human anymore . . .*

His arms, his arms almost looked—

"Wait!" she cried, but he didn't stop. The door swung shut behind him, and she rushed back through the house to the stairs. Her mind spun and she felt sick, and that cartoon from *The Hobbit* came back to her again. This time, it was as clear in her memory as if she had seen it yesterday. The fat black spiders weaving their cocoons around the dwarves, about to suck their blood, black hairy bodies and dripping fangs, and Bilbo Baggins leading them away with a song . . .

She reached the front door downstairs and saw Jonathan catch Helen at the Jeep.

It was then that he turned towards her, and she saw something that later she would refuse to face, something that she was determined to believe was caused by fright and exhaustion and the blow to her head:

Jonathan was no longer there. In his place stood a creature that seemed half human and half spider, its hairy arm locked around Helen's neck, its head a grinning skull that looked impossibly like Jonathan and yet so much more. It held a bloodied steel blade and its fangs were bared and glistening.

She screamed, and the spider-thing pulled away from Helen for one quick second. Then suddenly it was as if the very earth had exploded beneath Amanda's feet. *Gun.* She threw herself to the snow.

The gun roared again, and Amanda looked up in time to see the second bullet hit Jonathan Newman in the temple. The back of his skull burst outward in a tattered mass of red and gray matter, spattering the snow behind him as he fell with a thump into the soft powder, all but disappearing into its depths.

Helen Pierce slumped to the ground. Everything was silent. Amanda began to cry.

After what seemed like forever, someone helped Amanda to her feet. It was Dan Flint.

Flint glanced back at the fallen man again, half expecting him to rise and pull himself up through the snow like a demon from hell and extend a bloody, gore-smeared hand out for the knife.

But he didn't do that, of course. He was dead.

At that thought, relief flooded through him, and suddenly his arms felt weak and shaky and he realized he had been holding the gun out all this time *(All this time? How long—two, three seconds?)* He let it drop to the ground. Little wisps of smoke escaped the barrel and were lost in the wind. *Funny the things you notice when you've just shot a man,* he thought. The world didn't seem quite right, not at all the way he had expected it. He thought he would feel relieved, vindicated, but he didn't feel any of that. He felt empty, dead inside.

He stood up from the cold ground where he had been kneeling and went to help Amanda. After a minute, they both went down to the woman.

She lay against the runners of the Cherokee, crumpled in an awkward position, and for a moment, he thought she was dead. But then he saw her chest move. He managed to pick her up and get her onto the porch, all the while keeping an eye on the figure half-buried in the snow.

He's done, he can't get up, not anymore.

A minute later, he left the two women on the couch and went back to look for Bobby. He found the man lying in the snow around the far corner of the house. His throat had been brutally cut ear to ear, the skin hanging down like peeling wallpaper.

Flint went back inside and found some blankets upstairs, wrapping the two women in them. He didn't know how badly Mrs. Pierce was injured, but she was alive.

I should get us out of here; I should start that Jeep and drive . . .

But he didn't.

He just sat and stared at the wall across from the chair, noticing the cracks and markings *(little bloody fingerprints on the railing upstairs?)* of the wood. Soon, people would come to help them; soon, the police would clear the snow drifts to the front door. Somebody would come.

Now he just sat and stared at the wall, and at the two women, wondering how it had all happened. Nobody spoke for a long time, they just sat in silence.

After a while, he could make out the thin, whiny buzz of a snowmobile engine in the distance.

EPILOGUE

The baby was kicking today.

Helen Pierce could feel him deep in her belly, odd little points of pressure, tremors that felt like mild indigestion. But this feeling was a good one. It made her happy again. It had been a while since she had been happy, and she hardly remembered what it was like.

David was in Washington with Dan Flint, testifying in the indictment against Michael Olmstead. Even with his help, the lawyers cautioned them that it was possible Olmstead would face a light sentence, time served and probation. The only shot they had at something more was to try him on an attempted murder charge, and that meant proving that he had firsthand knowledge of the chemical's effects and sent Jonathan Newman to the plant with intent to kill.

Any records that might have existed to prove that point had been destroyed. Flint said that even if they didn't get a conviction, at least the bad publicity would keep him from finding another job for a while.

The whole thing made her sick, but she hardly dared think what it was doing to David. Flint too; she had talked to him quite a few times since last winter, and he just didn't seem to be the type for all this bureaucratic bullshit. Helen gave him another six months, and then he would get out. She could feel it.

The baby kicked again. "Hold your horses," she said, and limped to the fridge. Maybe he wanted something to eat. She made herself a peanut butter and jelly sandwich, and sat down at the kitchen table to eat it. Holding the sandwich was still a little awkward. She had gotten some frostbite on her toes and two of the fingers of her left hand, and had lost three of the toes and one finger to the first knuckle. It made it hard for her to hold things in that hand. Still, she realized, that was just a small reminder of what she had been through the day of the storm.

That's not exactly all of it, she thought. There were other, less visible scars. She knew that the image of Jonathan's body in the snow would stay with her forever, a cross for her to bear as she tried to find herself again. David and Jessie had even deeper emotional scars than she did, but they would heal, in time. She had to believe that they would.

The sandwich finished, she wandered into the living room and sat on the cream-colored sofa. Their new house was located in Santa Barbara. It was a pretty little ranch with a flowerbed running around three sides and a two-car garage. Most of Hydro Development's assets had been frozen while the trial was being prepared (besides the money paid out for the cleanup), but David had received a healthy bonus and a promise of a later settlement for his trouble from the members of the board, who had no knowledge of Olmstead's actions. David had been amazed and unwilling to believe that Thompson had been innocent of everything, but it appeared that he was not guilty of anything other than being an asshole. Which, Helen thought, was indictment enough in her book.

She stared out the window at the California sunshine, thinking of Jessie. She had started kindergarten a month ago, and seemed to be doing fine. They had been frightened at first; she hadn't spoken for three days after the storm, and then one morning, she woke up and started again. She was a different girl, though, quieter and more thoughtful. All her laughter, all her *childhood* had been snatched from her. But at least the visions had stopped. Either that, or she just wasn't telling anyone anymore.

It was hard for Helen to face what had happened, even now. When she thought about how close they all were to death, and when she had heard about the bodies found in the mine buildings and shafts, the deputy, a hunter and even the little girl from the poster (what was her name? Marie) . . .

She shuddered, and pulled a blanket around her shoulders, though the temperature outside was a balmy eighty-seven degrees. It did her no good to sit here and think things like that. They were starting over now, with a new home, a new baby on the way, a new *life*. This new life had little room for the old regrets and fears.

But why did they have to carry along so much goddamned baggage?

David had been hit hard by all of it too. He felt responsible for what had happened. He had experienced severe mood swings for weeks after they left. Even now, he had some sort of dark side that didn't want to go away, and Helen knew that he often hid things from her, things that he couldn't understand himself.

Amanda had been wonderful through all of it, helping them personally through the hard times, but a psychiatrist could only do so much. And Helen suspected that she had her own scars to deal with, and that they kept her up at night. Something had happened those last few seconds before Jonathan had been killed, something that Amanda wouldn't discuss with anyone. She had mentioned one thing that Helen thought rather strange, and only after she had been pushed and prodded by one of the doctors. "Do you believe in ghosts?" she said. And then, looking slightly dazed, "The mind plays the strangest tricks . . ."

The baby seemed to be enjoying the peanut butter and jelly sandwich. He had quieted down and seemed to be waiting for something else to happen, perhaps a new kind of delicacy to be delivered to him through her womb. Helen patted her stomach gently. Jessie would be getting home soon, and they would go pick up David at the airport. He was due in at three thirty. That would mark the end of their involvement in the whole thing. Finally, it would be time to put the winter and Hydro Development behind them. Helen stood up slowly, wanting to find the car keys before Jessie got home.

The mind plays the strangest tricks . . .

Why had she thought of that again? *Of course the mind plays tricks*, she thought. *All kinds.* Sometimes it made them up on its own, and sometimes it got a little help along the way.

Helen went upstairs. Each step was a small triumph. As she was searching for her car keys among the junk on the top of the dresser, she was reminded of that one other thing Amanda had said. And as she thought about it, she could swear she heard a voice, faint and distant; it sounded like her father.

Do you believe in ghosts?

NATE KENYON

"A voice reminiscent of Stephen King in the days of *'Salem's Lot*. One of the strongest debut novels to come along in years."
—*Cemetery Dance*

A man on the run from his past. A woman taken against her will. A young man consumed by rage…and a small town tainted by darkness. In White Falls, a horrifying secret is about to be uncovered. The town seems pleasant enough on the surface. But something evil has taken root in White Falls—something that has waited centuries for the right time to awaken. Soon no one is safe from the madness that spreads from neighbor to neighbor. The darkness is growing. Blood is calling to blood. And through it all…the dead are watching.

BLOODSTONE

ISBN 13: 978-0-8439-6020-4

Bram Stoker Award–Winning Author of *Castaways*

BRIAN KEENE

"One of horror's most impressive new literary talents."
—*Rue Morgue*

When their car broke down in a dangerous neighborhood of the inner city, Kerri and her friends thought they would find shelter in the old dark row house. They thought it was abandoned. They thought they would be safe there until morning. They were wrong on all counts. The residents of the row house live in the cellar and rarely come out in the light of day. They're far worse than anything on the streets outside. And they don't like intruders. Before the sun comes up, Kerri and her friends will fight for their very lives…though death is only part of their nightmare.

URBAN GOTHIC

ISBN 13: 978-0-8439-6090-7

Five-Time Winner of the Bram Stoker Award

GARY A. BRAUNBECK

Hoopsticks will get you if you don't watch out!

More than three decades ago high-school senior Andy Leonard snapped. When he stopped shooting, thirty-two people were dead. But not little Geoff Conover. Andy spared Geoff for reasons no one ever knew. Now, all these years later, tragedy has struck again. Bruce Dyson too has gone on a murder spree, leaving nine dead in his wake. Even though they never met, there's only one person Dyson will speak to—Geoff Conover. And what he tells Geoff will shake him to his core. With one word, Dyson will reveal that he knows the dark truth behind the legendary bogeyman used to terrify local children for years, the deformed creature known as Hoopsticks…and the final, shocking secret of Cedar Hill, Ohio.

FAR DARK FIELDS

"Braunbeck's fiction stirs the mind as it chills the marrow."
—*Publishers Weekly*

ISBN 13: 978-0-8439-6190-4

ROBERT DUNBAR

Author of *The Pines*

As a winter storm tightens its grip on the small shore town of Edgeharbor, the residents are frightened of much more than pounding waves and bitter winds. A series of horrible murders has the town cowering in fear. Mangled victims bear the marks of savage claws, and strange, bloody footprints mar the beach. A young policewoman and a mysterious stranger are all that stand between this isolated community and an ancient, monstrous evil.

"The Shore is every bit as much of a classic as *The Pines."* —Hellnotes

THE SHORE

*"*Among the classics of modern horror.*"*
—*Weird New Jersey* on *The Pines*

ISBN 13: 978-0-8439-6166-9

☐ **YES!**

Sign me up for the Leisure Horror Book Club and send my FREE BOOKS! If I choose to stay in the club, I will pay only $8.50* each month, a savings of $7.48!

NAME: _____

ADDRESS: _____

TELEPHONE: _____

EMAIL: _____

☐ I want to pay by credit card.

☐ **VISA**   ☐ MasterCard.   ☐ DISCOVER

ACCOUNT #: _____

EXPIRATION DATE: _____

SIGNATURE: _____

Mail this page along with $2.00 shipping and handling to:
Leisure Horror Book Club
PO Box 6640
Wayne, PA 19087
Or fax (must include credit card information) to:
610-995-9274
You can also sign up online at **www.dorchesterpub.com**.
*Plus $2.00 for shipping. Offer open to residents of the U.S. and Canada only.
Canadian residents please call 1-800-481-9191 for pricing information.
If under 18, a parent or guardian must sign. Terms, prices and conditions subject to change. Subscription subject to acceptance. Dorchester Publishing reserves the right to reject any order or cancel any subscription.